T0267266

"There is an overall lack of novels about mermaids, and I'm pleased to see Enclave working to remedy this situation. If you long for such stories, L.E. Richmond has you covered. Swim into *The Mermaid's Tale* where music can be magic. There you will discover a story packed with mystery and high-stakes adventure in a fascinating underwater world where danger lurks behind coral reefs and in dark caves. Richmond's story adds a twist to the familiar and delivers an ending that promises more to come. Perfect for fans of *The Little Mermaid* and Catherine Jones Payne's Broken Tides series."

— JILL WILLIAMSON, Christy Award–winning author of *By Darkness Hid* and *Thirst*

"L.E. Richmond has crafted a fascinating underwater world in *The Mermaid's Tale.* Not only full of mermaids, but of curses, fish tails, legs, and wild undersea adventure. And just the right dash of forbidden love. An excellent addition to mermaid lore!"

— AJ SKELLY, best-selling author of The Wolves of Rock Falls

"A fresh, new take on *The Little Mermaid!* Richmond springboards from the beloved classic into a vivid undersea civilization where one smitten mermaid's decisions have unleashed generations of consequences. Characters as timeless as they are complex leap from the page, drawing readers into their captivating journey of love, treasure, curses, and mystery. Whether you're a fairytale devotee, hopeless romantic, or seafaring adventurer, *The Mermaid's Tale* won't disappoint. Book two can't come soon enough!"

— LAURIE LUCKING, award-winning author of *Common*

THE MERMAID'S TALE

THE MERMAID'S TALE

L.E. RICHMOND

This one is for the man who will still
jump through ocean waves with me if I ask him to,
who has always been a rock of steadiness
and wisdom when life's storms hit.
I love you, Dad.

Mediterranean Kingdoms

Undula

Mount Oro

★ Aquaticus

Darin's Wreck

"What kind of man is this? Even the wind and the waves obey him!"

MATTHEW 8:27 (NCV)

LOCKLYN

"I LOVE YOUR TAIL, LOCKLYN."

I look down and shock thrills through me. My legs are gone. In their place is a supple, blue-green tail like Amaya's. I look up at Darin in confusion.

"I don't understand."

"The enchantress took away the curse."

"What? But why?"

I look down again, and for some inexplicable reason, my heart sinks. I've wanted a tail all my life—ever since my parents abandoned me in the reef when I was born with legs. But now that I have it, it feels foreign, strange.

I glance up at Darin again, but he is gone. In his place, Amaya flutters excitedly up and down, a bundle cradled in her arms.

"Locklyn! You have a tail!"

I stare at the swaddle she holds, confusion and hurt rising inside. "You had the baby? But . . . I was supposed to be there."

Amaya ignores my words, continuing to bounce up and down in the water. "Maybe now Darin will finally fall for you!"

Heat flares in my cheeks, and I open and close my mouth wordlessly, shame swelling inside. I've never told my sister how I feel about her brother-in-law, Darin Aalto. Not only is he eight years older than I, but he is the most famous Treasure Hunter in Aquaticus. He could have any Mermaid in the city for the asking.

"I . . . How did you . . .?"

"Beck will take you to see him!" trills Amaya. "He's out harvesting a wreck."

I look around and see I am in the front hall of Beck and Amaya's house. Beck, Amaya's pale, silent husband, drifts out of my nephews' room and opens the front door, beckoning me to follow.

"I should really go check on my dugongs. They shouldn't be alone so long," I say helplessly, but Amaya waves me after Beck.

"This might be your only chance, Locklyn!"

But Darin has never minded my legs.

Slowly, I follow Beck, struggling to adjust to the feeling of having my legs tied together. We swim out through the city gates of Aquaticus and begin wending our way through the reef. The farther we venture from the city, the greater my feeling of unease grows. "Beck," I say to his back. "We should wait for Darin to return. You know it's dangerous to swim out into the open sea alone."

Beck turns and I scream, throwing myself backward in the water. The face looking at me has haunted my nightmares for years. Gaunt and pale, framed with curtains of stringy black hair, with a huge, puckered pink scar slashing across the left cheek. The palace guard, Blackwell, is leering at me.

"But, love, I want to be alone with you."

He moves toward me, and I lurch away, groping the back of my pants for my coral knife. But I'm not wearing pants. I have a tail now. And my knife is gone.

I turn and streak through the reef toward the city gates.

Just a little farther.

Almost there.

But just as I reach the end of the reef, Blackwell appears in the gap between the two coral spikes in front of me, blocking my path.

How did he get there?

I whip around and swim madly in the opposite direction. I can hear Blackwell's tail churning through the water behind me, and I swim faster, bursting out of the reef and into the open ocean.

Where should I go?

Darin. Amaya said he was harvesting a wreck. I need to find him.

I am about to start swimming when I hear chittering and turn to see my herd dolphin, Darya, hovering in the water on the reef's edge.

"Darya, what are you doing here? Where are the dugongs?"

Darya twitters happily, flicking her sleek gray tail back and forth.

Blackwell bursts out of the reef behind her, and my heart jumps into my mouth. I begin to sing, a soft, wordless melody, inviting Darya to return home.

Blackwell's eyes widen as he looks from me to Darya, who turns at my command and flits away into the reef. Most Merpeople can't sing. The way their throats are constructed gives them the ability to breathe both air and water, but makes singing impossible. "You little witch," he mutters, backing away.

Relief floods through me, but only for a moment. As I turn to swim in search of Darin, I catch sight of a black shape speeding in my direction out of the corner of my eye. Terror freezes my voice in my throat. The black, ghost-like form of a giant squid is flying through the water, tentacles pulsing. I turn to flee, swimming as quickly as I can, but strong, rubbery tentacles wrap around me from behind. I struggle frantically, terror echoing the beat of my heart.

I have to get away!

But the tentacles are squeezing more and more tightly.

Ahhhhhhhh . . .

My eyes fly open as my entangled legs churn desperately against my scratchy, posidonia-fiber blanket.

Legs.

I have legs.

I flop back on the stone shelf that serves as a bed and wait for the pounding of my heart to subside.

A dream.

It was just a dream.

Amaya doesn't know about my feelings for Darin.
Blackwell hasn't come back.
And the Sea Enchantress's curse remains unbroken.

2

LOCKLYN

"LOCKLYN!" THE VOICE BEHIND ME makes me give the elastika rope, with which I am trying to lasso a spur of rock, a jerk that causes me to miss the spur by a few feet. I glance over my shoulder just in time to see Darin, the older brother of Amaya's husband, Beck, grab my biggest dugong calf and swing her effortlessly over his shoulder. With one flick of his muscular copper tail, he shoots away into the dark water.

After last night, I'm too tired for this.

But at least I am getting one more confirmation that this rope was a good investment.

It is impossible to use ordinary seaweed ropes as lassos. They are too light to be able to fly through currents without being knocked off course. But when I was twelve, a merchant caravan from Atlantis visited Aquaticus. As soon as I heard a salesman shouting the praises of elastika, a metal-infused fiber the Atlanteans had developed to be attracted to the magnetic fields of organisms, I knew I had to have one. This lasso cost every moonstone I had saved in two years—plus a little from Darin, which I insisted on repaying. But I have never regretted the purchase.

I twirl my elastika loop twice over my head and then launch it after him. The rope snags, and I jerk hard to tighten the noose.

Puckering my lips, I whistle a simple command, and Darya comes dancing through the water toward me and begins to circle the herd of dugongs as they graze. Keeping a firm grip on the rope—which has begun to twist and jerk—with one hand, I reach down with the other and pull my coral knife out of the sheath on my belt. Then, kicking as hard as I can, I swim toward the spur of rock I was originally trying to lasso.

It is tough. Darin is fighting as hard as he can on the rope's other end, and since he is a lot bigger and stronger than I am, swimming as hard as I am able is only just keeping me from being dragged backward toward him and away from the stone spur. But I have an advantage he doesn't. I begin to hum and then sing—a merry, wordless tune. The seaweed rope goes slack for a moment, and I know the baby dugong in his arms has begun to struggle, trying desperately to obey my musical command to join me. It's all Darin can do to hold her. Putting on a burst of speed, I strike out for the spike and manage to latch on. Bracing myself with my legs wrapped tightly around the jagged structure, I begin to reel in my line.

Darin is still fighting, but I continue to sing, and eventually he and the baby dugong are close enough. I knot my rope around the rock spur, leaving a long end dangling, and dart at him, wielding my knife. He is hampered by the calf under his right arm, but as I swim toward him, his tail whips up, whacking me hard in the shoulder. Tumbling through the water, I see from the corner of my eye he has drawn a knife and is trying to use the point to unravel my knot. I dart at him again, fingers latching onto the arm wielding his knife. Using a move he taught me, I twist his arm behind his back and use a chopping motion to bring the knife's pommel down on his wrist. He gives a grunt and releases his weapon, which drops to the sand beneath us. Still holding his left arm pinned to his back, I wrap my other arm around his throat and allow the tip of my knife to prick his neck.

"Drop the calf," I say in my deadliest voice.

His grip slackens and the little dugong wriggles through the water to hide behind me, its head butting against my shoulder. I loosen my grip on Darin and turn my head ever so slightly, chirruping to the baby. Taking advantage of my momentary distraction, he rips his left arm free and catches me around the waist. At the same time, he ducks free of my arm around his throat and chops me on the wrist with his unencumbered right arm, robbing me of my knife. I struggle fruitlessly, but his muscular arms are like manacles.

"How many times have I told you," he asks, "not to get close to an opponent who is bigger than you?"

I sigh and drop my head, going limp in his arms. The moment I feel a relaxation in his hold, I kick out at his stomach and wriggle desperately, managing to squirm free. I dart jubilantly away from him, but the next second, I feel something wrap around my ankle and jerk me to a halt. Darin had used the long end of my own rope to lasso me. Now we are both tied to the spur by different ends of the rope.

As he swims toward me, I raise my hands in surrender. "Well done."

"You weren't focused," he accuses, stopping a few feet away.

I sigh and reach down to stroke the baby dugong, who is nuzzling at my leg. "Off day, I guess."

"You don't have off days, Locklyn. What's wrong?" He swims closer, and as I look up into his tawny golden eyes, they soften. Darin has known me all my life. He and Beck were Amaya's best friends growing up, and they helped her care for me after I was abandoned in the reef. If Amaya taught me basic survival skills, Darin was the one who taught me how to protect myself and those around me. He showed me how to weave nets and ropes out of seaweed and kelp. He gave me my first coral knife and taught me to slash the gills of the sharks who came to attack my herd of dugongs. He trained me in hand-to-hand combat so I would be able to fight off the Nebulae women who frequently raided the outskirts of Undula looking for food.

When Beck and Amaya married, I was even more thrilled to have Darin join the family than Beck. The effortless comradeship he and I possess is a rare gift. And he is one of three people in the world whom I trust implicitly.

"The castle kitchens told me they would only be interested in buying two of my bulls this year."

His eyes widen. "Don't they normally get six?" I nod miserably. "Did they tell you why?"

I shake my head. "No, just that they will only be 'requiring' two this year. Maybe they've finally decided they'd rather not do business with a Crura."

Darin's eyes harden. "Their loss," he says after a moment, his voice measured. "You raise the biggest dugongs in Undula." His lips twitch upward into a smile. "I think your calves like being sung to."

I grin back at him. "That's what Amaya says. I think she's a little irked she gave me the initial cow to start my herd, which is now bigger than hers. But," I sigh and gesture moodily toward my legs, "it seems only fair I should get some compensation for being the one in our family to draw the short straw. Being Vocalese and a Crura is better than just being a Crura. People think you're gifted if you can sing. If you have legs, they think you're a dangerous mutant."

Darin raises his eyebrows, and I raise a hand quickly to forestall him. "Don't, Darin. Don't tell me again I shouldn't care what ignorant, prejudiced people think."

Darin looks as though he is going to argue for a moment, but then he closes his mouth and shrugs, looking away. Silence stretches between us, guilt eating at me for my sharpness. But he doesn't understand. How could he?

I'm not the only Merperson I know who has legs. But I could count the number on one hand (or foot). Most Crura can trace their legs to a genetic abnormality resulting from having a Land Dweller somewhere in their ancestry. My legs are a result of my great-great-grandmother Llyra double-crossing the Sea Enchantress.

Their deal was that after Circe gave Llyra the potion which would make her human, Llyra would swim to The Surface, drink it, transform into a human, use her beautiful voice to make Marcus fall in love with her, and then seal her voice in a magic locket and sail to a spot in the sea directly above Circe's lair. There she would throw the locket overboard, thus paying the enchantress. This deal meant Llyra would live her entire life on land as a mute, but she was so desperately in love with Prince Marcus, she agreed to Circe's demands. However, after becoming human and joining her prince on land, Llyra began to have second thoughts. After all, what could the Sea Enchantress do to her now? So the deadline for her payment came and went. When Circe discovered Llyra had reneged on their bargain, she went into an irate rage. In her fury, she declared that, until the end of time, one of Llyra's descendants in every generation would be cursed, at home neither on land nor in the water. Nine months later, Llyra gave birth to a baby boy with webbed hands and feet. The child could not speak. Devastated, Llyra and Marcus struggled to raise their son until one day, when he was fifteen years old, he dove off a cliff and swam away, never to return.

He, like his mother, had found forbidden love. He married the Mermaid who had enticed him away from his human parents and settled beneath the ocean, falling in love with the world his mother had sought so desperately to escape. In the isolated settlement called Ondine where he and his wife lived, no one cared that he had legs. But in Undula, King Triton, mad with vengeance and grief over the loss of his beloved daughter, passed harsh laws forbidding any contact with Land Dwellers and fear and hatred of Crura began to spread.

Meanwhile, on land, Llyra, beside herself with grief, believed Circe had taken her son as payment for her treachery. As time went on, she became convinced Circe would give her son back if she fulfilled her end of the original bargain. After persuading Marcus, who was equally distraught over the loss of their child, to go along with her plan, she loaded a ship with treasure and, using the spell Circe had originally given, sealed her own voice inside the magic locket. She planned to throw all of the treasure, in addition to the locket, overboard above Circe's lair as a kind of interest payment.

But she and Marcus never reached their destination. A vicious storm sank their ship three days after they set sail.

The fabulous treasure on Marcus and Llyra's ship became legendary. On land, kings from many countries outfitted expeditions in search of it. But as the years passed and nothing was ever found, interest in the lost treasure began to wane, except as a fantastic story with which to dazzle children. Under the sea, however, Merpeople are still searching avidly for Llyra's Treasure.

Darin's voice breaks into my thoughts. "Are you going to be alright this winter if the palace only takes two bulls?"

I shrug one shoulder ruefully. "It's not the end of the world. Obviously, I won't starve, but my place really needs some repairs, and I was hoping to get Amaya some new baby clothes when the baby comes. The ones she has left over from Fisk are worn to shreds. And, besides," I flash a smile at him, "we might get a niece this time."

"We definitely will if Amaya gets her wish," he says. "I think Beck secretly wants another boy, though. Since we didn't have any sisters growing up and he currently has three sons, I think he's scared he won't know how to handle a girl."

"I think he'll do fine," I say. Beck is gentle and so quiet that he rarely says more than three words in succession. Perhaps that is why we've never really been able to get close. I struggle to relate to silent people.

I glance at Darin. He's as different from his brother as saltwater is from fresh. Beck is small and slight with short, blue-gray hair and eyes so colorless they're almost clear. His tail is a dull blue-green color, the most common shade among the Merpeople. Darin, on the other hand, is the most unusual looking Merperson I have ever seen. His blond hair alone would have set him apart from most other Merpeople, but combined with his copper-colored tail and golden-brown eyes, it makes him completely distinctive. And Darin carries it well. He wears his hair in a long seahorse tail that billows behind him when he swims, and the white shirts he normally wears make his coppery tail appear to glow.

But, despite their differences, he and Beck have been inseparable since they were children. Maybe it is because Darin likes protecting people, and he has always been the one to stand up for his little brother. Or maybe he enjoys having someone in his life who doesn't talk back to him as much as I do.

We sit in silence for a moment, watching my dugongs drifting lazily above the seafloor, nibbling at posidonia. Eventually, he says, "I have something I want to talk to you about."

I glance sharply at him, and for a split second, I imagine him saying the words I spent my entire sixteenth year dreaming he would say. But sixteen came and went. And seventeen. And eighteen. And nineteen. On the night of my twentieth birthday, after he gave me a new knife with the words—To My Little Sis—engraved into the hilt, I had promised myself, through the tears streaming into my pillow, I wouldn't hope any more. Darin could have any Mermaid in Aquaticus. Why under the sea would he want a freak and social outcast like me?

I feel Darin's golden eyes fixed on me and look hurriedly away, terrified he will read my thoughts in my expression.

"What's wrong?" he asks.

He knows me too well.

"Oh, nothing," I mumble, feeling blood rising into my face. "What was it you wanted to talk about?"

"On Beck and Amaya's first anniversary, he told me that with Mermaids, 'nothing' never means nothing," he says gravely, but I can hear the suppressed laughter in his voice.

"Well, I suppose I'm not a typical Mermaid, now am I?" I say lightly.

For a moment, I think that he is going to continue to rag me, but then he says, "It's about a job."

I glance at him in surprise. He never talks to me about his work. I think he doesn't want me to know how rich he actually is. Darin is a freelance Schatzi, the Mermish word for Treasure Hunter. He scours all of Undula looking for wrecked ships. When he finds one, he assembles a crew of diggers and "harvests" the bounty, bringing it to the palace, where he receives a sizable cut of the profits. Being a Schatzi is extremely dangerous work. It requires being willing to swim the seas during the wildest of storms watching for wrecks. The ability to fight off predators and rival Schatzi is crucial.

Darin is one of the most respected Schatzi in Undula. Not only is he extremely skilled at locating and harvesting wrecks, he is also known to be scrupulously honest. Most Schatzi and their diggers skim some treasure off the top of their haul before delivering it to the palace. Darin, however, is known to be very vocal about his aversion to the practice and has fired diggers whom he caught pilfering treasure.

"What kind of a job?" I ask.

He rubs the back of his neck slowly before answering. "Obviously, I can trust you not to say anything about this to anyone, Locklyn?"

"Obviously," I say quickly.

"Yesterday, I found a huge wreck. And when I say huge, I mean *huge*. The ship in question must have been returning from a successful trading expedition. It is full of wine, silk, amber, and oil. And, Locklyn, there are ten chests full of uncut rubies."

My eyes widen and I blow out a bubbly whistle. Rubies are the most valuable commodity in the Seven Seas. "Not really."

"Really." He pauses a moment. "But the wreck is directly on the border between Undula and Nebula."

I purse my lips. "Ah."

"You understand. By law, half of the treasure is due to the crown of Nebula. But if I turn the treasure over to King Malik, I would bet every last urchin in the Mediterranean that Queen Ginevra will never see a single ruby."

I nod slowly. King Malik is not known for his honesty at the best of times, and there is no love lost between Nebula and Undula. "But if you tell the palace you discovered the treasure on the border between here and Nebula, then you've discharged your duty, haven't you? I mean, if they choose to behave dishonestly, that isn't your fault."

"I suppose," he agrees reluctantly. "But I'm worried about more than that, Locklyn. If Ginevra discovers Malik stole a treasure of this size from her, there will be war between Nebula and Undula. Unless . . ." he trails off, staring into the distance.

"Unless what?" I say, my heart beginning to tap out a quicker cadence against my breastbone.

"Unless Malik has a scapegoat," Darin says, turning to look me full in the face. "If Ginevra finds out about the treasure and approaches him, claiming he stole an enormous amount of treasure from her, he can claim that I, the Schatzi who found the treasure, told him the wreck was entirely located in Undula territory. It will be my word against his. I will be found guilty and sentenced accordingly."

I stare at him as the full horror of his words sinks in. In a country as poverty-stricken as Undula, theft is a heinous offense. Ordinary stealing is punishable by a life sentence working on Oro, the volcano located beneath the Strait of Gibraltar, making tridents and weapons. Although exile to Oro is legally described as a life sentence, death sentence would be a more apt description. The work is extremely dangerous, since the laborers are required to get as close as possible to the simmering craigs in order to melt metal to fashion into weapons, and there is often no warning before the volcano erupts, spewing boiling magma over everything in the vicinity. However, if Darin was found guilty of stealing from the crown, he would be lucky to get the chance to go to Oro. Offenses against the crown are normally punishable by death, usually by being locked in a chamber with a blue-ringed octopus. Not only are these creatures extremely aggressive, but their venom is potent, killing victims in under a minute. There is no known antidote to their poison.

"Darin," I say, clutching his forearm hard, "stay away from that wreck. Let someone else find it."

He turns away from me, but I swim in front of him, forcing myself into his line of vision. "It's not worth it, Darin! I know this would be the biggest find of your career, but it's not worth it. If the Nebulae find out—and they probably will—you'll be finished."

He stares at me, his amber eyes inscrutable. I know any

reasoned argument I can give will weigh little in the balance of his thirst for adventure. For fame. For recognition. With an inarticulate sound of frustration, I push away from him, swimming back toward my dugongs. Darya darts toward me, flicking her tail in ecstasy, desperately reminding me how well she has guarded my flock for the last hour.

"Locklyn." I swirl to face him. "Don't be like that," he says, swimming toward me with his hands outstretched.

"Why did you bother asking for my advice if you weren't planning to listen to it?" I snap.

"I am listening," he says patiently. "I haven't made up my mind yet."

"What's to make up your mind about, Darin? If this gets found out, your best option is a life sentence on Oro and your worst is dying with blue-ringed octopus poison coursing through your veins! How can any amount of treasure be worth that risk? It's not like you need it!"

"It's not about me needing it, Locklyn."

"I know," I say. "It's about the glory of being the one to find the biggest wreck in a hundred years."

He makes a frustrated sound in his turn, running a hand through his blond hair. "Well, when you put it like that."

My conscience stabs me as I realize how terse I've been. I swim forward, reaching out to lay my hand on his forearm, and he looks down at me. "I'm sorry," I say softly. "It's not that I don't understand. I do. You know I do. There are so many days I want to go and sign up as an octopus wrestler, just because I want to be remembered for something other than being a freak outcast who struggled to survive as a dugong shepherdess all her life. I know I'll probably die, but sometimes it feels like those few minutes of glory, with the crowd screaming your name, would be worth it. But then, I remember Amaya. I remember Beck and Zale and Ren and Fisk. I remember old Hali who can only afford dugong milk because I discount the price for her. I remember I promised the little beggar girl near the Shark's Fin that I would teach her to weave kelp nets next summer. I remember you. And I know that I can't leave. That I can't just throw my life away. Because there are people who need me. People whose lives would be ripped apart if I chose momentary glory. There are even more people who need you. You know there are, Darin."

He sighs and closes his eyes for a moment, then looks down at me again, something unreadable in his gaze. "When did little Locklyn become so wise?"

I laugh and give his shoulder a push. The somber moment is over. I know I've won. "I've been dropping pearls of wisdom for years. You just haven't noticed because you think of me as a child."

"You are a child," he retorts. "When I found my first ship, you were barely able to swim straight."

"Well, how does it feel to have a child teaching you responsibility?" I mock, swimming backward and wiggling my eyebrows.

Laughing, he opens his mouth to respond, but at that moment, Zale, my oldest nephew, comes bursting through the reef's entrance.

"Aunt Locklyn, Uncle Darin," he gasps.

"Zale, what are you doing here?" Darin asks sternly. "You know you aren't supposed to play in the reef—it isn't safe."

"But . . . Mama . . ." he is still gasping from having swum so quickly.

Darin's eyes meet mine, and a spark of fear flashes between us. "What's wrong with your mama, Zale?" I ask as calmly as I can.

He gulps water, finally managing to get a sentence out. "I can't find Papa anywhere . . . and the baby's coming!"

There is a moment of stillness. Then Darin and I both leap into action. I whistle a snappy march and my dugongs, shepherded by Darya, begin meandering toward the opening in the coral reef. Darin swings Zale up onto his back.

"I'll find Beck and the midwife," he calls over his shoulder as he shoots through the reef's opening.

"I'll be with Amaya," I yell back. As soon as every last dugong is in the reef and Darya is chivvying them homeward, I streak toward the city.

3

DARIN

"IS YOUR DAD AT WORK, LITTLE MERMAN?"
he asks Zale as they dart through the dim streets of Aquaticus, his
nephew's arms clasped tightly around his neck.

"That's where he went this morning, but he wasn't at the net shop
when I went to look for him," Zale says. There is a pause before he
adds, with a slight quiver in his childish voice, "Uncle Darin, I'm
scared for Mama. She was looking really bad."

"It's hard work bringing life into the world," he replies, reaching
behind his back to give Zale a reassuring squeeze. "She'll be alright.
She had you and Ren and Fisk, didn't she?"

"But I can remember her having Fisk," Zale says. "And she didn't
look like this."

"And how is that?"

"White as foam with her teeth clenched together. And before I
knocked on her door to see how she was doing, I heard this awful
moan. It scared me, Uncle Darin."

Pace quickening, he veers down a side street. "Don't worry,
buddy. We'll fetch your great-aunt Chantara and send her to keep
your mom company while we go and get your dad. Chantara's
delivered hundreds of babies. Your mom will be in good hands."

He gives his nephew a poke. "Want to know what I saw while out hunting today?"

"What?" Zale asks, his voice slightly more animated.

"A line of silver glinting from the sand next to a big rock."

"And what was it?"

"Let me tell my story, boy!" Zale giggles. "Where was I? Oh, yes, I saw a line of silver next to a big rock. So, I began to dig. First, a long silver paddle with curved edges emerged, but it was attached to something, so I kept digging. Turns out the paddle was attached to a collar made from the same metal, and when I pulled on the collar, out came two more blades. It was a submarine propeller."

"What's a submarine?" Zale asks breathlessly.

"Some sort of metal ship. They make them in Atlantis."

"Why don't we make them here?"

"There you have me," he replies. "It would sure be nice not to have to wait to catch a ride on a blue whale to get places. But we're here." He hammers on the wooden door of Chantara's small stone hut, and it flies open in a moment. Chantara hovers in the doorway, her deep purple hair pulled up into an ivory-colored scarf. He recognizes the scarf. It was his gift to her from the first wreck he ever harvested.

Crinkles appear at the corners of her dark eyes as she surveys Darin and Zale. "It's Amaya's time, isn't it?" Darin nods and she darts back into the house, returning with a basket full of supplies balanced on her hip.

"We haven't been able to find Beck," Darin tells her as they turn toward Amaya's house. "Can Zale go back with you while I go look for him?"

"Of course," Chantara says briskly, shifting her basket to the other hip and holding a hand out toward Zale. "Come, my Z."

Zale glances up at Darin as he takes her hand, his pale little face pinched with anxiety. "Don't worry," Darin assures him. "I'll find your dad soon. Just keep Ren and Fisk out of trouble so your mom can focus on having that baby, alright?"

Zale manages a small smile before setting off down the street with Chantara. Darin turns the other way, heading toward the net shop where his brother works. Zale said he already checked there, but Beck might have been out on a delivery so they missed each other.

When he reaches the shop, it is dark and shuttered. With a muttered oath, he pauses, tail churning against the water. It is quite late by now, and it seems unlikely that Beck is still out making deliveries. After a moment's hesitation, he turns in the direction of Amaya's house. Perhaps Beck has returned home. Even if he hasn't, Locklyn should be there by now.

When he pushes the door to Amaya and Beck's cottage open, his heart leaps at the sound of his brother's voice coming from the bedroom at the end of the hall. But, just as quickly, it plummets again. Beck's voice is frantic and accompanied by a horrible keening. Chantara says something, her calm voice much sharper than usual.

Heart hammering, he taps lightly on the door of the small bedroom to his right and pushes it open. His nephews are huddled on Zale's bed. Ren has his eyes shut tight and his fingers in his ears. Zale is cradling little Fisk in his arms, mumbling comfort in a shaking voice.

"Little buddies!" he says with forced heartiness. Ren's eyes fly open, and he bounds from the bed, catapulting himself into Darin's arms, Zale and Fisk right behind him. "But where is Aunt Wyn?" he says, using the name Zale gave to Locklyn when he was a toddler.

"She hasn't come yet," Ren says with a shrug.

"What?" he responds so sharply that all three boys stare up at him with wide eyes. "Sorry," he says quickly, thoughts tumbling.

She should be here by now.

"You boys stay here." He gently detaches his nephews' arms from around his midsection. "I'll go look for her."

"Stay, Uncle Darin!" wails little Fisk, trying to glom onto him again, but Zale grabs him and holds him back. Fisk bursts into tears and begins to beat Zale's chest with his tiny fists. "I want Mama! Let me go to Mama!"

"You can't, Fisky," Zale says, his voice gentle as the surf in the early morning, stroking its way up a gray, cold beach. "But I'll let you play with the new sea snail shells Dad brought me. That'll be fun, won't it?"

Fisk's wails subside into whimpers, and he blinks up at his older brother. "The orange ones?"

"I'll be back," Darin says softly to Zale over Fisk's head, and the boy nods as he turns and whisks out of the room.

His heart is beating a tattoo of panic by the time he emerges into the dark streets again, a glowing length of seaweed he snatched from the entryway closet wrapped around his wrist. Curfew was over an hour ago. Where is Locklyn?

Could she have misunderstood and thought she was supposed to go for the midwife? He streaks back toward Chantara's house through the dark streets. He has to go down a side street one time to get away from a patrol of night guards, and to avoid explaining why he is out so late. When he reaches Chantara's, he grabs the door handle and wrenches, but it is impossible to open. She must have locked it behind her.

Whipping around in the water, he starts back toward Amaya and Beck's, his golden tail casting a bubble-encrusted path through the water. When he pushes open the front door, Amaya's continuing wails strike him again.

Wave Master, help her.

For a moment, he considers knocking on the door to see if they need anything, but decides Chantara would have sent Beck for anything desperately needed. Silently cracking open the door to his nephews' room, he sees the three of them sprawled on the floor, playing with a pile of vibrant orange sea snail shells. Zale glances up and meets his eyes, but he puts a finger to his lips and doesn't say anything as his uncle eases the door closed.

Darin bursts into the streets again. Locklyn wouldn't have willingly let anything keep her from being with Amaya at a moment like this. Can something have happened to her? Did the gates shut before she had a chance to come through? But she was right behind him. She should have been on time.

For an instant, he considers going to the gates, but then he dismisses the idea as useless. If the gates were shut by the time Locklyn reached them, she would just have gone home.

As he begins to swim at random, eyes skimming for a sight of Locklyn's familiar slender white shape and dark blue hair, worst-case scenarios chase each other through his mind.

Locklyn lying unconscious in the coral reef with a bleeding lump on the side of her head after swimming into a coral spur.

Locklyn dragged off to the palace jail by the night watchmen for being a Crura out in the streets so late.

Locklyn jerked into the dark doorway of a building by a faceless Merman.

His mind spins, remembering the look on her face in the reef today when he said he wanted to tell her something. For a fleeting instant, the mad impulse to blurt how he felt about her had crossed his mind. But he'd hesitated and the moment had slipped away. She had listened to his problems and then given him wise advice—advice he'd needed to hear. After he'd given in, they had laughed and were back to being friends.

Friends.

Cursing inwardly, he turns onto the next street, catching sight of a watchman swimming slowly toward the far end of it. "Hi!" he shouts, and the watchman turns. Drawing closer, he recognizes him as one of the palace guards he regularly delivers treasure to.

"Aalto," the guard says in surprise. "You're out late."

"Clyde," he says without preamble, "have you seen Locklyn Adair in your rounds tonight? The dugong shepherdess who supplies the castle kitchens?"

Clyde's lips twist into a sneer. "The Crura?"

Anger flares inside Darin—so hot he can almost taste it. "My brother's wife's sister," he says levelly, staring into Clyde's eyes. "My sister-in-law is in labor, and she was supposed to be coming."

Clyde's gaze flickers before Darin's glare and he looks away.

"I—I haven't seen her," he mumbles. Something moves at the end of the street. "But Blackwell was guarding the gate," Clyde adds, motioning toward the dark figure swimming into view. "You should ask him. Oy, Blackwell!"

The figure turns and swims slowly toward them. As it draws level, the seaweed's ghostly light illuminates a pale face surrounded by greasy black hair and throws the ugly scar on the Merman's left cheek into sharp relief.

"Blackwell, Aalto here is looking for the Cr—I mean, the young shepherdess who sells dugongs to the palace kitchens. We were wondering if she came through the gates."

Blackwell looks up at Darin. Something about his face breeds dislike within him, though he has never seen the scarred Merman before. "The little blue-haired spindle-shanks?" Blackwell says in a sneering voice.

Darin's hand snakes out, closing around Blackwell's upper arm. The Merman gives a yelp of surprise and pain as Darin's fingers dig into his skin.

"I'd prefer you didn't use that word in front of me." His voice is sharp.

Blackwell glares malevolently up at him through his greasy bangs. There is a pause before he snarls, "I let her in just before the gates closed, alright? Happy?"

Locklyn is somewhere in the city?

"I need to go," he says abruptly, releasing Blackwell's arm. Without another word, he turns and darts away.

Hours pass as he scours the streets of Aquaticus, checking every place he can possibly think of that Locklyn has ever mentioned going. But the market square is empty and deserted. The palace guard hasn't seen her. She isn't at his house waiting for him. The bartender of the Shark's Fin shakes his head silently when questioned, then resumes wiping empty glasses.

As he swims slowly back toward Amaya and Beck's house just as a clanging bell announces the morning opening of the gates, exhaustion dulls the edges of his panic. There is no point in continuing to search without getting some rest. Unexpected, irrational anger flashes across his consciousness and his jaw clamps in frustration.

If Locklyn doesn't have a good excuse for putting me through the most harrowing night of my life, she is going to wish she was still lost whenever I manage to find her.

4

LOCKLYN

AS I WEAVE TOWARD THE GATES, I KNOW
I'm going to have problems. It is impossible to tell time by light or
darkness here, but I can see that the huge sand-filled hourglass
standing next to the gate is nearly empty. Two guards are in the
process of shutting the enormous shell-studded gates. I fly toward
them.

"Hello?" I yell. "Excuse me? I need to get in before you shut
those, please!"

One of the guards turns, and I catch sight of the jagged scar
slicing along his right cheekbone. My heart sinks into my toes.

"Well, well, well," drawls Blackwell. "If it isn't the Dugong
Princess herself."

"Blackwell," I say, inclining my head in a stiff nod. I come to a
stop in front of the barely open gates. Every instinct screams for me
to dart for the opening, but I force myself to stay where I am. After
everything I said to Darin, getting crushed in the gates of Aquaticus
might seem a tad hypocritical.

"Could I slide through before you shut the gates, please?" I
make my voice as pleasant as possible.

"What's the hurry, Crura?" Blackwell asks silkily.

I clench my teeth to keep from shouting. I have been at every single one of Amaya's births. If he makes me miss this one . . .

"My sister is in labor," I say. "You probably just saw my brother-in-law and nephew come through."

Blackwell glances at his companion, a pale Merman with gray hair and a long, ashen tail, and a wicked smile twists his lips. "We haven't seen anyone come through, have we, Alun?" he says. "I think you're lying, Crura."

My eyes flicker toward the hourglass. By my calculations, it looks like there are less than five minutes remaining. Blackwell knows as well as I do that the gates must be shut before the last grain of sand falls to the bottom of the hourglass, or the gatekeepers will be severely punished.

I decide sweetness is getting me nowhere. "It isn't actually any of your business why I want to go into the city, Blackwell," I say brusquely. "The hourglass still has a few minutes, and until it has run out, any Merperson is free to come and go as they please."

"Any Merperson, yes," Blackwell says, staring pointedly at my legs. "Which you aren't. We don't want your kind in the city."

So much for diplomacy. I reach for the sheath at my ankle and yank my coral knife free. "I've given you one scar already," I say softly, staring into Blackwell's pale blue eyes. "Don't make me give you another."

His hand twitches involuntarily toward the long, jagged wound on his cheekbone and fury fills his eyes. "Shut the gates," he snarls at the other guard. Alun, who seems transfixed by the sight of the sharp coral blade in my hand, doesn't move. Blackwell turns with a flick of his dark tail and reaches for the gates himself.

"No!" I cry, lunging toward the opening. Trying to push past Blackwell, I thrust out an arm and scream as I feel the huge door crunch against my forearm. Blackwell pushes against the door, and I bite back another scream as pain shoots through my trapped limb. Laughing, Blackwell swims so close that the bubbles of his breath brush my face. A prickle of fear races up my spine. My free hand still holds my coral knife, and I thrust it at him so that he backs away.

"Don't you dare touch me," I say.

He gives me a slow smile that makes my skin crawl. "Come now," he says, his tone oily. "I think we can reach some sort of agreement. There is no way you can open the gate yourself. But Alun and I might be persuaded to open it and let you through if we were sure of a proper show of gratitude. Perhaps a little kiss for each of us?"

Disgust causes bile to rise in my throat. I did give him the scar, two years ago when he came to my hut in the reef and propositioned me in a similar fashion. When he'd refused to leave, I had given him a flesh wound to show I meant what I said. I hadn't expected the wound to leave a lasting mark, but it got infected. From what I had heard, the story he was spreading around town was that he had been attacked by a hammerhead and had killed the brute after a terrific struggle in which his face had been wounded. I knew he didn't want to admit to anyone that he had been making romantic advances to the outcast shepherdess from the reef.

"You're disgusting," I say. "You don't even think I'm a person."

He swims closer and I tighten my grip on my knife. The arm caught in the door is throbbing badly now, and I know it will soon go numb. "What does that matter, love?" he says. "You can be a lovely creature without being a person, can't you?"

Anger boils inside me, like magma rising to the surface of Oro, but I clamp it down. "Careful," I say, "or I might give you a matching gash on the other cheek. I'm sure you'll be able to explain why a hammerhead shark was considerate enough to keep you looking symmetrical."

Blackwell stares at me, his face twisting with fury. "You think you're so clever. The Crura maiden who managed to stay alive after being abandoned. The one who has wormed her way into town by selling her bea-utiful dugongs. You aren't one of us. You're a monster and a freak and people shudder behind your back, all while keeping smiles pasted on their faces in order to buy your love-ely dugongs."

I stare blankly back at him, careful to keep my face expressionless. He's not telling me anything I don't already know. But that doesn't take away the dull sting of his words' truth.

Alun tugs at Blackwell. "We need to get inside," he says, glancing nervously around. "I don't fancy meeting the critters that come around here after nightfall."

Blackwell continues to stare at me for a moment, and then his eyes light up. "We should get inside, Alun," he says brightly. "After all, the gate is closed."

Dread pools in the pit of my stomach. Alun's eyes flicker to me again. "But," he gestures helplessly, "the . . . the . . . girl . . ."

"Oh, I'm sure nothing will be able to slip past her," Blackwell says.

He turns and begins to swim toward the small guard door to the right of the gates.

"Wait!" I call, unable to stop myself. "You can't leave me here."

He pivots. "Oh, can't I?" His voice drips with malice. "Since you're such good friends with hammerhead sharks, I'm sure they won't harm you when they show up. Come, Alun."

Alun gives a last helpless look and then swims after him. Blackwell unlocks the guard door with a small, pointed shell hanging around his neck and gestures Alun through.

"Blackwell!" I bellow desperately.

But he only turns long enough to say, "Sweet dreams, love." The door clicks shut.

I flatten myself against the doors, staring into the gloom around me. Glowing algae grows on the walls of the city, creating an eerie blue shimmer in the surrounding water. My heart thuds dully against my breastbone as I scan my surroundings for any signs of movement. Having lived in the reef all my life, I know the waters are dangerous after nightfall. And I don't even have both of my arms to fight attackers.

I struggle fruitlessly, trying to free myself, but the gate is much too heavy for me to move with one arm, and the movement only causes more stabbing pains. I slump back against the gates. I'll just have to wait until morning when a new pair of guards will open them and pray no predators swim close enough to notice me trapped here.

Time crawls by. My eyelids begin to creep shut. I wriggle and the ensuing tendrils of pain jerk me into wakefulness. I stare into the shadows and my heart stops. A larger patch of darkness slips through the water toward me. I grip my knife so hard, the rough coral handle cuts into my hand. In sick fascination, I glance down to see a cloud of scarlet rising from my palm.

Terror flashes through me just as I look up into the eyes of a massive tiger shark. Time seems to slow as the creature slices through the water nearer and nearer. I hear Darin's voice in my head, "Eyes and gills, Locklyn. Go for its most vulnerable areas."

Its mouth opens, revealing row after row of razor-sharp teeth. I twist as hard as I can against my trapped arm, trying to put myself at an angle where I can reach the side of its head, but I can't move enough.

In my mind's eye, I see a beggar hovering outside the door of the Shark's Fin, the stump of one arm wrapped in dirty bandages. He was the victim of a shark attack. How would people respond to a Crura with only one arm?

My heart gives one sharp thump of horror, and then reality clarifies and sharpens around me. I know what I must do. I begin to sing a soft nonsense song that I've crooned to wounded dugongs and to each of my nephews when they were little. Singing does not give you complete control over wild creatures, but most are affected to some degree by the mood of the music. For one dreadful moment, I think this tiger shark is too aggressive, too maddened by the scent of my blood, but then the giant, undulating body slows and stops, hovering inches from me.

I continue to warble, infusing as much tranquility into the song as I can, while my fingers fumble with my elastika rope, which is looped through my belt, attempting to knot the free end around the knife I have clamped between my thighs. I try to focus on the music, rather than the impossible task, in a desperate attempt to force down my panic, but some of my emotion must bleed into my voice. The shark quivers as though awakening from a trance, then bares its teeth.

The knot finally tightens. I yank the rope free and twirl it over my head to give it some speed. As the shark charges, I whip the knife at its snout. My aim is not perfect, but the impact of the knife's hilt is enough to knock the animal off course. I reel in my weapon, then dart forward as far as my trapped arm will allow and slash viciously at its momentarily exposed gills.

Unlike many large sea creatures, sharks are voiceless. But their complete silence only adds to their ghostly menace. As my blade makes contact with rubbery flesh, I wish desperately that the animal would roar to let me know how deadly of a wound I managed to inflict. Warm red liquid clouds the water as I huddle back against the door, expecting the beast to turn and attack again. But instead, it glides away into the dark water, leaving a carmine trail shimmering in its wake.

For an instant, I slump back against the doors in almost painful relief. Then panic jolts me upright again. The bloody trail of my victim will lead other sharks straight to me. I position myself into the most defensive stance I can muster, moaning as agony screams through every nerve of my trapped arm. This is going to be a very long night.

The waiting is the worst. More sharks come and I manage to fight each of them off, adrenaline coursing through me for the few moments each altercation lasts. But in the intervals between, pain returns. The adrenaline drains only to be replaced by a tingling dread that spikes into panic every time I see a dark shadow slicing through the water.

Minutes creep by and in the unchangeable darkness, I have no idea how much time has passed. It feels as though I am trapped in an unending nightmare of emptiness and complete silence. The smell of shark blood lingers, and in my despair, I wonder when my blood will mingle with theirs. My reflexes slow as weariness overwhelms me. It is only a matter of time before one of them gets a bite.

My thoughts drift to my sister, writhing in the agony of bringing forth life, and I whisper a prayer to the Wave Master, begging Him to protect her and that I would live long enough to see the new baby. Faces swim before me. Amaya. Darin. Beck. Zale. Ren. Fisk. Chantara. Each image sends a shot of liquid courage through me. I will not die tonight. I will not give Blackwell that satisfaction.

Music wells up inside, and I begin to sing—softly at first, then loudly and confidently—my voice oddly magnified in the still, red-tinted water. I sing the marching song that the Vocalese perform whenever a raiding party goes out. I sing a love song Chantara taught me about a dugong shepherdess who married a prince. I sing a children's song about a hunt for lost treasure. I sing an old hymn about the Wave Master calming tempests at sea.

I sing and sing and sing. The music wraps around me and becomes a shield, pushing back the horrors that lurk on the edges of my vision. Time blurs into eternity and the music is my only reality, along with one thought that pulses over and over in my brain.

I will not die.

Not tonight.

Not tonight.

Not tonight.

5

LOCKLYN

WHEN THE GATE FINALLY CREAKS OPEN
and I slip downward in the water, it takes me a moment to realize
I am free. My arm lost all feeling hours ago.

"'Ey!" a voice barks behind me and I spin on the spot, raising
my bloody coral knife out of habit.

A middle-aged Merman with silver hair and an obsidian tail
darts backward with a curse. "What is wrong with you, spindle-
shanks?" he spits.

Angry words bubble up behind my lips, and for a moment I
hover in front of him, contemplating how satisfying it would be to
spew my spleen all over him. Instead, I lunge past him, streaking
away up the main street of Aquaticus. His shouts echo behind me,
but I don't slow down. I need to see my sister.

I am almost to Amaya's door when an arm grabs me roughly
from behind. "What do you think you're doing?" a furious
voice demands.

Something inside me snaps. "I'm going to see my sister!" I
bellow, thrashing and kicking at my unseen attacker with all my
might. "And neither you nor anyone else, including all the sharks
in Undula, are going to stop me!"

Despite my frantic struggles, the iron grip on my arm has not slackened, and I am jerked around to face my assailant. Darin's blond hair fans out around his face in a tangled mass and his breaths are heavy. "Where have you been?" he growls.

Feeling returns to my injured arm, the same one he grabbed. The pain makes me look down, and my throat convulses at the sight of my mottled purple and green forearm laced with lines of red where the rough edge of the gate cut into it. I swallow and glance up as Darin stares in transfixed horror at my arm.

"Locklyn, who did this to you?"

I swallow again as a lump rises in my throat.

He catches me by the shoulders and gives me a little shake. "Talk to me," he says desperately.

Forcing down the lump, I manage to croak out, "Blackwell trapped me in the front gate . . . all night . . . tiger sharks," before I break down completely.

Darin's arms wrap around me, and he pulls me gently against his solid chest. Sobs rack me and I lean into him, not even trying to restrain them.

He doesn't say anything for a long time, just holds me, rubbing one hand soothingly up and down my back.

Finally, gulping, I push away from him and swipe my uninjured arm across my eyes. I know I must look horrendous. Merpeople don't cry salt water like Land Dwellers. We cry acidic green tears that leave inky trails which don't wash off for days. I see the black trails of my tears splattered across the front of Darin's white shirt, and I can only imagine how my face must look.

"I'm sorry," I mutter with a sniff, gesturing to his shirt front.

His expression flickers, but then he says lightly, "It's not the first time you've ruined a shirt of mine. I swore I would never hold you again after you ruined my favorite shirt with tear stains when you were eight weeks old. My resolution lasted all of two days."

I choke on a laugh. "I'm sure you regret that now."

"Absolutely," he agrees solemnly. Silence stretches between us, and I know he is staring at me with concern. But I don't want to relive last night right now. Not even for him.

"So," I say, with a stab at airiness, "niece or nephew?"

"I don't know."

"What?"

"I was out all night looking for you," he says quietly, and for one mad moment, I think I hear his voice tremble before dismissing the thought as impossible.

"Well, what are we waiting for?" I say heartily, unable to meet his eyes for some reason. "Let's go find out."

But as soon as we push open Amaya and Beck's door, I know something is wrong. None of the usual happy sounds of a family with a new baby greet us. Instead, I hear quiet, nervous voices and broken weeping. Darin and I exchange a glance just as a door to our left creaks open and my youngest nephew, Fisk, peers out. When he sees us, he darts into the hall and flings his arms around me, burying his head in my waist.

"Little Merman, what's wrong?" I say, wrapping my arms around him and hugging him close.

He raises a pale, pointed face, streaked with black tear tracks, and stares at me beseechingly with huge turquoise eyes. "I don't know," he whispers, and another steaming green tear slides down his cheek. "I'm scared, Wyn." All of my nephews have called me this, from the time Zale first pronounced my name Wockwyn. "Mama keeps crying and Papa sent us to our rooms. They haven't let us see the baby at all."

My heart gives a painful thud. *Is the baby dead?* "Have you heard the baby crying, Fisk?"

"Yes." He makes a face. "Very loudly."

The knot unravels and I give him a squeeze. "Everything will be alright," I say.

Fisk looks from me to Darin, who ruffles his hair.

"I'm sure you'll get to see the baby soon," he says. "Try not to worry, buddy."

"Where are your brothers?" I ask.

"They're sleeping. We were up almost all night." Fisk puffs out his chest importantly.

At that moment, the door at the end of the hallway creaks open and Beck appears in the doorway. The sight of his face turns my stomach to lead. Beck has always had a youthful face, round and babyish. People who don't know them often mistake him for Amaya's son rather than her husband. But now he looks old. So old.

Fisk darts toward his father. "Papa!"

Beck puts out his arms almost absently and Fisk swims into them, burying his head against his father's chest. Beck stares glassily at us over the top of his son. When he speaks, the words sound as though they require tremendous effort. "Amaya . . . wants . . . to . . . see . . . you."

I want to ask what is wrong, to mentally prepare myself for what I will encounter when I go through the door, but I know I can't in front of Fisk. I swim to the door and squeeze past Beck, who seems unable to move.

Amaya is lying on her bed, a new sealskin blanket tucked around her. My heart warms. Beck might speak slowly, but he has always treated my sister like a queen. Sealskin blankets are a luxury since they have to be imported from the Isja people who live off the coast of Norway, and I know Beck must have worked overtime for weeks to pay for this one. But they are well worth the extra expense for those who can afford them. The alternative are the coarse blankets woven from posidonia fibers, which provide little warmth or comfort.

"Amaya," I say, and she looks up from the bundle nestled against her breast. Apart from the fact that she has a beautiful, supple blue-green tail, Amaya and I look very similar. We have the same pale, heart-shaped face and long, bluish-purple hair. I never saw my father, but Amaya told me on the day he died that she and I had both inherited his shifting eye color—one day our eyes are aquamarine blue, the next emerald green, the next stormy gray. Right now, her eyes are a blue so dark they are almost black and are swimming with steamy green tears that well up and spill over as she looks at me.

"Locklyn," she whispers.

I dart forward and slip my arm around her, gazing down at the bundle she cradles. "What's wrong?" I fight to keep my voice steady.

In answer, she gently pulls back the blankets wrapped around the baby sleeping in her arms.

My niece is beautiful. Her tiny body is perfectly formed, with flawless ivory skin and light blue fuzz all over her scalp. Her lips pucker as I watch, and she blows out a stream of bubbles in a whistling snore before curling closer to her mother as the water brushes against her exposed body. And, as I look at her, I get the strangest sensation, equal parts tremendous joy and terrible pain.

Because my niece is like me. Instead of ending in a tail, her torso tapers into legs, each tiny foot with webs between the toes. I reach down to stroke her downy little head, and my heart contracts hard as I catch sight of the mottled flesh of my own forearm.

This innocent little creature will be hated before she knows how to swim. She will have to fight her way through life because of something she had no control over. When I think of her being attacked, being shut in the city gate to fend off murderous sharks through the night, having to ward off the advances of Mermen like Blackwell who view her as a soulless mutant, emotions pulse through me so strong, I can almost taste them.

Gently pulling the blanket back around her daughter, Amaya looks up at me, the tears now pouring down her face. "I'm not . . . It's not for me . . ." she chokes, drawing her daughter closer. "I l-love her beyond measure. But, what kind of a l-life will she have?"

I sense Darin swim up beside me. When I glance at him, I see a sheen of green sparkling in his eyes. Beck must have told him. Wordlessly, he reaches out and Amaya places the baby in his arms. Darin cradles our niece against his chest, his large blond head bent down over her tiny blue one. The baby looks ludicrously tiny against the bulging muscles of his chest and arms.

Amaya makes a sound that is half sob, half laugh. "I remember you in the middle of the reef, crooning to Locklyn when you were eight years old."

Darin gives me a little smirk and I roll my eyes. But the

momentary brightness dies out of Amaya's expression, and she buries her face in her hands, shoulders heaving. Beck swims into the room, shutting the door softly behind him. Without a word, he moves to his wife and gathers her in his arms, his face gray with misery.

For a long moment, there is no sound in the room but Amaya's choking sobs. Darin's eyes meet mine and they reflect the helplessness I feel. There is no place in regular Mermish society for Crura. No school will accept our niece. She will never be able to leave the house unaccompanied, for fear of an attack. Amaya and Beck will be shunned by the majority of their acquaintances when it becomes known they have given birth to someone like me.

Finally, unable to take the silence anymore, I open my mouth, but Darin beats me to it. "What are you going to call her?" he asks.

Silence follows again as Amaya gulps on sobs and Beck rubs her shoulders, staring at the ground. When it becomes apparent his wife cannot speak, he says slowly, "We were thinking Avonlea."

"Avonlea," Darin says, running a gentle finger along the baby's minuscule nose. "I'm your Uncle Darin, little Mermaid." A tiny hand waves vaguely out of the blanket, batting at his large one. Eventually, Amaya's sobs subside, and she manages a watery smile as she watches Darin cooing over her daughter. Beck murmurs something in her ear, and she snuggles her head against his shoulder.

"Can I hold the baby?" I ask, feeling a little left out.

"Not yet," Darin retorts, cuddling the baby closer. "She's happy."

"Darin!"

"I've only had her for a couple of minutes," he protests.

I resist the urge to appeal to Amaya, knowing that doing so will make me look like a child begging its mother to arbitrate a dispute with a sibling. I content myself with giving Darin a dirty look.

A loud rap sounds at the outer door. Not a neighbor or relative's knock.

We startle and stare at each other. "Who could it be, Beck?" Amaya gasps.

Zale's voice sounds through the wall. "Papa, someone's at the door!"

Beck gets up slowly and swims out into the hall. Amaya, Darin, and I remain silent and still behind him, straining to hear. In a moment, Beck returns.

"It's a night sentry," he says in his slow voice. "He says he heard rumors of a disturbance at the city gates last night, and an eyewitness says Locklyn was involved. He'd like to speak to her."

My heart gives a painful squeeze. It's Blackwell. I know it. Darin's eyes meet mine. "I'll go with you," he says quickly, swimming after me as I head toward the bedroom door. It is only as I open the door that I notice he is still holding Avonlea.

"No!" I hiss so sharply that he recoils.

"What?"

"You can't bring her out there!" I whisper frantically, pushing at him.

He stares at me for a moment, and then his eyes widen in comprehension. "Good thinking," he whispers back and turns to hand Avonlea to her mother.

Out in the hall, I suddenly hear Fisk's voice, loud and childishly carrying. "Mama, can we see our new baby sister now?"

My heart plummets as my nephews wriggle past us into the room, swarming toward their mother's bed. At the end of the hall, through the half-open front door, lurks the hovering form of Blackwell. I feel Darin's hand at the small of my back, and he guides me quickly out the bedroom door before shutting it firmly behind us. The door muffles the sounds from within but does not shut them out completely. The rotting wood desperately needs to be replaced, but Darin hasn't had time to salvage new wood from a wreck, and Beck and Amaya are too poor to afford a door made from metal or shell.

Darin and I make our way to the front door. Blackwell's leer changes to a grimace when he catches sight of Darin behind me.

"My brother-in-law said you would like to speak to me," I say, staring at him coolly. Darin's big, golden presence behind me seems to infuse me with courage, and I am grateful he allows me to do my own talking.

"Yes," Blackwell says, a slight sneer twisting his features as he looks me up and down. Heat rises inside me as his eyes linger on my discolored forearm, the shark blood soiling my clothing, and the black tear stains streaking my face. "I heard rumors you might have witnessed a disturbance at the city gates last night, and I wanted to collect your . . . official statement regarding the incident."

I force my voice to remain level. "What kind of an incident exactly? The only thing I remember that might interest the law would be an attack perpetrated by two watchmen on a Mermaid who was trying to come into the city." I smile my sweetest smile. "I would love to give you descriptions of them—it might aid you in your search for these thugs." Blackwell's jaw clenches, and I hurry on. "One was fairly nondescript, but the ringleader had greasy black hair that needed a trim." Blackwell's fingers inch toward the ends of his hair. "A scrawny build." Darin gives a well-timed snort behind me and Blackwell flushes. "A dark tail—I can't remember what color—and a horrible scar that looked like a knife wound, disfiguring his whole face."

Blackwell's complexion has gone from its usual pasty white to a nasty puce color. He is extremely self-conscious about his appearance. With a visible effort, he twists his expression into a painful smile. "It sounds like congratulations are in order," he says silkily. "Your sister must have had her baby last night."

I feel Darin shift behind me and force myself not to look back at him for help. What should I tell Blackwell? No one must know that Avonlea is a Crura until Amaya and Beck have decided how to protect her. But people will start to ask questions if the baby never leaves the house. I can't even lie and say the baby hasn't been born yet since Blackwell almost certainly heard Fisk talking in the hall.

I hesitate too long. Blackwell's eyes start to glitter. "Rumor has it your family is cursed to have one Crura in every generation, spindle-shanks. Did your sister just give birth to a mutant?"

I am frozen, but Darin darts past me, his fingers closing hard on

Blackwell's upper arm. "If you call anyone spindle-shanks in front of me again," he says tersely, "you are going to regret it." Blackwell gives a small squeak as Darin's fingers dig into the flesh of his arm. "And I believe you have outstayed your welcome." With a final dig, Darin releases Blackwell, who flashes me a look of pure loathing before swimming away.

Darin steers me back into the house. The moment the door closes, I grab him. "Darin!"

"I know," he says heavily.

"The whole city will know by nightfall."

"I know," he says again.

I give his arm a little shake, desperation coursing through me. "We have to do something."

"The easiest thing would be to take out Blackwell," he mutters.

"Darin. We need a real plan." Silence descends as we hover in the hall, both racking our brains. I struggle desperately to come up with something, but instead the memory of an awful story I heard about a Crura baby being kidnapped and fed to sharks hammers through my head over and over. Finally, I say numbly, "Maybe nothing terrible will happen. Maybe she'll just grow up like me, shunned by normal society."

Darin's eyes suddenly widen. "Locklyn. What if she could live in a society where she was normal?"

I stare at him, feeling heat rush into my face. "You mean . . .? Darin, you're brilliant."

"Why, thank you."

Then the rising bubble of happiness inside me pops. "But how are we ever going to get enough money to send her? If I sell every dugong I own, it won't be enough to pay tuition for a year."

He looks at me. "There's a way."

I stare back at him, feeling dread pool in the pit of my stomach. "You're going to claim that wreck, aren't you?"

"Yes."

I know he knows the risk he is taking. But he's not doing it for the glory. He's doing it for a little blue-haired girl and the brother he loves. In that moment, I want to tell him what an amazing brother and uncle he is and how much I admire him. But I can't find the words. So, all I say is, "Be careful, will you?"

He looks down at me for a moment, and there is something in his eyes that sends warm tingles shooting down my arms and legs. But all he says is, "I'll be back."

The door thuds behind him, and I stay in the hall, staring at it and wishing I could go with him because I want to do something, anything, to help send little Avonlea to Atlantis.

LOCKLYN

EVEN LAND DWELLERS KNOW ABOUT
Atlantis. But to them, it is an island that sank beneath the waves of the
Atlantic Ocean thousands of years ago. A lost civilization. A legend.
A myth. To Merpeople, it is the paradise of the underwater realm.

Most Land Dwellers do not know it, but there are ways for humans
to survive underwater long-term. Plants like respira give the ability to
breath underwater when consumed. Certain jellyfish can be coaxed
with food to envelop the human head, creating an air bubble around
the face. These methods, combined with devices the Atlanteans had
invented for deep sea diving, allowed many to survive after the island
sank to the ocean floor. Many of these humans intermarried with
Merpeople, resulting in the largest population of Crura anywhere
under the sea. In Atlantis, Crura are not despised mutants. They are
respected members of society.

There is a boarding school in Atlantis for Crura children from
other parts of the ocean. This school allows them to grow up as
normal children, rather than being constantly bullied and harassed.
They receive a phenomenal education and grow up to become
teachers, musicians, and doctors rather than as societal outcasts who
perform the most menial work in order to survive. It is the dream of
every loving parent of a Crura in the underwater realm to send their

child to Atlantis. But the price tag is exorbitant. Usually only the nobility can afford to send their Crura children there.

Not only is Atlantis a haven for the Crura, it is also a prosperous trading hub and the center of undersea education, culture, and invention. When the island sank to the seafloor five hundred years ago, its storehouses were filled with gold, silk, weapons, wine, and oil, all extremely valuable commodities underwater which can usually only be obtained from wrecks. The city was also home to some of the most brilliant Land Dwellers ever to live—Sosthenes the Inventor, Cassandra the Vocalist, Plato the Philosopher, and many others sank to the seafloor with Atlantis and devoted their considerable talents to life underwater.

Every Merperson in Undula dreams of going to Atlantis someday. But the trip is expensive and dangerous. It takes fifteen days to reach the sunken island if you can catch a ride with a passing blue whale. If not, the trip goes as quickly as you can swim. And swimming alone through thousands of miles of deserted ocean is courting death. But if Darin claims the wreck he found, there will be more than enough money to secure passage on a blue whale for Avonlea, and to pay tuition for her to attend the school.

I tell myself this over and over as I clean Amaya and Beck's house, play with my nephews, and prepare food for everyone. But fear is a constant undercurrent to my thoughts. I can't shake the feeling that Darin should stay away from that wreck and that something very bad will happen if he doesn't. I tell myself I'm being stupid. I try to believe it.

Shortly before the gates close, I leave the city to check on my dugongs and catch a few hours of rest. I'd promised Amaya I would be back in the morning to help out. As I swim sluggishly through the reef, fatigue washes over me. When I reach my hut, I barely manage to keep my eyes open long enough to milk my dugongs and mumble a few words of praise to Darya for being a good watch dolphin, before I fall onto my bed and sink into an exhausted sleep.

"Locklyn!"

The shout jerks me from my slumber. I sit up dazedly, and focus on the wild face of my brother-in-law.

"Whaaa . . .?" I stammer. Beck has a spectacular black eye and blood dribbles down his face from a cut on his cheek. He holds a bundle in his arms, which he thrusts at me.

"You have to take her," he says wildly.

I accept the bundle. I look down uncomprehendingly at the fuzzy blue head poking out. "Beck." My voice is coated in sleep. "I don't understand."

"I have to go back," he calls over his shoulder, already swimming out the door. "I have to make sure Amaya and the boys are safe. Take care of her, Locklyn." The battered wooden door Darin made from shipwreck wood slams shut.

Still half asleep, I stare at the bundle for a few minutes. Then I lay on my bed with my niece snuggled into my chest, and drift back to sleep.

A few hours later, I am awakened by a mewling cry next to my ear. The cry is muffled, and when I look down, I see that Avonlea has thrashed around until her head was completely buried in the sealskin blanket wrapped around her. Quickly, I sit up and unwrap her. Her tiny face screws up as she flails her fists and wails.

"Don't worry, I feel like that most mornings too," I tell her as I stand and rock back and forth, jiggling her and crooning under my breath. She quiets for a moment, but the instant I stop singing, she begins bellowing again. I suddenly realize she is probably hungry, so I swim out to the niche near the dugong pen where I keep the pails of milk overnight. At first, I have no idea how to give her the milk since I don't have a baby bottle, but as her shrieks increase in volume, I dip a corner of her sealskin blanket into the bucket of dugong milk and offer it to her. I am relieved when she sucks happily and then squeals for more. After drinking a substantial amount of milk, she falls asleep in my arms still sucking on the corner of her blanket.

I carry her back into the hut and lay her on my bed, then I look around. I still have no idea why I have my niece. Beck's night visit swims hazily through my memory, and my heartbeat quickens as I recall the injuries on his face. Clearly, something bad has happened. Fear jabs through me as I think of Amaya and my nephews. Are they alright? I want to go into the city and find out, but I know I can't bring Avonlea back into Aquaticus. I also can't leave her alone out here.

Hours drag by as I force myself to go through my daily routines. I would usually take the dugongs into the open to graze, but I don't want to bring Avonlea into the dangerous waters outside the reef, so I feed them some of our stored posidonia. Avonlea wakes again and howls for more milk.

"Demanding little princess, aren't you?" I chirrup to her as I feed her more milk off the corner of her blanket. After her second feeding, she seems more awake, so I wrap her in her blanket and tie her to my front with a length of rope before swimming into the reef to look for pieces of coral to make into knives.

The busyness of caring for her helps keep my mind off her family, but as evening draws near, the dread gnawing at my stomach becomes heavier and blacker. I am sitting on the edge of my bed, singing softly as she stretches a tiny fist, when there is a knock on my front door.

The thought flashes across my mind that it could be someone from the city coming for Avonlea. I glance quickly around my bare hut. Where do you hide a baby? The person outside knocks again. I yank open the door to the cupboard where I keep most of my food and gently lay my niece on the empty bottom shelf.

"Shhhh," I whisper as I softly close the door and swim to the front of my hut. Groping with one hand for the coral knife I always carry in my belt, I fling open the front door with my other hand. Beck hovers outside.

"Beck," I gasp in relief, reaching out a hand to draw him inside. "Are you alright? Amaya? The boys? What has happened?"

He sinks onto one of the sitting ledges next to the door, concern in his gaze. "Where is Avonlea?"

"She's here." I swim to the cupboard and retrieve my niece.

"Great blue whales, she's fallen asleep. I wasn't sure who you were," I explain as I gently place the little one in her father's arms. "I was afraid you were someone from the city."

He nods and cuddles his daughter into the crook of his arm, looking down at her. I sit cross-legged on my bed and watch them, fighting the burning questions longing to escape my lips.

Finally, he looks up. "Locklyn, a group of Mermen attacked the house last night." My mouth falls open in horror. "They burst in demanding we hand 'the Crura child' over. There were five of them, and I knew I couldn't fight for long, so I grabbed Avonlea from Amaya and fought my way through them to the front door. I swam out and hid near the city gates until dawn. As soon as the gates opened, I brought Avonlea to you. Amaya and the boys are safe, praise the Wave Master. The Mermen chased after me and Avonlea, and when they lost us, they didn't return to the house."

I stare in silence at my brother-in-law as he bends his thin, pale face over his sleeping daughter. Rage sloshes inside me like pounding ocean waves. I have occasionally felt angry over how people treated me. But never like this.

I clench my teeth and my fists, making a silent vow—the rest of Avonlea's life will not be like this. She will not spend her life being hunted and harmed because of something she cannot help. She will not struggle to make ends meet until the day she dies. She will go to Atlantis. And she will grow up safe and happy and respected. She will not be me.

A knock sounds on the door and Beck looks up, his eyes alarmed. I leap to my feet and swim silently behind the door, drawing my knife as I go. If this is Blackwell looking for Avonlea, I swear I will give him another scar. Gladly. "Who's there?" I call.

"Darin," answers a voice I recognize. My heart leaps and I yank the door open. Darin has purple circles under his eyes, and he is hovering lower in the water than usual. He looks exhausted.

"How did it go?" I demand as I pull him into the house.

He sinks onto the edge of my bed and rubs his eyes. "No problems. Yet. It took me all of yesterday to assemble my team, but the actual work was extremely quick since I told everyone involved I would pay them double if we could harvest the entire wreck before the gates closed for the night. We delivered the last load of treasure to the castle fifteen minutes ago."

Relief courses through me and I smile widely. "This is it then! Did you get your cut?"

"Yes."

The way he says it makes me study him more closely. He isn't just sagging with exhaustion. His jaw is tensed, and I can see that his fingers tremble slightly when he brushes the hair out of his face. I catch his eye, trying wordlessly to ask what is wrong, but he shakes his head slightly and turns to his brother.

"They're about to close the gates, Beck."

Beck nods and rises. He swims to me and lays Avonlea tenderly in my arms, then moves slowly away. "Amaya will come tomorrow if she is strong enough," he says. "Thank you. Both of you."

The door closes behind him. But for once, his laconism fails to bother me. The look on his face as he bent over Avonlea was worth a thousand words.

"Darin," I say as the door bangs behind Beck. "What happened?"

He runs a hand through his hair. "Nothing happened," he says hesitantly. "But something was missing."

I perch on the bed beside him, cradling Avonlea, my heart pounding, though I don't yet know why. "What do you mean?"

"There was a harp," he says. "It was very distinctive. Wood inlaid with gold and pearls. I noticed it the first time I visited the ship because when I was planning to harvest the wreck, I remember thinking I should request it as part of my cut and give it to you to play with your singing." He pauses, and I give him a small, tight smile. "But when we arrived at the wreck yesterday morning, it was gone. I questioned my entire crew after we harvested the ship. None of them had seen anything like the instrument I described. They're honest men, Locklyn. Someone else must have found the wreck and taken the harp, probably as evidence to show their queen."

My heart squeezes as I realize what he is saying. "It might just have been a scavenger," I say as evenly as I can.

"Maybe." His tone is flat, and I know he doesn't believe it any more than I do. He rises, fumbling in the money pouch at his waist. "Since the harp was gone, I brought you this instead."

His fingers brush the palm of my hand as he gives me the gift. Interlocking silver chains sparkle with chips of sapphire the same color as my hair, and my smile is as wide as a fringehead's when I look back up at him.

"It's an anklet," I say.

"Wear it," he says. "Make all the other Mermaids wish for a pair of legs."

Then he is gone.

7

DARIN

SITTING AT THE BAR OF THE SHARK'S
Fin, fingers wrapped tightly around the cup in front of him, he
stares down into the rubicund liquid. With the gold clinking in his
pouch after his visit to the palace, he could easily afford the best
the inn offers. But cheap wine gets you drunk just as quickly as
the expensive stuff. And tonight, oblivion croons his name with an
irresistible siren song.

"Rough day?" a voice says beside him, and he turns slightly
to see a Mermaid with purple, shoulder-length hair. She is pretty
enough, with her large, dark eyes fringed with long, silky lashes,
and her slender torso curving into an aquamarine tail sparkling
with adhered pieces of sea glass. It isn't her fault that to him, beauty
is a pale, heart-shaped face framed with wavy blue hair and eyes
that change color with every mood. *I'm really not into girls with
tails anymore.*

"You could say that," he responds, turning back to his drink. She
moves closer, and he stares pointedly into the clay cup in his hand.

"I know the Shark's Fin isn't exactly high class, but they sell
better drinks than that." She leans casually against his shoulder.

"I know," he says, not bothering to look at her as he lifts the cup,
draining it in one gulp. He catches the bartender's eye and nods

slightly, inviting him to top it off again. The big Merman, who has been using shell tongs to squeeze juice from a succulent plant into a proofing jar, pauses. He carefully places the succulent in the middle of an orderly row at the front of the bar, halfway between a fattig plant, which produces the cheapest wine, and a traub plant, whose juice is used to make lecker, an underwater delicacy. Reaching under the counter for a jug of fattig wine, the bartender swims over, but before he can start pouring, the girl places a hand over the cup's mouth. She is wearing several rings made of sea glass, and her hands are soft and smooth. Clearly, she comes from the upper classes.

"Let me get you something better," she says, a smile sparkling in her voice. "I can afford it, and then I won't have to stand by and watch you drink muck like this."

He jerks the cup from beneath her hand and fixes his tawny, golden eyes on her. She startles backward, and a crimson blush colors her cheeks.

"Since I just claimed the biggest wreck in a hundred years, money isn't a problem for me." His voice is so low, it is almost a growl. "But I only drink expensive wine when I *want* sparkle added to the world around me." Glancing pointedly at her scintillating tail, he turns back to his refilled cup. He expects her to swim away, crushed by his harshness. Instead, her fingers clamp onto his bicep.

"Master of the Waves!" she gushes. "You're Darin Aalto! My father bought a diamond ring for my mother from that wreck you found near Stargazer Ridge. I've wanted to meet you for so long—"

She breaks off mid-gush as he rises and pushes his way toward the door at the back of the room.

"Darin! I'm sorry! I didn't mean to imply anything about your financial status. I just wanted to buy you a drink!"

Without a backward glance, he thrusts his hand into the pouch at his belt and drops a golden coin into the hand of the Merman at the door, before shoving it open with his shoulder. A roar of sound hits him as the door bangs shut. A Merman holding a crab shell in one hand and a squid-ink pen in the other darts forward.

"Care to take a bet on the outcome of the fight, sir?"

He stills his breath. "Who's fighting?"

"We have four different octopi here tonight—a mimic, a blanket, a common, and," he pauses for dramatic effect, "a blue-ringed."

"What?"

The man gives a delighted chuckle, wiggling his tail ecstatically. "I know!"

"Who would be fool enough to go up against a blue-ringed?"

The man taps his pen on his shell importantly. "That you will see for yourself in a moment. We've just had a volunteer. He's beaten all three of the others. Easily. Less than two minutes per fight."

Darin turns and searches the crowd of jostling Merfolk. At the center of the room, a tightly woven kelp net floats in a dome, creating a circular arena. A slim figure bobs in the heart of the ring, undulating black tail keeping him aloft. His back is to Darin, who catches a glimpse of a thin string wrapping around the back of the stranger's skull, barely visible in his wavy dark hair.

What?

Then the octopus wrestler turns, lifting his hands in acceptance of the crowd's screaming adulation. Darin sees he is wearing a close-fitting silver mask, studded with black opals around the eye sockets. Clearly, business has been lucrative.

"Sir?" The bookie taps his pen against the rim of his crab shell pad expectantly.

Darin glances back at the slim dark figure. Wrestling a blue-ringed is insanity. But tonight, insanity doesn't sound so bad.

Untying the money pouch at his waist, Darin holds it out to the bookie. "I'll bet on him," he says, jerking his head toward the Merman in the arena.

The bookie's eyes go wide. "All of it, s-sir?"

A cynical smile twists the corners of Darin's mouth. "All of it," he says. "I have a feeling that money is going to be the least of my problems in the near future." And he swims away, pushing through the crowd toward a slightly emptier spot at the arena's edge.

Glancing to his left, he sees a Merman wearing thick walrus-hide gloves, struggling to hold a small octopus whose golden hide is sprinkled with black-rimmed azure circles, giving it the hideous look of being covered with hundreds of wide, unblinking eyes.

His insides clench, and for a moment, he closes his own eyes. The weight that settled deep within as he handed in the last of the treasure to the king's steward at the palace gates has only been growing, pressing on his insides with a cold, heavy ache. He had hoped a few drinks might melt the dread, but as he opens his eyes to gaze unseeingly before him, it is heavier than ever.

Maybe Locklyn was right, and the harp was taken by scavengers. But his gut says otherwise. The harp was by no means the most valuable piece of treasure on that ship. So, what scavenger would take it and leave everything else?

Dark thoughts crowd his mind. Arrest. A trial. Charges of treason. Conviction. A windowless room. Ricocheting flight from wall to wall of the tiny room to escape the pursuit of a small golden octopus. The inevitable sleep with no waking.

I am not afraid of dying. Death is just a door, leading to the realm where we will see the Wave Master face-to-face. But what of those he would leave behind? Amaya and Beck, who are barely able to feed their children, even with the shark meat he brings every few weeks, which is the only help they will accept. Fisk and Ren and Zale, who will never have the courage to try anything but weaving seaweed nets like Beck if they see their uncle end his life as a convicted criminal. Avonlea, who will be bullied and harassed every day of her life by people who cannot see how beautiful she really is.

Locklyn.

Locklyn, who has never let him protect her as much as he wanted to.

A shout rises, bringing him back to the present. The handler has released the blue-ringed into the arena, and it immediately darts at the masked Merman waiting in the center of the enclosure. In the open ocean, octopi are not usually aggressive, but wrestling octopi are specifically bred to be ferocious and hostile.

He drifts closer to the enclosure, intrigued in spite of himself.

The black-tailed Merman stays perfectly still as the octopus charges. Then at the last possible moment, he darts to the side, catching the animal by one of its groping tentacles and flinging it with impressive force so it smacks into the kelp ropes surrounding the arena. For a moment, the blue-ringed hangs limply from the kelp net and then disentangles itself and drifts back toward the Merman, who still waits at the center of the ring. It is moving more slowly this time, clearly aware its last tactic had not worked with this particular opponent. Moving in a gradual circle, legs waving, almost carelessly, it slips through the water around the Merman, who is forced to turn as well in order to keep it in view.

After a moment, the octopus darts again, but this time, as the Merman reaches out to grab the tip of a tentacle, it wraps around his wrist. He sucks water in through his teeth as the tentacle jerks, yanking the Merman's captured arm toward the beaked mouth hidden between the octopus's legs. If the blue-ringed can get a bite in, this fellow is finished.

But, with impossible speed, the Merman's free hand closes around the octopus's head. With a shout, he wrenches backward, biceps straining, and rips the rest of the octopus away from the tentacle still twined around his wrist. Then he hurls the seven-legged creature into the kelp netting so hard, it hits with a splatting sound and slides limply to the floor.

The room erupts in gasps and screams. His cheers are among them, admiration swelling. *He should be a Schatzi, though he clearly has a promising career as an octopus wrestler. I would love to work with a man like that.*

The octopus wrestler turns in the center of the arena, arms raised as he waves to the cheering crowd. As he faces Darin's side of the room, the wrestler suddenly freezes, posture faltering as he stares at something beyond Darin. Whirling, Darin sees the group of soldiers pushing their way through the crowd. Toward him.

For an instant, he considers trying to fight his way back to the door. But there is a chance, however slim, that the guards are not coming for him. Darin moves gradually to the side to let them pass, one hand stealing beneath his shirt to the hilt of the coral knife strapped across his chest.

The soldiers don't stop. They swim past, straight toward the netted dome, where the octopus wrestler has darted through the enclosure door, attempting to make his escape. But his fans press around him, clamoring congratulations as the soldiers close in. Turning at bay, he seems to be arguing with the head soldier, who is gesticulating toward his mask. Finally, with a growl of frustration, he reaches behind his head and wrenches the ties apart, letting the mask fall through his fingers onto the seafloor below. He crosses his arms and glares sullenly around the room at the audience, which has gone completely silent. Darin stares at him, jaw dropping. *I know him.* No wonder the mask looked familiar. *The little brat got it from me, after all.*

It's Prince Conway.

8

LOCKLYN

THE SOUND OF CONCH SHELLS JERKS
me awake. My head snaps up and I stare wildly around, my eyes
taking in the dugongs grazing peacefully on all sides. Panic surges
and I grope at my midsection, my heart rate slowing as I feel the
small body tied securely with a sealskin blanket. I softly stroke
Avonlea's downy little head.

"I can't be lying down on the job like this," I tell her. "If you
wanted to actually rest at night, that would be a big help. I know
you don't understand, sweetheart, but most of us aren't as lucky as
you—able to laze the whole day away after missing a night's sleep."

Darya curves through the water toward us, chittering. "I know,
I know," I say, scratching her nose as she nuzzles against me.
"You've been a superb watch dolphin. I really do appreciate it."

As my mind clears, I suddenly remember what woke me in the
first place and peer into the dark water. Conch shells? No one uses
those except . . . except . . . My heart thuds against my ribs as I hear
the deep, melodious sound wavering toward me again, nearer this
time. I leap to my feet and whistle as softly as I can, the same march
I use to bring the dugongs home every night. The beasts raise their
ponderous heads, mouths still chewing posidonia, before starting

to drift slowly through the water. I whistle slightly louder, with more urgency, and they grudgingly pick up the pace.

"Darya, take them home," I whisper, patting her sleek tail.

She gives a farewell chitter and zooms after the retreating dugongs, chivvying the stragglers.

I kick upward from the sandy ocean floor and paddle toward the edge of the reef. I can hear the conch shells getting louder and a rustling, swishing sound draws near, as if a large group of people swims behind me. Heart hammering, I swim faster. If this is who I think it is, I don't want to be caught alone outside the reef with a Crura baby strapped to my chest.

Legs burning, I kick as hard as I can and cover the last few yards to the reef. Darting behind a sizable outcropping of coral, I press myself against the rough surface, trying to quiet my breathing. The next time the conchs sound, they are so close that I know I must have barely reached the reef in time. Slowly, I peer around the edge of my hiding spot.

A chariot pulled by six enormous seahorses cuts through the water, surrounded by an entourage of more than twenty Merpeople. More specifically—Mermaids. Their skin is deep brown, and their hair and tails are mostly shades of green or black. Except for the Mermaid on the chariot. Her silvery-white hair is tied back in seven complicated braids that flow through the water behind her, and the scales of her tail are a white so pure, they seem to shine in the dark.

I don't need the sapphire-studded silver circlet in her hair to identify her. This is Ginevra Kaveri, who became the Nebulae warrior queen when she was ten years old. I have taken some pains never to meet her or any of the Nebulae face-to-face. Nebula and Undula have been enemies for centuries. Only by turning a blind eye to the frequent raids on the outskirts of his kingdom by the tribe of warrior women has King Malik managed to keep a tenuous peace. On the other hand, Ginevra has been itching for a fight for years, and it has long been known in Aquaticus that the Nebulae would attack given the slightest provocation.

And, I realize, my stomach plummeting to my toes, Ginevra

would almost certainly regard a richly laden wreck on the edge of her kingdom being harvested without the Nebulae as a much more than slight provocation.

Ginevra turns her head suddenly, staring straight at the shadow of the coral spike where I lurk. Our eyes meet and my heart leaps into my throat. Her eyes are a brown so dark, they are almost black. And they are cold. As cold as the ice caps I've heard float on the waves in the North Sea. For an instant we stare at each other, and then I duck backward into the shadows of the coral outcropping, one arm wrapped tightly around a sleeping Avonlea. My free hand gropes for my coral knife. But I know I can't fight them all off, so I pray to the Wave Master with everything I have that they will not stop.

Minutes tick by and I stay frozen, hovering in the shadows, not daring to look out again. My thoughts skip around like dolphins bouncing on the ocean's surface.

I need to get to Darin.

But I can't leave Avonlea. And I can't bring her into the city with me.

Could the Nebulae be here for another reason? Is it possible they don't know about the treasure?

Finally, deciding they must be gone, I leave my hiding place and streak through the reef. As soon as I near my hut, I begin to sing softly, calling Darya. Almost instantly, she appears from the direction of the dugong paddock, her tail fluttering in welcome. I am already working at the knots in the sealskin blanket.

"Take her into the house and keep her safe," I croon to Darya, using the long ends of the blanket to tie Avonlea snugly around the dolphin's middle. Opening the door to my hut, I shoo her inside, duck in after her, and rummage in a drawer for the bottle Darin gave me. Such things only come from wrecks, and I know he must have spent a fortune on it, but since it was for Avonlea, I accepted (not to mention the fact that feeding with a blanket corner was growing cumbersome). I curl my niece's tiny hands around the bottle and nuzzle the nipple against her lips until she begins to suck. With a last glance over my shoulder, I slip out the door again, cringing inwardly at the thought of what Amaya would say if she knew I was leaving her precious daughter in the care of a dolphin. But Darya cares for my baby dugongs all the time. And I have no choice.

Five minutes later, I am banging on the metal door of Darin's house. He lives in a neighborhood near the palace, on a street lined with Schatzi mansions. His house is much smaller than I know he can afford. He claims he doesn't want to pay to have a massive house cleaned, but I know he hates the arrogance and pretension that characterizes most of his fellow Schatzi.

When there is no answer, my heart skips in fear. It is impossible that Ginevra could have arrived at the palace and lodged her complaint with King Malik in time for him to blame Darin and have him arrested before I got here. But where is he?

Memory strikes and I dart toward the large orange sea anemone clinging to the porch pillars. I gently stroke its tentacles so that it folds in on itself. When it reflexively reopens, I plunge my hand into its squishy interior, releasing a satisfied *ah* as my fingers brush metal.

The key opens the front door in a trice, and I speed down the hall to Darin's bedroom. The door bangs as I fling it open and burst in. Darin sits up in bed, rubbing his eyes. With his blond hair sticking out in all directions, and his eyes crinkled from sleep, he looks younger somehow. His sealskin blanket slides down and my heart flips as I see he is not wearing a shirt. Many of the more toned Mermen don't, but Darin always does. Though, as I can clearly see, he has no need to be ashamed of his physique.

Blood rises in my face and Darin glances down at himself, then yanks the blanket up to his chin, his own face going red. "Locklyn," he croaks, "I don't remember letting you in."

I snort a laugh and the tension breaks. "I heard you telling Beck where the spare key is. And I did knock for about five minutes first." The fear that had receded for a moment comes swelling back as I remember why I was pounding on his door in the first place. "Darin, the Nebulae are here!"

He was sitting with his head in his hands, like he had a headache, but now he glances up. In the bluish-green light of his seaweed lamp, his face pales to an eerie, glowing white.

I remember Ginevra's tail and my heart squeezes.

Darin just lowers his head again. "Not really," he says quietly.

"No, I'm kidding!" I snap at him. "Because jokes about you getting arrested and tried for treason against the crown are really hilarious right now!"

He swears under his breath, shaking his head, and then stops abruptly, as though the motion hurts him. "Of course not," he agrees. "I just hoped you might be a figment of my hungover mind."

I stare at him. Amaya told me Darin drank heavily in his younger years, but that he stopped as soon as Zale was born. He said he wanted to set a good example for his nephew. He meets my eyes and his shoulders sag.

"Don't look at me like that, Locklyn."

I open my mouth and then close it again. "Okay."

With a frustrated growl, he pushes himself out of bed and scoops a gray, long-sleeved shirt off the floor, pulling it over his head. Then he faces me, arms folded across his chest, brow thunderous. "Say what you want to say, Locklyn."

I bite my lip, then give a little shrug and say lightly, "You know I'm not a big proponent of alcohol as a problem solver. I've seen too many emaciated Crura begging anyone who passes by for money because they've become enslaved to drink, unable to see that rather than solving their problems, it is adding to them."

His frown deepens. "Do you really think I'm somehow enslaved to alcohol? It was a one off."

I hate it when he's angry at me. "No, no," I say soothingly. "I just . . . don't want you to make choices you regret the next day." I swim toward him, putting on my most winning smile. "Come on, Darin. I'm practically your sister. You must admit I have the right to nag you a little."

I reach out to put my hand on his arm, but he turns away. Hurt, I retreat, completely taken aback by the fact that he looks even angrier than he did before.

"It won't happen again," he says shortly. "You're right. It's weak to try to forget your problems."

"Darin . . ." I start, wanting to apologize for offending him.

"I have to go." The words are abrupt. "I need to find as many of my team members as I can so they can vouch that I told the steward the wreck was on the border between Undula and Nebula. And it will increase my chances of being heard if I go to the palace, rather than waiting to be hunted." He turns toward the door.

"Darin!" I manage to grab hold of his shirt. "Darin, I'm sorry. You have enough on your plate without me telling you off. I should have kept my mouth shut. Please, forgive me." My voice cracks. "You can't leave like this. Not with what might happen. Not before we're friends again."

He pauses, then looks back at me. "There's nothing to forgive, Locklyn," he says. "And as I've been your friend since the day you were born, nothing you can ever say or do is going to make me stop." He gives me a sad but sweet smile, the deep grooves of his dimples carving lines in his handsome face, and then he swims out the door and down the hall.

Blinking back sudden tears, I follow him, my heart heavy. As I exit the house, I see a sight that makes me stop in my tracks. Darin is surrounded by a group of soldiers who are chaining his hands behind his back. He glances up at me through the blond hair still falling around his face and jerks his head ever so slightly, motioning me back inside.

But before I can slip out of sight, the lead soldier looks up and sees me. His face twists into a sneer. "I see how it is, Aalto. Spending the time you aren't committing treason against the crown with a spindle-shanks in your bed." Darin's face darkens with fury, but he says nothing. The captain glances between him and me. "Take her too."

"What?" The word explodes out of Darin as he twists to glare at the captain. "She's done nothing!"

"Her kind don't need to *do* anything, Aalto," the captain says smoothly. "The guests visiting King Malik from the kingdom next door hunt Crura for sport. Maybe they'll be interested in putting on a little show for us."

I see Darin's biceps strain against the chains binding his wrists as two soldiers grab me and loop chains around my wrists as well, pulling them so tight the metal cuts into my flesh.

Fear should be uppermost in my mind. But I feel strangely calm. Darin is here. And I think part of me will always believe he is able to prevent anything truly terrible from happening.

Darin leans toward the captain, his voice low, but still audible. "Listen, my storeroom is full of Land Dweller treasure. You and each of your men can take your pick if you let the girl go."

The captain glances sharply at Darin for a moment and then coughs out a scoffing laugh. "That would be nice, if all of your property weren't forfeit to the crown, Aalto. But it's good to know you have a soft spot for the wench. If you prove troublesome, she will provide us with some excellent leverage." He turns to the rest of the soldiers. "Let's go. They're waiting for us at the palace."

9

DARIN

MY WILDEST NIGHTMARE COULD NOT
have compared to this. Ever since finding out about the missing
harp, a part of him had known they would come for him. But he
never could have foreseen that Locklyn would get arrested as well.

Locklyn's face is set and still and she betrays no sign of fear,
but a slight flicker remains behind her eyes, which have shifted to
a pale, almost opaque, gray. He thinks of Blackwell's treatment
of her. There is no way Locklyn can expect to receive justice—not
with the hatred most Merfolk bear toward the Crura. And there is
nothing he can do to protect her.

They are hustled through the streets toward the palace, a
towering structure constructed of pure white stone that glows
eerily in the dark water. Locklyn and her guard swim ahead, and
rage stabs through Darin as he sees the guard purposefully moving
too quickly for her, jerking the chain around her wrists so that
it cuts deep, leaving red welts. Suddenly, she wrenches sideways,
wrapping her legs around a seahorse hitching post. Her guard is
pulled to a momentary stop.

"Zale!" she yells. "Zale!"

Pivoting, he sees his oldest nephew huddled in the shadow of a
nearby building, eyes filled with terror. The guard utters an oath

and yanks Locklyn's chain, pulling her slightly forward, but she tugs back, pulling them to a halt once more.

"Zale, tell your father to go to my house!"

Zale's eyes widen with sudden comprehension, and understanding dawns on Darin as well. Locklyn must have left Avonlea there. His nephew gives a jerky nod and shoots off toward home.

Locklyn's guard has been trying to drag her forward, but with her clinging like a barnacle to the post, he has had little success. As she relaxes, watching Zale zipping away, the guard wrenches her toward him and slaps her so hard that her head whips to the side.

"Hold us up again and I'll give you worse than that!" he screams in her face.

The slight trickle of blood from the fresh cut in her lip nearly causes Darin to lose control. He wants to sink an elbow into his guard's stomach and make a break for it. But there are too many guards. And he has a plan that, if it works, might not save himself, but will definitely save Locklyn.

They are dragged through the double doors at the front of the castle, which are gold-studded with shells and precious stones. But he notices several divots that mar the gold, making it look as though someone has dug gems out. It seems the whispers about the royal family's financial status are more than just idle gossip.

As he and Locklyn are hustled toward the silver doors which lead into the throne room, a young Merman swims out, his face suffused with anger. Darin ducks his head, hoping the youth will swim past, but the motion catches the other's eye, and he turns. A smirk tilts his lips.

"Aalto. Fancy meeting you under these," the Merman glances at the guards and then at Darin's chains, "circumstances."

"Your Highness, if I remember rightly, the last time we met in these circumstances, our positions were reversed."

A flush rises up the Merman's cheeks toward his wavy hairline. "Given your current position, Aalto, I'd watch your tongue."

Darin begs the Wave Master to help him control his mouth. Now is not the moment to antagonize the royal family. Not if he wants to save Locklyn. Inclining his head slightly, he forces his lips to form words. "I apologize, Prince Conway. I spoke out of turn."

For an instant, the cocky coolness in Conway's eyes wavers, and the insecurity that has controlled the eighteen-year-old prince of Aquaticus since he was old enough to feel it, peers out. But then the moment passes, and his eyes fill with disdain once more.

"Don't let it happen again," he says and sweeps up the curving staircase to the left.

The guards chivvy Darin and Locklyn through the silver doors and into a long hall lined with statues of the previous monarchs of Undula. Blown-glass orbs filled with glowing seaweed hang from the ceiling at regular intervals, casting clear, white light over the scene.

King Malik sits on a throne of scarlet coral at the end of the hall, one hand gripping the symbolic golden trident, the other stroking his black beard, which is threaded with gray. The last few years have taken their toll on him, but his shoulders are still broad, and his muscular green tail glistens in the light. In the throne beside him—once occupied by Queen Kendra before she died giving birth to Conway's younger brother Etan—lounges Ginevra, her pearly tail tapping lightly on the dais, impatience written in every line of her face.

As the silver doors swing shut, her dark eyes sweep the prisoners and widen when they land on Darin. He stares back at her, forcing himself not to look away, unable to read the emotion in her eyes. She is beautiful, with an exotic beauty seldom seen in Aquaticus. After a long moment, she turns and addresses Malik.

"So, this is the Treasure Hunter?" Her voice is a surprise. For a queen famed throughout the underwater realm for her ruthlessness, it is strangely high and clear, like a little girl's.

"Yes," Malik says, sitting straighter on his throne and fixing Darin with a look of mingled indifference and disdain. "He and a team harvested the wreck we were speaking of and brought the treasure here. I had no interaction with him personally, but my steward swears he never said anything about the wreck being on the border with Nebula."

Darin's eyes flick to the left of the throne, where the steward, a small, ferrety Merman named Wyre, hovers in the shadows. Avoiding his gaze, the steward says in a squeaky voice, "It's true, Your Majesty. Darin Aalto never mentioned the location of the wreck to me."

His hands form a fist, forcing himself to stay calm. Saving Locklyn. That's all that matters now.

"And what have you to say, Treasure Hunter?" Ginevra asks.

"He cannot be trusted, Ginevra," Malik interrupts. "There is no reason a thief should not be a liar as well. Rest assured he will be dealt with."

Ginevra turns back to him and lifts a hand, which glitters with silver rings. "And how will the rest of this situation be 'dealt with,' Malik?"

Malik's eyes flicker for an instant. "Of course, now that we know where the wreck was discovered, we will deliver half of the treasure over to the Nebulae at once." He makes a small gesture to Wyre, who snaps his fingers. A door below the dais opens, and a group of servants enters carrying a chest. At a sign from the steward, they set it down before the throne and throw back the lid. Ginevra leans forward slightly to survey the contents.

Curious, Darin leans in as well, craning his neck to catch a glimpse of the chest's contents. The sight of what is inside almost makes him burst out laughing. He catches Locklyn's eye for a moment before she looks away, lips tightly compressed.

The pile of treasure in the chest is pitifully small. Ludicrously small. If Ginevra received a report of the wreck's size that was in any way accurate, she will know instantly how badly she is being ripped off. He looks toward the dark young woman sitting on the dais, and the sight of her expression causes the laughter to die in his throat.

Silence swells and billows like an icy current as Ginevra continues to gaze into the chest. Malik begins to shift uncomfortably on his throne, but he cannot seem to find the nerve to speak. Darin catches Locklyn's eye again and mouths, "I have a plan."

To his surprise, she gives him a wry smile and mouths back, "So do I."

His heart drops, but before he can do anything to communicate that she must not, under any circumstances, try some crazy scheme that puts her in danger in order to save him, Ginevra leans back in her throne.

"This is half the treasure you received from the wreck that was harvested this week?" Her voice is still high and young-sounding, but there is a menace in it that sends chills racing up and down Darin's spine.

Malik's free hand tightly grips the arm of his throne, and his eyes dart momentarily to Wyre, who avoids his gaze, staring at the floor beneath him. There is another long moment of silence, and it is unclear which horn of the dilemma Malik will choose to impale himself on—admitting he lied and accepting the consequences, or continuing to espouse a story that is so patently false.

At length, Malik says with an unconvincing heartiness in his voice, "Of course, it is not half the treasure! My son, Conway, had some—ahem—pressing debts that needed to be settled—young blood, you know—and since we weren't aware at the time that all the treasure was not ours to dispose of as we saw fit, we used a little over half to deal with them. What you see now is merely a deposit. We will, of course, pay the difference as soon as another wreck is discovered." The smile he flashes toward Ginevra does not reach his eyes.

"I'm afraid that isn't satisfactory." Ginevra's voice is still light and pleasant, but her dark eyes shine like chips of obsidian. "My people have no reason to trust that we would receive our fair share. Indeed, it seems very much as though you were attempting to pass this," she waves contemptuously at the open chest below her, "pittance off as half of what was described to me as the most fabulous wreck to be discovered in a century. And as someone wisely told me, there is no reason a thief should not be a liar as well."

Malik's face flushes an ugly, blotchy red. "I would watch your tongue, if I were you. In case you hadn't noticed, my girl, you and your retinue are alone in Undula territory. I would recommend refraining from unfounded accusations."

Ginevra laughs in his face. Her laughter, like her voice, is clear and lilting, completely at odds with the aura of menace she exudes. "And you really think if you dared to lay a finger on me, every warrior in Nebula would not be at your borders tomorrow and razing Aquaticus to the ground the day after that?"

The muscles in Malik's face tighten. He is cornered. His eyes narrow. "What exactly do you want?"

Ginevra smiles. The expression does nothing to enhance her beauty. "What I want," she says softly, "are rubies the size of my fist, overflowing chests of gold, innumerable barrels of honeyed mead, and bolts of silk piled as high as this palace. According to my sources, that is the share Nebula is due. So, this is what I propose, Malik." She points at Darin. "You claim this Schatzi discovered the original wreck and lied to you about the location. My offer is this—if he can find another wreck of comparable worth, harvest it, and return with the contents in a month's time, I will leave your city standing. If not, I will return and exact payment from every man, woman, and child in this city, starting with you and your worthless offspring."

A harsh laugh echoes through the room and Darin turns his head to see that Conway has reentered the hall and now hovers near the doors, a contemptuous smirk on his face. "Still bitter that I refused your proposal, Ginny?"

At Conway's words, Ginevra pales. For an instant, her lips part as though she is about to spew venom all over him. Then with visible effort, she turns back to his father, and says, "Unlike you, Malik, I tell no lies. These are my terms. Take them or not—it matters little to me. If you refuse, my people will merely attack your kingdom a month earlier."

Malik glares at her for a moment and then looks at Darin. "I hope for your sake that the Wave Master tosses another wreck into your lap, Aalto. Because if you fail, I promise that every member of your family, from the oldest doddering fool to the youngest infant, will spend the rest of their short lives toiling over the flames of Oro."

Relief floods through Darin. He was not forced to play his trump card. And if this quest is successful, Locklyn will still go free. Before he can say a word, a voice says loudly, "I challenge the accuser."

He swivels to Locklyn, who gazes up at the dais, her eyes clear and steady.

"What?" Malik blusters, but Ginevra has gone completely still, her black eyes fixed on Locklyn's gray ones.

"I challenge the accuser," Locklyn says again, lifting her head. "You," she points at Ginevra, "claim Darin lied about the location of the wreck he harvested and that as penalty he must find and harvest a wreck of equal or greater value for you. But I say that Darin is not the one guilty of lying, and in accordance with the laws of the Nebulae, I challenge you to mortal combat, staking my life upon his innocence."

Mortal combat. Locklyn, what have you done?

Ginevra regards Locklyn, her eyes taking in Locklyn's waving, cloth-clad legs. The corners of her mouth rise. "How is it that you know our laws, Crura?"

"Does it matter?" Locklyn says coolly.

Admiration flashes momentarily in Ginevra's eyes, but then it vanishes. "No," she says. "I accept your challenge. As I am sure you know, I, as the one being challenged, get to select the time and place of our battle, as well as the weapons with which we will fight. I declare this duel will take place immediately, in the central square of Aquaticus, and we will battle with nets and spears, in the manner of my people."

She'll be killed.

With a yank, Darin pulls away from his guard, dragging the chain through his slack hands, and throws himself at Locklyn's guard, using his still manacled fists to punch the Merman hard in the face. The guard drops Locklyn's chain as he staggers away from her.

"Go!" Darin shouts.

"No!" she retorts and doesn't move. "You told me a wreck that big hasn't been found in over a century! I'm not letting you go on some hopeless quest that will probably get you killed. Not if I can stop it."

Frustration mounting, Darin suddenly feels a hand on his arm, and he flips his tail backward as hard as he can, sending the guard spinning away through the water. "Believe it or not, I can take care of myself, Locklyn," he says. "Take the chance and leave. Now!" He lunges between her and the two guards who are closing in to seize her again.

"I'm not a child, Darin." She remains steadfast and her words pierce him.

I know, Locklyn. Wave Master as my witness, I know.

Her voice changes, almost breaks. "And I care about you. Which is why I have to do this." She darts forward, her small white hands latching onto his wrists just above the cuffs. He could throw her off easily. But as he stares down into her eyes, which are now a deep, vivid blue, all he can feel is the pressure of her fingers on the inside of his wrists, sending warmth rippling through his body. There is no way to dislodge her without hurting her. And he would never hurt her.

Other hands, rougher than hers, close around his biceps from behind, and he is yanked backward, away from Locklyn, whose eyes are full of determination and sadness. She turns toward the guards approaching her, laden with a large seaweed net, weighted with small chunks of sandstone and a long, metal-tipped spear.

Ginevra swims down from the dais, collecting her own net and spear from a Nebulae attendant, and heads toward the doors, ignoring Conway, who blows her a mocking kiss as she passes.

At the doors, she turns back, looking around the throne room with her dark, fathomless eyes. "Come," she says, her voice almost bored. "Let's get this over with."

IO

LOCKLYN

AS I LOOK INTO THE DARK EYES OF THE woman across from me, one thought beats through my mind over and over.

Will I kill her?
Will I kill her?
Will I kill her?

With a horrible sinking sensation, I am at the city gates again, my arm trapped between the coral doors as a dark shape slices through the water toward me. I knew then that, in order to stay alive, I was willing to mortally wound the approaching tiger shark. But I have never killed a person before. And I'm not even sure if I can.

Another scene comes to mind. Myself at twelve years old, weeping over the body of a giant squid I had just killed when it tried to snatch one of my dugong calves. Darin had found me and had been terrified I was injured.

"I'm not hurt," I had sobbed to him. "I don't know what's wrong with me."

A strange look had come into his golden-brown eyes as he patted me gently on the shoulder. "You're not a killer, Locklyn," he had said. "And there's no shame in that."

But Nebulae duels are fights to the death, which means someone will die today. And if I don't have the spine to kill Ginevra, that someone will be me.

Malik's voice rings out over the crowd that has gathered on the edges of the city square. "Are both contestants ready to commence fighting?"

Ginevra assents in the same bored voice she used earlier. "Yes."

"Wait," I say suddenly. I grab the slender shaft of the spear in both hands, bring it down hard across my knee, and snap it so I am holding a spearhead with a short wooden handle. Now it's similar to the knife I am used to wielding.

"Now I'm ready." I don't look toward Malik. Darin waits next to him, surrounded by guards, and I can't bear to see the fear on his face. If Darin, who taught me everything I know about combat, thinks I will lose this fight, I really don't stand a chance.

"You may begin." Malik has barely finished his declaration when Ginevra shoots toward me with impossible speed. I throw myself to the side, but I am not quick enough. The folds of her net settle over my body, the weight of the sandstone pieces on the edges dragging me down to the sandy ocean floor. Looking up, I see Ginevra's white tail for an instant before it slams into my side. Stars explode across my vision as I roll over and over across the ocean floor, becoming more entangled in the net, the sounds of the spectators' jeers ringing in my ears.

Terror seizes me a moment before it's obliterated by anger. I am not going to die in the first thirty seconds of this fight. Out of the corner of my eye, I catch sight of the sparkling white of Ginevra's tail again and throw myself sideways, rolling in the opposite direction.

I can barely move my arms because of how tightly the net is wrapped around them, but I manage to wriggle my hand around and use my shortened spear to slash a hole in the seaweed. Thank the Wave Master it is not kelp, which would require minutes of sawing to break through. Thrusting my arm through the hole, I am just in time to slash my spear across the fins of Ginevra's tail, before it smacks into me again. She screams and though the blow is more glancing than it might otherwise have been, I am sent spinning through the water again.

My head spins along with my body, but I continue to hack desperately at the seaweed, thrashing as the strands part, freeing my torso. I feel, rather than see, Ginevra coming at me again. Time to go on the offensive. Instead of trying to evade her, I use my still trapped legs to push off from the ocean floor. As I shoot toward her, I stab my spear toward the shining white mass of her tail. But, to my horror, instead of penetrating her glossy white scales, my shortened spear glances off and falls to the sand below.

I turn my head to see Ginevra's spear hurtling as if in slow motion toward my face. Throwing myself sideways again, I wrap both hands around the spear handle as the head grazes my cheek. Then using Ginevra's momentum against her, I plant both of my feet into her stomach and kick out, wrenching the spear from her grasp.

Righting myself in the water, I see her charging again. I use the spear's shaft to hit her in the side, but it is the wrong move. She is larger and heavier than I am, so instead of reeling end over end through the water, she merely flinches and latches onto the shaft, attempting to wrench it out of my hands.

In my mind, I hear Darin's voice saying, "How many times have I told you not to get close to an opponent who is bigger than you?" So, instead of allowing her to use the spear to drag me toward her, I abruptly let go and drop to the ocean floor, crouching low and scooping up my fallen spear. Because of her lack of feet, she will only be able to get so close to the bottom, so I wait until she dives headfirst, her spear aimed and ready. At the last possible second, I push off the bottom again, slashing her shoulder as I speed past, while the force of her attack causes her spear to embed in the ocean floor.

Turning sharply in the water, I look back to where Ginevra struggles to pull her spear out of the sand. The water around her is tinged with red from the wounds on her shoulder and fins. My heart catches. Now is the moment when I should dart forward and bury my spear into her exposed side.

I can't. You were right, Darin. I'm not a killer.

A thought occurs and I dip downward again, scooping up my broken spear shaft. Stuffing my shortened spear into the back of my pants, and wielding the shaft with both hands, I flash forward and bring it crashing into the back of her skull with all my might.

She lets out a moan and flounders, sinking toward the ocean floor. I watch her crumple and relief courses through me. The spear shaft slips from my limp fingers and I face Malik. My eyes meet Darin's, expecting to see relief and elation, but instead they reflect anxiety as they fix on a point just below me.

Fingers latch around my ankle. Trying not to panic, I quickly pull my spear from the back of my pants, reaching down to slash at the attacker, but she grabs the blade with her free hand, wrenching it out of mine, despite the self-inflicted cuts she suffers.

She yanks my leg hard, wrapping both arms around my torso, and uses her superior weight to push me down, against the ocean floor. There she presses me, one hand around my throat, the other trailing dots of blood while holding my blade high, poised to deliver the death blow.

I thrash, attempting to throw her off, but she squeezes my throat and black spots swim near the edges of my vision. Stilling, I look up at her through the haze. Her teeth are bared, but when our eyes meet, something shifts in the depths of her dark gaze. And, for one mad moment, I wonder if Ginevra, the warrior queen of the Nebulae, is not a killer either.

Then the look is gone, and I close my eyes, thanking the Wave Master that death will almost certainly be swift. But the blow doesn't come. Instead, I hear shouting above me, and my eyes fly open as Ginevra drags me upright, pressing the spear's tip into my side.

"Don't come any closer," she warns.

To my dismay, I see that Darin has broken free of his captors and is streaking toward us, chains trailing behind him. I feel the knife's point penetrate and clamp my teeth to keep from crying out.

Darin jerks to a halt as the misty cloud of red spreads away from my side. "Stop!" he demands. "You must not kill her!"

I feel Ginevra's blade pushing deeper and can't restrain the moan that escapes my lips. "Oh?" she says. "And why is that?"

His face contorts, but his voice is steady as he answers. "Because she knows where the Lost Treasure of Llyra is. And she is going to lead me there."

DARIN

THIS WAS THE PLAN. FROM THE
beginning, he had intended to use this claim as leverage to force
Malik to release Locklyn. Then Darin could go treasure hunting
rather than have his "treachery" punished with blue-ringed venom
or a trip to Oro.

Before Locklyn challenged Ginevra to mortal combat, he had
intended to say he was the one who knew where Llyra's Lost
Treasure was. It would not have been a lie, nor is the claim that
Locklyn knows the location a lie either. They both know someone
who knows where it is.

He tenses his whole body to keep still, while the water around
Locklyn becomes tinged with scarlet. Her face is so pale, it looks
like the reflection of the moon he once saw rippling on the waves
when he visited The Surface.

Everything inside him longs to throw himself at Ginevra, wrest
the spear from her hands, and free Locklyn. But the most likely
thing he would accomplish by such an attempt would be Ginevra
plunging her blade into Locklyn's heart. He hovers in place,
watching the queen of the Nebulae's face. Darin ignores the guards
behind him, who wait for a signal from Ginevra to seize him again.

Ginevra considers him. "That is a bold claim, Treasure Hunter."

He flicks his tail. "A bold claim is only bold until it is backed with the most fabulous treasure the Undersea Realm has ever seen. Then it becomes a reality overlaid with gold."

Her mouth quirks slightly. Then she pulls the point of her spear from Locklyn's side and shoves her toward Darin.

With his manacled hands, he is unable to catch her, but Locklyn wraps her arms around his neck, tendrils of her blue hair drifting up to tickle his cheeks. Inwardly cursing his chains, he awkwardly props his forearms beneath her, supporting her weight.

"As you can see, the lady is injured." His tone is polite but icy. "Are we free to go?"

Malik's voice slides through the water, and Darin turns to face the king, careful not to dislodge Locklyn. "Not entirely, Aalto. You and the Crura may return to the palace, where you will remain as my *guests*," sarcasm taints the word, "until you are ready to set out on your quest. We wouldn't want you to—ahem—disappear, before you even have a chance to begin."

With that line of reasoning, we might just disappear.

Malik's smile widens, teeth gleaming, as though he has read Darin's mind. "I am sure you won't disappear while on your quest," he says. "Blackwell, one of the gate guards, tells me you've just had an addition to your family. I'm sure you will be most anxious to return and see all of them. In your absence, my soldiers will make it their priority to ensure they are kept . . . safe." He lingers on the word, eyes fixed on Darin's.

He wills his expression to remain neutral. Faces flash through his mind, but unchecked emotions accomplish nothing. Instead, Darin refuses to break eye contact with Malik, willing the king to read his thoughts.

I will be back for my family.

And if I find that you have harmed them in any way, I will make it my life's mission to bring you and your family crashing down from the gilded throne on which you sit.

Malik is the first to look away. "You may go," he says, waving a hand before turning to Ginevra and engaging her in conversation.

Ginevra glances over at Darin with Locklyn dangling limply around his neck, both of them surrounded by the misty red cloud of Locklyn's blood. Ginevra's expression is unreadable. The memory of her pearly tail smashing into Locklyn's slight frame over and over makes him want nothing more than to snatch a knife from one of the nearby guards and send it hurtling to find its mark in the gleaming skin of Ginevra's torso. Maybe that would generate some emotion on her expressionless face.

His thoughts must be visible in his eyes, because Ginevra looks away, the faintest flush of pink rising in her cheeks.

He turns to the guard behind him. "Could I have the use of my hands? I promise I won't disappear."

The guard glances toward Malik, who waves an impatient acquiescence without looking. The moment Darin's hands are free, he loops one arm under Locklyn's legs, cradling her body against him. She looks up, giving him the faintest smile, before closing her eyes and allowing her head to drop onto his chest. She doesn't make a sound, but as he looks down at her, Darin sees an inky tear leak from one eyelid, tracing a green trail along her cheek.

By the time they reach the palace bedroom assigned to her, Locklyn's face is chalky white, streaked with sooty black stains. As he draws back the sealskin blanket on the bed and gently lays her down, she cries out.

"Fetch the palace physician, please," he says tersely to the maid drifting near the door.

Hovering next to the bed, he tries vainly to find words of comfort, while still wrestling with his desire to upbraid Locklyn for getting herself into this state in the first place. Gradually, he notices Locklyn's black shirt has an enormous patch of greater darkness growing on the left side, above her wound. He pulls off his own shirt since cutting the palace's sealskin blankets up for bandages doesn't seem like a good idea under the circumstances. Wadding it up, he presses it hard to Locklyn's side. She moans again.

"I'm sorry," he whispers, glancing toward the door. *Where is that blasted doctor?*

She shakes her head, still not opening her eyes, and reaches to cover his hand with her own, as if to say she knows he is trying to help and not hurt her. The feel of her weak hand covering his and the bravery of the mute suffering etched into her face are too much. He stoops down, brushing the soft, navy strands of hair off her forehead, and presses his lips gently to her clammy skin.

Her breath catches and her hand tightens over his, but just then, a voice sounds from the doorway. "Is this the individual who was injured in a duel?"

Turning, Darin sees a small Merman with mint hair and a wispy goatee hovering over the threshold, a basket of supplies slung over one arm. It is clear from the dull sheen of his scales he is not young.

Locklyn opens her eyes and tries to sit up, but Darin restrains her. She attempts to speak, then stills for a moment again. "Cut in my side," she finally says between breaths. Her voice strengthens with her next words. "Anything else will heal on its own."

The doctor gives her a cursory glance, then turns to Darin. "Was the blade that inflicted the wound straight or serrated?"

"I'm thinking your patient is now perfectly capable of answering any questions you might have, Doctor."

The doctor busies himself with supplies, not looking at Locklyn. "Well? Was it straight or serrated?"

"Straight," she answers.

The doctor sets several vials, a needle, a spool of jellyfish thread, and a knife on the small table next to the bed. "You may wait outside," he tells Darin.

He looks at Locklyn, but when she nods toward the door, he swims slowly out into the hallway, closing the door and propping himself against the wall to wait. Leaning his head back, he closes his eyes, trying to block out the sounds from the next room by pushing his brain to map out a plan to ensure that he, Locklyn, and Beck's family all make it out of this situation alive.

The first move would be to get into and out of the castle tonight undetected. Ginevra gave them thirty days to locate a wreck of equal or greater value. He should start preparations tonight so that he and

Locklyn can set out as soon as she is fit to travel, hopefully in the next day or two.

The next step is to contact Beck and Amaya, to make sure their family is safe and, on the very off chance they are not already being watched, to persuade Beck to move the family out to Locklyn's place and catch a ride on the next blue whale.

After that, Darin should go back to his house and collect any treasure not yet impounded, for journey expenses, and for bribes.

And, finally, he must visit a certain Mermaid. Hopefully she was not exaggerating when she told four young Mermish children stories of her uncle, the greatest Schatzi of all time, who, she claimed, had discovered the location of Llyra's famed wreck.

The door opens, and Darin jerks upright, opening his eyes. The doctor emerges, clutching his basket, distaste on his face.

"How is she?"

The doctor's sour expression morphs into a look of fearful respect as he takes in the bulging muscles of Darin's torso and the tooth-shaped scars that cover his chest and back. "She'll live," he says shortly. "Now, if you'll excuse me."

After the doctor swims off up the hall, Darin enters Locklyn's room.

"Hey," she says, trying to push herself higher up on her pillows.

"Hey," he says, zipping toward her. "Just lie back. You need to rest."

"Stop fussing, Darin." She leans against the headboard and reaches up to push her hair out of her face, wincing as she raises her arm.

"Locklyn, seriously," he says, unable to help himself. "Lie back down. You look awful."

"Thanks," she says flatly.

"I didn't mean it like that. You just got brutalized by that harpy."

"I got in a few good cuts of my own."

Her tone says she's upset about something. "Of course, you did." He grins, hoping to lighten the tension. "But I'm sure she is actually listening to her elders and resting."

Her lips tighten, and she turns away.

He moves closer. "Locklyn?"

She doesn't turn her head. "A 'thank you' would be nice, Darin."

He blinks, completely confused. "Thank you? For what?"

"I didn't just let myself get cut open and tail-thrashed for the sheer joy of it." She sounds irritated. "I did it for you."

"Well, thank you, Locklyn, but if you really want to do something for me, I'd prefer that you never let yourself get tail-thrashed or cut open again." He tries to force a smile into his voice.

There's no reply, so he reaches out tentatively to touch her shoulder. She shrugs his hand away and curls tighter onto her side, pulling the sealskin closer around her shoulders.

An ache grows inside him as he looks down at her hunched form. "Locklyn? What's wrong?"

"Nothing," she says. "I think I'll try to rest, like you suggested."

He hesitates, running a hand through his hair. "Locklyn, I didn't mean to hurt—"

She flips toward him, her face twisting in pain, her eyes a vivid, poisonous green as she glares. "Don't you dare say you didn't mean to hurt my feelings, Darin Aalto. I'm not three."

He opens and closes his mouth, then opens it again. "I know you're not three."

"Do you?" she says, still glaring.

"What? Of course."

"You could try acting like it."

"Locklyn, I have no idea what you're talking about."

Her voice is one of forced calm. "I know you've protected me since I was little, Darin. But I'm not that baby abandoned in the reef anymore. I don't need you to always try to stand between me and the world. Believe it or not, I can look out for myself. And, once in a while, I'd like to be the one risking my life for my friends, not the perpetual protectee."

An exasperated laugh escapes him. "Locklyn, if this," he gestures toward her battered body, "is the result of you 'looking out for yourself,' I think you'll understand why I'd rather be the one looking out for you. You remember spending the night with one arm caught in the city gates, don't you?"

The moment the words leave his mouth, he wants to take them back.

Locklyn's eyes fill with tears. "Well," she says, "I guess it's a relief to learn that you despise me too."

Bewilderment and panic churn as she turns her back on him again, pulling the blanket tightly around her shoulders. "Locklyn," he says desperately. "I didn't mean it like that. I'm sorry, I—"

"Just leave me alone, Darin."

"Locklyn, please. How could you think I despise you? I—" He breaks off a second time.

"What part of 'leave me alone' is unclear?" Her voice freezes his blood.

For a long moment, Darin stares at her small form, curled in on itself as though to guard against further hurt. Hurt he unintentionally inflicted—hurt, apparently, much worse than the wounds on her body. Confused, he turns and silently leaves the room.

LOCKLYN

I LISTEN TO HIM LEAVE, EYES SQUEEZED shut against the burning tears, cheek pressed into the softness of the caddis worm silk sheets. His words pound over and over in my brain, the burning sting of their meaning undiminished by repetition.

If this is the result of you looking out for yourself, I think you can understand why I'd rather be the one looking out for you.

You remember being locked in the city gates all night, don't you?

If you really want to do something for me, don't let yourself ever get tail-thrashed or cut open again.

Stay helpless, Locklyn.

Stay a child.

Because that's how he sees me. As a child. Which is not how I want him to see me anymore.

I want him to see me as a Merwoman. Someone strong. Someone capable. His equal.

I know I'm overreacting. I know he doesn't despise me. He is my friend. My best friend. And because he is my best friend, I wouldn't mind him looking out for me if he would let me do the same for him.

I want him to love and respect me in the same way I do him. Not view me with the indulgent fondness one might have for a seal pup or dugong calf. The fact that there is no one I have a higher opinion of than Darin makes his dismissal hurt even more.

The moment before the doctor came in, when he kissed my forehead, I felt something stir inside me. A warmth. A question. Like the tentacles of a sea anemone unfurling to reveal the softness inside. Feelings I thought I had starved out of existence.

All the time the doctor spent stitching up my side, barely able to hide his disgust at touching a Crura, the pain was background noise in my consciousness, as my soul waited in breathless anticipation for . . . I'm not quite sure what.

But when Darin returned and began to act the concerned older brother, something inside me broke a little. While I wasn't entirely ready to admit what the questioning warmth inside me had been waiting for, an older brother most certainly wasn't it.

The door creaks. I close my eyes tightly, my emotions a weird mix of annoyance and relief. "You really are the most persistent person I have ever met in my life," I say, not turning around. "Some people might find it annoying."

"Why, thank you," says an unfamiliar male voice behind me.

Heart pounding, I launch myself out of bed, hand groping beneath my pillow for my coral knife as I turn to confront the dark figure hovering in the center of my room. "Who are you?"

There is a rustling sound, and a blue-green glow fills the space, emanating from the seaweed in the hand of a dark-haired young Merman with a pale, narrow face. For a moment, I think he is the prince, Conway, but then I see, with a jolt of something halfway between pleasure and surprise, that he is standing on the floor. He is not a Merman. He is a Crura. Like me.

He moves a step closer, and I grip the handle of my knife more tightly, fear replacing the momentary feeling of pleasure. "Who are you?" I repeat.

His lips twitch toward a smile. "Don't you know?"

"I'm not in the habit of asking questions I already know the answers to," I snap. "Would you prefer that I screamed for the guard?"

"The guard let me in," he says. "He's a friend of mine."

My heart sinks. Would the guard have let someone in to take their way with me? I am a prisoner, after all, not a guest.

The dark-haired boy's smile widens and he moves past me, throwing himself down on my bed and propping himself up on his elbow. "I'm surprised you haven't seen me in the parades. My father always insists that I go."

I gape at him, incensed by his air of superiority. "I don't particularly enjoy parades," I say.

"Something else we have in common," the young Crura says, gesturing toward my legs. "I'm Prince Conway."

I stare uncomprehendingly at him for a moment and then shake my head. "Very funny. Who are you really? Conway's Crura twin brother who's been hidden in the castle since birth?"

The boy who claims to be Conway raises his eyebrows. "Because that's more likely than me actually being Conway."

"It is, actually," I say. "Since Conway happens to have a tail."

"Oh, I do have a tail," he replies. "I just don't have it on me at the moment."

I'm starting to think this boy might be insane. "Look," I say, as gently as I can, "I'm pretty tired and I have a long journey tomorrow. Was there something you needed my help with?"

The boy sits up, and for the first time since entering my room, his face wears a serious expression. "Why, yes. I was hoping I could persuade you to let me come with you on your journey."

I stare at him. "I think you must have me confused with someone else."

He smirks. "Oh, sure. Because this castle is full of injured Crura maidens who are supposed to set out tomorrow to find Llyra's Lost Treasure."

I open my mouth, but no words emerge. I take a breath and ask, "Why under the sea would you want to come on a journey that is almost certain to end with the deaths of everyone involved?"

He leans toward me conspiratorially. "Because, they say Llyra's wreck is near the den of the Sea Enchantress."

I almost laugh out loud. According to most legends, Circe's den is the reason no Schatzi who has gone looking for Llyra's Treasure has ever returned. I have no idea who the boy in front of me is, but he is clearly disconnected from reality. Slipping my knife into the back of my pants, I paste a smile on my face. "Hey," I say, "is your room somewhere nearby? I can help you get back there. Going to look for the Sea Enchantress is an idea I would definitely sleep on."

The boy laughs. "You think I'm crazy."

I bite my lip, unsure how to respond. "It sounds to me like you haven't really thought this through," I say at last.

His jaw tightens, erasing the laugh lines from his face. "Oh, believe me, Locklyn, I've thought this through. I've thought about nothing else for years." His use of my name jolts me. He pats the bed beside him. "Sit down." At the look on my face, he raises his hands in a gesture of surrender. "Or don't. But it's a long story, and I thought you might want to be comfortable."

I scrutinize him for a moment, hearing Darin's voice in my head. *Never let yourself be lulled into a false sense of security.* The boy is considerably taller than I am, but he is slender and doesn't appear to be carrying a weapon. I'm pretty sure I could take him in a fight, even if still recovering from the last one. Then again, I, as a short, frail-looking Crura girl who happens to have impressive combat skills, should know looks can be deceiving.

"I think I prefer to stand."

The boy eyes me for a moment, one corner of his mouth quirking up in a smile. "You're really something, you know? No one would guess by looking at you that you could give the most famous warrior queen in the Undersea Realm a swim for her money in a fight."

Heat spreads up my neck, accompanied by a pleasant, tingling feeling.

See, Darin? Someone appreciates the fact that I'm not completely useless at taking care of myself.

The boy leans back, eyes half closed, the blue light from the seaweed giving his face an almost ghostly look. "Much as I wish you were right about the whole Crura twin theory," he says, "the truth is that when their firstborn child was born with legs, my parents decided Undula was not ready for a Crura crown prince. So, they put out the rumor that I was delicate and unable to leave the palace. They then sent messengers secretly to Aenon in Atlantis, whose teacher, Deniz, was a student of the great Sosthenes himself. They commissioned the strangest work that Aenon had ever created—a mechanical, child-sized tail that could be worn over legs and be controlled via a series of levers in the bottom of the contraption.

"When the tail arrived two months later, my parents discovered that Aenon's reputation was well-deserved. The tail was a masterpiece, and when they put it on me, no one, not even my servants and tutors, could tell I had not been born with it. As I grew, my parents commissioned three more tails from Aenon, the last of which I currently wear." His expression changes. "The secret of my 'abnormality' has been well-kept. The handful of people who have accidentally discovered the truth have been shipped off to Oro without delay."

I gasp.

He glances up at me, cocking a brow. "That surprises you? I have begged my father since I learned to talk to send me to Atlantis. My dearest wish is to abdicate the throne to my younger brother and go to a place where I will not have to hide who I truly am. I have never had a real friend. How could I when I would have been forced to lie to them every single day, or else risk them receiving the worst punishment imaginable for the heinous crime of knowing the truth?"

"But why?" I say. "Why won't your parents let you abdicate in favor of your younger brother?"

He frowns. "If you ever tell anyone what I'm about to tell you, you'll end up on the next shipment to Oro."

A chill runs through me. "Got it."

"Etan has hemophilia."

I draw my breath in sharply. "I thought that was a Land Dweller's disease."

Conway coughs out a laugh. "How do you think I got these, love?" He gestures to his long, black-clad legs. "My great-grandfather had a little fling with a peasant girl from a hamlet a day's journey south of here, and when his wife, the queen, was unable to produce an heir, he summoned his son to court and made him king. The peasant girl was—you guessed it—the daughter of Llyra and Marcus's son, Severin."

I stare at him, my mind whirling as I try to process this information. "But," I say slowly, "wouldn't you and I be part of the same generation? How can both of us be cursed?"

He gives a mirthless smile. "Unfortunately, genes apply to everyone. Even if my legs are not a direct result of 'the curse,'" he exaggerates the words, "they could simply be the consequence of being descended from a Crura. And the traces of Land Dweller blood flowing in Etan's veins chose to manifest themselves in an even more unfortunate way. He can never be king. If he bumps his elbow, his entire arm swells up and turns black. If he bites his tongue, blood pours out of his mouth for hours afterward. He could never lead the armies of Undula. He could never make state visits or travel to The Surface. If he accidentally started bleeding for any reason on the trip, he would attract every shark in the Mediterranean."

Another point of his story strikes me. "You said you've never had a friend," I say. "But when you first came into my room, you said the guard let you in because he is a friend of yours."

Conway looks bemused. "That was your takeaway from all of this?"

I flush. "No, I just—"

He waves me off. "You'd be surprised how many friends you can make with a fat pouch of gold coins. Though, to be honest, that avenue of making friends won't be open to me much longer."

Words of the past float to the surface of my mind—words whispered in the marketplace with subtle winks, snide laughter. "I had thought those stories were just idle gossip," I say.

His mouth looks as though he just tasted something sour. "You mean the stories that say the prince of Undula has squandered his inheritance betting on every octopus wrestling match in the city? Oh, believe me, the gossips don't know the half of it."

I look at him with curiosity. "The prince of Undula doesn't sound completely satisfied with his choices."

His eyes flicker up to mine, and then he gives a rueful smile. "It's less the choices and more the fact I can't pick a winning octopus to save my life."

"Why keep betting then?"

He hesitates for a moment but then says almost to himself, "Oh, what does it matter?" He looks me square in the eyes. "I've told you far too much already. I needed the money to go to Atlantis."

I look into his dark gray eyes and understand. He wanted to run away. And there was no way his father would give him enough money at one time to book a passage to the fabled city. So, he had tried and tried to win enough, and failed over and over again, money trickling away through his fingers like sand.

"I am not the source of all my father's financial woes, as the rumors claim," he says, running his fingers back and forth over my sealskin blanket. "But I've certainly contributed to them. And the kingdom truly is in dire financial straits. The treasure from the wreck Aalto found was just enough to pay my debts and allow Father to replenish the castle storerooms. Obviously, he had hoped the queen of Nebula wouldn't find out about the wreck. Pity she did."

I glare at him. "Pity? Darin told your father where he found the treasure! And that"—I pause, fighting down the nastier names that rise to my lips—"good-for-nothing nearly allowed my brother-in-law to be locked in a room with a blue-ringed to save his own lousy neck!"

Conway cocks his head. "He's your brother-in-law? I didn't know Aalto was married."

"He isn't. He's the brother of my brother-in-law if you want to be technical about it."

Conway smirks. "I'm sure he does want to be technical about it."

"What?"

Conway suddenly raises his hand, making a shushing motion. We listen as a Merwoman's voice sounds from outside the door.

"Has Prince Conway come this way by any chance? I'd like a word with him."

"I haven't seen him, my lady," the guard answers smoothly.

"Really?" the female voice replies, just as smoothly.

There is a pause, and my straining ears catch a clinking sound. Conway's eyes widen, and he sits bolt upright on the bed. The guard lowers his voice, but we can still hear every word. "Well, now that your ladyship has jogged my memory, I believe I did see him." There is silence again, and I imagine him jerking his head toward the door.

"Whose room is this?" The female voice holds a sudden urgency I don't understand.

"It's the room of that Crura, Your Highness. The one you defeated in the arena."

There is a sharp thunk, like a tail smacking wood, and then quiet. Conway slumps back on the bed, slapping his hand against the mattress. "Blast!"

"Why was Ginevra looking for you?"

He lifts an eyebrow. "All the ladies come looking for me eventually." His eyes glint wickedly, and I burst out laughing.

"Fat chance."

"Because of the brother of your brother-in-law?" he mocks.

"No," I snap as heat rises in my cheeks. "Because my family is cursed. And until I can bring a child into the world without being terrified they would be better off never entering it, romance is off the table for me."

His smirk widens into a grin. "Good."

Too late, I realize how what I just said sounded. My face feels like it is on fire. "And I wouldn't come looking for you, anyway."

"Uh-huh," he says, still grinning. "Well, luckily for you, I have a plan to break your curse."

Embarrassment forgotten, I look at him eagerly, anticipation rising inside. "You do? How?"

"Why did the Sea Enchantress curse your family in the first place? Because Llyra broke her word about giving Circe her voice. But the way the story goes, Llyra sealed her voice inside the locket before setting sail on the voyage that ended her life. Which means the locket is on the wreck we are going to find. And since Circe's den is supposed to be near the wreck, I was thinking maybe we could cut a deal with her. The locket with Llyra's voice inside for an end to our family's curse. Which will hopefully mean a tail for me as well."

"Are you giving up on Atlantis then?" I ask curiously.

"Atlantis is just a place where I could fit in," he says. "But if I had a tail, I could fit in anywhere. And I'm tired of being slower and weaker than almost all the other Mermish men I know. If I had a tail, I could thrash . . ." he trails off.

I glance down at my own legs. They do look slightly pathetic, drifting in the water below me, like ghostly strings of kelp. But they're mine. "I don't think I want a tail," I say slowly. "I want the curse to end, so children in my family will stop having to come into the world as outcasts. But I guess I'm used to being an outcast now. And the people whose opinion I really care about have never minded my legs."

Conway gives me a disbelieving look, then shrugs. "I'm sure Circe won't mind leaving you your legs since you like them so much. So, what do you say? Will you allow me to join your treasure hunt?"

"I'm not sure it's my permission you need," I say. "Your father and Darin are your bigger problems."

Conway surprises me. "My father has already agreed. I didn't tell him my real reason for wanting to go, of course. During our conversation, I focused on my regret over my irresponsible living, and my desire to make amends by finding a treasure that would more than replace all the gold I had squandered."

I raise my eyebrows, and he gives me an unconvincingly innocent look. "And Darin?" I ask, fighting a smile.

Conway's mischievous grin reveals perfectly straight white teeth. "Oh, I don't think Aalto should be a problem. Not now that you're on my side." And with those words, he rises and heads for the door, winking as it swings shut behind him.

13

DARIN

THE DARK STREETS OF THE CITY BLUR into each other as he swims through them, but it doesn't matter. The place Darin is going is one he has visited so often, he could swim there in his sleep. Getting out of the castle was even easier than he had thought it would be. Apparently, the royal family's financial woes had resulted in staff pay cuts at the palace, and it had only taken the promise of a silver and opal necklace to convince the guard outside his room to turn a blind eye as Darin slipped away. The servants' entrance where he normally brought his loot was unguarded—a security oversight so egregious, it was a wonder the royal family had not yet been murdered in their beds.

The darkness presses around him, as heavy as the memory of Locklyn's tears. He hadn't meant to cast that night at the gates at her. The words had just slipped out—a response to his helplessness in the face of her suffering.

And now, the words he hadn't meant to say might have ruined his chances of ever saying the words that had been hovering inside him for years, bursting to be shared.

He had started falling for Locklyn when she was sixteen. He was twenty-four at the time, eight years her senior. His feelings remained unchanged as years passed. And he waited, the fear that she would fall in love with someone else the constant backdrop of his life. Romance for Locklyn would spell the death, not only of his hopes, but of their friendship as well. No husband would want a tall, blond, golden-eyed brother-in-law hanging around his wife.

When her twentieth birthday passed without a lover in sight, tiny shoots of hope burgeoned in his heart. But the months continued to go by. And, still, he said nothing, sure that if he were to wager their friendship against a chance at love, he would lose both.

Glancing around, he jerks to a stop. He has passed his destination. Reversing course, he heads for the small house nestled against Aquaticus's city wall. A bluish tint illuminates the windows. Chantara is still awake.

When Darin raps on the door, a low voice calls, "Come in," and he drifts inside, gazing around the house he has visited regularly since he was eight years old. Luminous ropes of seaweed are woven into a net that dangles from the ceiling, casting azure light over the room below. A small Mermaid with eggplant-colored hair and starfish feet wrinkling the corners of her eyes chops the leaves of a dark green plant. She adds them to the pot slung over the glowing, red-gold crack of bubbling lava in the corner of the room. Beside it, a tiny narwhal lies curled on a pile of posidonia, fast asleep.

"You really shouldn't tell people to let themselves in, you know," Darin says to Chantara's back as she continues to work, her fingers deftly sweeping chopped leaves toward a corner of the cutting board.

"I recognized your knock," comes the reply. "How are Amaya and the baby doing?"

Chantara is Locklyn and Amaya's aunt, and the city's most sought-after midwife and herb woman. The rich of Aquaticus employ the services of physicians, but most of the poor Merfolk seek Chantara for all their medical needs, from an infected cut to a toothache to childbirth.

"I'm not sure." He draws near and watches the motion of her fingers, chopping and sweeping, chopping and sweeping. The effect is strangely cathartic. "I was arrested this morning."

Chantara still doesn't pause. "Oh?"

"You're the most unsatisfying person to share news with. I don't get arrested every day."

The corners of Chantara's mouth tilt upward. "When you've lived as long as I have, Darin, and you have seen as many fingers burnt until the skin is black and bubbling and tail fins suspended by a thread of skin and babies so small and blue, you're certain they won't live through the night, you'll realize you don't have the emotional capacity to get excited about every little thing."

"Well, how's this for a little thing? Locklyn nearly got killed by the queen of the Nebulae in a duel today, and we're supposed to set out tomorrow to look for Llyra's Lost Treasure. And, if we don't find it in thirty days, Malik is going to send Amaya and Beck and the children to Oro."

Her fingers pause, and she looks up with fathomless, black eyes. "No one has ever found the Lost Treasure of Llyra, Darin."

He studies her for a moment. "When we were young, I remember you telling a story about your uncle, who had met Lief Orwell, the great explorer and Schatzi. You said he had told you the way to his secret home, in the mountains to the west. If anyone would know where Llyra's Lost Treasure is, it would be Lief."

Chantara continues to survey him for a moment, then shakes her head and resumes her chopping. "I can tell you what my uncle told me about how to find Lief Orwell," she says. "But I do not like to think that the lives of both my nieces and their family depend on you reaching him."

"Thanks for the vote of confidence," he says dryly.

"It's nothing personal. No one has seen Lief Orwell in living memory."

"What about your uncle?"

"He's dead," she says shortly. "Ran afoul of the monarchy. Ended his days at Oro."

"I'm so sorry," he stammers. "If I'd known—"

"You couldn't have," she says more gently. "I don't like to talk about him. Generally, I only use the stories of his treasure-hunting adventures to entertain children. Come." With an almost impatient gesture, she sweeps the entire pile of chopped leaves into a small jar and places it on a shelf above the burbling lava pit. With a flick of her amethyst-colored tail, she perches on one of the short stools beside her kitchen table, pulling a large tablet made of driftwood and wax toward her.

Withdrawing one of the long, thin, wooden pins securing her hair, she twirls it between her fingers and then begins to trace it through the wax. "According to Uncle Moses, Lief Orwell lives in the heart of the Rayan Mountains, seven days of hard swimming from Aquaticus. No towns exist between Aquaticus and the mountains, so it is imperative to bring enough provisions to last a minimum of fourteen days."

Darin nods. "There and back, of course. Go on."

She continues, "There are two ways to reach the heart of the mountains. It is possible to swim upward and enter from above. However, the mountains are so tall, it requires a day and a half to crest them. It sounds like you do not have that kind of time." She taps a point at the bottom of the spikey, upside-down V's that denote the mountains. "The other way is through the Douglas Pass. The problem is that at the mouth of the pass is a bottleneck, barely wide enough for a Merperson to squeeze through, and in the crags above it lives an Anakite crab."

He whistles through his teeth.

Most Merpeople are too frightened to speak about the Anakite—enormous, ghostly white crabs that stand tall enough for a full-grown Merman to swim between their legs. Not that any Merman in his right mind would try. Their razor-sharp pincers can easily cut through scales. One old Schatzi had told him, voice quivering with horror, how he and his partner had strayed too close to an Anakite den. The crab inside had grabbed his partner, shearing him cleanly in half.

"Yes. My uncle called him Nimrod."

"Your uncle named him?"

She gives him an exasperated look. "No. Lief Orwell named him."

Darin laughs. "Of course, he did. Lief Orwell has a monstrous, Merman-eating Anakite as his personal watch crab."

"That's not all." The laughter dies in his throat. "Uncle Moses says when he swam to the entrance of the pass, he didn't know about Nimrod. As he was starting to enter, he looked down and saw the ground rising toward him. What he had taken to be the floor of the passage was actually the largest stonefish he had ever seen. He barely escaped the passage without getting impaled. Apparently, he decided to swim over the mountains after that. He never even saw Nimrod—he just heard about him from Lief."

"So, it sounds like swimming over the mountains is by far the best option."

Chantara glances up from her scratching stylus. "Haven't I made it clear, Darin? There are no good options. Uncle Moses managed to make it over the mountains, but he was attacked twice by scalloped hammerheads and nearly ran into a smack of Portuguese men-of-war. It took him a day and a half of straight swimming to make it over the range, and he was big and strong, even for a Merman. If Locklyn is joining you, it will take longer. And there is nowhere to rest along the way."

"Locklyn's strong. She'll be fine."

Chantara huffs. "Locklyn's stubborn, you mean. I think that's the real reason she's survived all these years."

"We had a fight," he blurts. He is not sure what made him do so, but something about Chantara had always invited confidences.

Her black eyes watch him as she waits for him to continue.

"She says that I treat her like a child."

"Do you?"

He looks away, suddenly unable to meet her eyes. "I don't know," he admits. "Sometimes, maybe. But she doesn't want me to protect her. Or to take care of her."

"And that is exactly what you want to do." The words are a statement, not a question.

He looks up again and sees her eyes have become softer, warmer.

"Yes," he says, knowing he wouldn't have given that answer to anyone except her.

She is silent for a long moment. Then she says, "Did you know I was married?"

His eyes widen. "No."

"When I was sixteen." Her voice is uncharacteristically quiet. "I was mad over him. But he left me a year after the wedding. To be the lover of an octopus wrestler's daughter, whose older husband wasn't giving her the marital satisfaction she craved."

"I'm sorry," he says, unsure how to respond.

She gives a small, sad smile. "I've always seen a lot of myself in Locklyn. Many people who suffer abandonment desire nothing so much as to be taken care of. But I am not like that. And neither is she. My husband's leaving fueled a deep desire in me to prove my worth. To show the world I was more than the Mermaid whose husband didn't want her." She traces one finger down the center of the tablet, creating a furrowed groove, and then smoothes it away. Her eyes, when they meet his again, are full of a strange, deep peace. "It took me many, many years to accept that as one of the Wave Master's creatures, I am worthwhile to Him. Once I truly believed that, proving my worth to everyone around me became much less important."

"My desire to protect Locklyn doesn't mean I think less of her. But she can't see that."

"Then show her," Chantara says simply. "When we truly love someone, we have to show them in a way they understand. Maybe to every other Mermaid under the sea, your protection would be the epitome of caring. But to Locklyn, it means you see her as weak. I'm not saying you shouldn't protect her," she says, raising her hand as he starts to interrupt. "You should. But that will not be what demonstrates your love to Locklyn. Rather, your encouragement of her strengths, your desire to see her succeed, your acceptance of her help and advice—these things will prove to her that you see her as an equal, that you desire her as a lover, as a confidant, as a friend. Not as a trophy or a pet."

A deep, booming clang echoes through the room, causing the little glass pots of herbs on the shelves to clink against each other. Darin slides off his stool. That bell marks the opening of the city gates. It is time to return to the palace.

"Thank you," he says to Chantara, indicating the tablet between them.

"What? For sending you to your death?" The undercurrent of sadness in her voice belies the wry humor of her words.

"You think I'm afraid of an Anakite crab and a giant stonefish? Please." He smiles broadly. "Everything's been so dull lately. I was hoping for a challenge."

She laughs a little at that, but the worry lines remain etched around her eyes. "Do try to come back, won't you?" she says. "And take care of Locklyn. Just remember what I told you, and don't let her see it."

"I'll remember." He starts for the door. On the threshold, he turns back. "You know that Merman, the one who left you?" he says. "He was a fool."

This time, the smile reaches her eyes.

14

DARIN

WHEN A GUARD ESCORTS HIM OUT OF
the palace the next morning to where their group is assembling for
departure, Darin's eyes find Locklyn right away. She stands next to
one of the pack dolphins, scratching it under the chin and ignoring
her guard, who floats offensively close. Darin starts toward her,
then suddenly halts.

The slender, dark-haired form of Aquaticus's crown prince
has appeared next to Locklyn and the dolphin. He waves a hand
languidly at the guard, who immediately withdraws. Locklyn looks
up at him and smiles, saying something that makes him laugh.

A boiling feeling swells inside Darin's chest, like the red-hot
veins of magma that course below the surface of Mount Oro,
waiting for the right moment to explode.

Locklyn seems to feel his gaze and turns, giving him a slightly
strained smile. She says something to Conway, then swims over.
"Hi," she says awkwardly.

"Since when have you and the prince been friends?" The words
burst out before Darin can stop them.

Her lips tighten. "We met last night," she says shortly. "And,
clearly, the conversation you and I had made no impression on you."

He pushes back his long, blond hair. "It did make an impression, Locklyn."

"Darin, like I told you, I can take care of myself. I don't need you monitoring my relationships."

"You just told me you met him last night! That's not a relationship!"

Locklyn gives him an annoyed look, then a laugh bubbles out of her. "Ever heard of love at first sight?"

"What?"

She shoves his shoulder, and her smile turns mischievous now. "I couldn't resist," she says. "Don't be gullible, Dar. But since he is coming on this month-long trip, I do anticipate us both getting to know him a lot better."

"What!"

Locklyn raises her eyebrows. "He told his father he wants to help undo some of the damage he's done to the kingdom's finances."

"And you believe that?" He is incredulous. Her gaze slides away. "Locklyn. Why is he really coming?"

"If you have a problem with him coming, I think you'd better talk to him," she says quietly.

She clearly knows something she's not saying, and the thought of her cozied up with Conway last night, sharing confidences, makes the red-hot twangs in his chest bubble harder, pushing to break free. "No, I do not want him coming," he says, so forcefully that a servant passing with a basket of provisions gives him a startled look. "And I personally find the idea of him doing anything so selfless as going on a dangerous treasure-hunting mission to help Undula laughable. So, I'd like to know what his real reason is."

Locklyn huffs out a sigh, her eyes tired. "Darin, would it hurt you, just for once, to stop trying to control everyone around you?"

He is stung into silence.

Locklyn looks at him for a moment, her eyes a deep, defiant green. Then she drops her head into her hands. "I'm sorry," she says at last. "That was uncalled for."

"But it is what you think," he says slowly.

She looks away, clearly struggling for words.

He looks up to see Conway watching them. It takes all his resolve not to swim over and tail-slap the smirk off the prince's face. "I'm going to help load up the supplies."

"Darin." Locklyn's plea is quiet enough that he can pretend not to hear.

Heart aching, he turns away and swims toward the servants. They tote baskets of supplies from the palace to load onto ten pack dolphins.

"Treasure Hunter," says a voice, and Darin spins to see Ginevra waiting near the castle steps. She is flanked by two Mermaids carrying the traditional Nebulae spears. To his surprise, all three of them are dressed for travel.

"Your Highness," he says warily.

The corners of her lips twitch. Toward a smile? A frown? It is hard to say. "I have decided to accompany you on your mission."

Clearly, he and Locklyn will be lucky to catch a single moment alone together on this trip. "Really?"

Her mouth twitches again. "Not a man of many words, are you, Treasure Hunter?"

This "Treasure Hunter" business is starting to get old. "I am called Darin, my lady."

A wry smile emerges. "And I am called Ginevra. But my occupation shapes who I am. As does yours. And, to me, you are the Treasure Hunter who is going to restore the riches stolen from my kingdom."

"Is that why you are coming?" he asks, brow quirked. "To make sure I don't double-cross you again?"

She draws herself up, eyes challenging. "I don't believe it was you who double-crossed me in the first place. But, yes, I am going to make sure my kingdom receives its due." Her eyes flick sideways, and he follows her gaze to where Conway talks to Locklyn. "Let us say I do not trust Undula's royalty. So, when I learned the crown prince and four members of the king's personal bodyguard were to accompany the expedition, I decided my sister could handle the kingdom for a month without me." Her lips pucker slightly as she surveys Conway and Locklyn.

"Just to make sure I understand," Darin says, and Ginevra's attention turns back toward him, "who exactly is going to be leading this expedition? I must confess I did not anticipate the honor of having two royals along on this trip. I am happy to allow someone else to direct our course, but I do not believe turning this mission into a power struggle will help me to save my family, or either of your kingdoms, to gain the wealth they crave."

Ginevra looks at him appraisingly. "You ought to have been a politician, Darin. I can make no promises for anyone else." Her glower returns as she glances toward Conway. "But I am willing to give you the final say in directing us. My goal in accompanying you is not to undermine this mission, but rather to ensure my kingdom is not cheated again."

"Thank you," he says, bowing slightly. As he turns away, her fingers close around his wrist, her grip as strong as a Merman's.

"Just so you know," she says, sounding for a moment like a young Merwoman rather than the monarch of a realm of warrior Mermaids, "if Conway Struan gives you any trouble, it would be my pleasure to beat him within an inch of his life."

He barks a laugh. "I'm not the crown prince's biggest fan myself, so you don't need to worry about me being too gentle with him. But if I ever need help getting a point across, I'll let you do the honors."

Her face breaks into a grim smile that mirrors his, just as his name echoes across the courtyard. Wyre beckons imperiously from the castle steps. He swims over to Darin and turns to survey the scene below.

Ten dolphins loaded with weapons, sealskin blankets, and medical supplies, as well as bags of dugong cheese, herring, and dried posidonia, float near the steps. A shirtless Merman with long, black hair, a slate-gray tail, and bulging muscles chaperones the pod. He silently observes Locklyn, encircled by the dolphins who chitter with delight as she croons a wordless melody, stroking their smooth, silver noses.

Conway talks idly to a guard, his eyes fixed on Ginevra—who is pointedly ignoring him—with an expression that is difficult to read. Two Nebulae women clutching spears flank their queen, glaring at Conway's entourage, which consists of three Aquaticus soldiers, one of whom—Darin's heart sinks—is Blackwell.

"Before you set out today," Wyre's reedy voice draws back his attention, "King Malik has asked me to inform you of the terms under which the mission is to be undertaken."

Darin arranges his face into a mildly inquiring expression, resisting the urge to roll his eyes.

"As you can see, the king is generously providing you with supplies—including enough food to last your group for thirty days if supplemented with hunting. Kai," Wyre indicates the black-haired giant, "the keeper of the king's dolphins, will accompany you to care for the pod. In addition," he waves a vague hand, "three members of the king's guard, Hurley, Clyde, and Blackwell, will accompany you in attendance to His Majesty, Prince Conway, who will be watching out for Undula's interests. In addition . . ."

Wyre's voice fades into the background as Darin's eyes catch on Locklyn, who is standing frozen in the center of the dolphin pod, staring at Blackwell.

"Steward," Darin says, cutting into Wyre's remarks, "I believe one of Prince Conway's guards is unsuitable. I know the man and he would be a liability on this mission. Can he be replaced?" He gestures toward Blackwell.

Clearly annoyed, Wyre squints shortsightedly across the courtyard, then shrugs. "To answer your question, Aalto, no, he cannot be replaced." Darin begins to protest, but Wyre forestalls him. "He cannot be replaced because none of the king's other guards are willing to undertake such a dangerous mission."

He looks across at Blackwell again and sees that the Merman is watching Locklyn, his mouth twisted in a leer that drags down the edges of his scar.

"Your brother and his family," Wyre continues, forcing Darin to face him again, "will be kept in custody at the palace during your absence. If you have not returned at the end of thirty days, bringing Llyra's Treasure with you, they will be sentenced to a lifetime of service on Mount Oro." The blandness of his voice is entirely incongruous with the menace in his words. Wyre rolls up the scroll he has been consulting throughout and tucks it into his belt. "That is all, Aalto. You will be expected in thirty days' time at the entrance to Aquaticus before the gates close."

He motions to the guards on either side of the palace's golden front doors. They dart forward to open them, admitting him, and then allow the doors to swing shut. The echoing clang causes everyone in the courtyard to fall silent and look up at the steps, eyes locking on Darin.

Darin meets the gaze of each of the eight people in the courtyard, one by one. Locklyn's eyes are a soft, pale blue, and the small smile she gives him causes warmth to expand in his chest.

"This is it," Darin informs them. "We are about to embark on the most dangerous mission undertaken in the Undersea Realm for a thousand years, seeking a treasure that is the stuff of legends." For an instant, he pauses, eyes flickering between the four Undulae soldiers and the three Nebulae women. "We may all die," he continues. The three Undulae guards shift nervously behind Conway. "And we may not find what we seek. But I am going, because the people who mean the most to me need me to go. However, only one of the rest of you is obligated in the same way." His eyes find Locklyn again.

She gives a small wave as if to say, "Guilty as charged."

"So, if any of you, after hearing the facts I have relayed, decide you do not wish to come on this mission, no one will think any less of you." One of the Nebulae Merwomen gives a contemptuous snort, and he levels his gaze on her, staring her down.

She flushes and looks away.

"You must decide now," he declares. "Because after we leave, it will be more dangerous to return to Aquaticus alone than to proceed."

There is a pause, and he surveys the group before him. The

fierce confidence in the visage of their queen is mirrored in the faces of the two Nebulae Merwomen behind her. Conway gazes down at the sand, his expression studiously unconcerned as he ignores the nervous movements of Clyde and Hurley, who look as if they would like to leave, but don't quite have the guts to say so. Blackwell's eyes remain fixed on the back of Locklyn's head, and the sight of the greed shading his face causes Darin's left hand to ball into a fist. Kai could be carved from stone if not for the movement of one of his massive hands, stroking the head of the dolphin nearest to him.

Darin forces a smile. "As the Schatzi say, friendship is the only treasure you cannot find aboard a ship. The unity we exhibit will very likely prove the difference between success and failure." He raises one hand and lets it slice down through the water, purposefully exaggerating the drama of the moment. "Thirty days. The hourglass has turned. The sand is already falling. Let's go."

LOCKLYN

I HOVER IN THE SHADOWS OF A CLUMP of rocks, one hand pressed to my aching side. We stopped once today for about ten minutes to bolt down some food. Other than that, we've been swimming nonstop since we left Aquaticus this morning. Already self-conscious about being the slowest swimmer due to my lack of a tail, I was terrified my injury would cause me to delay the group even further. To my surprise and pleasure, Conway spent the entire day swimming at the back with me. Sometimes we talked—him telling me about his childhood in the palace, me regaling him with stories of life in the reef—and sometimes we just swam in comfortable silence.

Does Conway want more than friendship? For the first time since I turned twenty and intentionally buried all my dreams of love, a tiny shoot of hope unfurls inside me. I have always been resistant to the idea of romance for fear of bringing a child into the world who will suffer in the same way I have my entire life. But Avonlea has taken the curse for this generation of our family. And, with Conway's Crura genes, even if I gave birth to a child with legs, their life would be completely different from mine. Conway would be king. Under his reign, things will almost certainly change for the better for the Crura of Undula.

I like Conway. He definitely has some growing up to do, but his wry humor and snarky irreverence light up every room he enters. And—my heart squirms guiltily at the selfish thought—he understands me. He knows what it is like to be different. To be defined by something you cannot control.

Unbidden, the thought flashes that he is not really my type. In my mind's eye, I see a golden figure with scales that glow like fire and hair the color of sunlight rippling behind him in the water.

I shake my head. I am being completely ridiculous. Number one, the crown prince of Undula is almost certainly not interested in a poor dugong shepherdess. Or—bile rises in my throat at the thought—he is interested in something I have no interest in giving him without a ring on my finger. Number two, the only golden-haired Merman I know views me as his little sister. And you don't fall in love with your little sister.

"Moonstone for your thoughts," a voice says behind me, and I jump.

"How about you keep your moonstones and I keep my thoughts?" I say.

"Fine." Out of the corner of my eye, I see Conway lean against the rock wall next to us, surveying me. "What is the dolphin-whisperer doing, skulking off here by herself?"

I smile slightly at his name choice, glance around to make sure no one else is within earshot. "The swimming didn't agree with the hole in my side."

He blows out his breath in an exasperated stream of bubbles. "Why under the sea didn't you tell us to stop so you could rest?"

It's my turn to blow out a stream of bubbles as I snort derisively. "And have everyone in the group despise me more than they already do? No, thank you."

"No one despises you," he says. I give him a look. "All right, fine. No one who matters despises you."

"By that definition, you and Darin are apparently the only ones who matter," I say, the corners of my mouth twitching.

"Ginny doesn't despise you." He raises his eyebrows at my

expression. "What? She's jealous of and threatened by you. That's not the same thing."

"Jealous? Of me?" I splutter, glancing involuntarily toward the group around the lava hole Darin discovered.

Ginevra leans on her spear, talking to Darin, her pearly scales shimmering iridescently in the dark water. With Darin's golden scales reflecting the lava's rosy glow, they are an eye-catching pair. The sun and the moon. The two most beautiful people I have ever seen. For some reason, the thought causes an unpleasant, prickling heat within.

Conway rolls his eyes. "Oh, come on, Locklyn. You actually caused her to bleed in a fight. You have a lovely voice, and she can't sing a note. You're surrounded by the mystic of being Llyra's great-great-granddaughter who knows where her lost treasure is. And you're beautiful."

I look at him sharply.

Something shifts in the depths of his dark eyes, and he slides closer. "What?" he says softly. "You are."

"Prince Conway!" Both of us spin to see Ginevra hovering a few lengths away, staring at the pair of us. I fight to keep my expression cool and nonchalant. Conway stares daggers at Ginevra, whose face looks carved from stone. "Darin wants to discuss his plans with us and," she pauses for the barest fraction of a second, "the girl who knows the way to the treasure."

She makes me sound like a map with legs. I bite my lips to keep from asking her what her problem is. Then I follow Conway to where Darin hovers on the edge of the main group.

As we approach, he drifts toward us, widening the space between us and the others before speaking. "I wanted to discuss our course with all of you," he says when we are out of earshot. "With the timeline we are on, there is no room for error. We will not have time for any redos." He takes a deep breath. "Our first stop is at the home of Lief Orwell to learn the location of Llyra's Lost Treasure."

Ginevra stiffens. When she speaks, her voice is icy. "I was under the impression the whole reason for this quest was because you already knew that."

Darin's eyes are hard as granite. "Actually, the reason for this quest is that you had a knife between my sister-in-law's ribs. I said what I had to say."

Sister-in-law. Why does that sting?

For a long moment, Ginevra and Darin stare at each other. Conway catches my eye and mouths, "Awkward," causing me to swallow a nervous giggle.

Finally, Ginevra nods curtly, breaking the tension. "How long will it take us to reach Orwell?"

For a fraction of a second, Darin's eyes graze mine. Then they flit back to Ginevra as he says, "Moving at this speed, it will take us eight days."

Ginevra's mouth twists in a slight smirk, and I realize, with a sinking in my gut, she did not miss the look Darin cast me. She knows I am the reason we are moving at this speed. "We weren't moving particularly quickly today," she says smoothly. "I'm sure we could all pick up the pace and shave off a day or two."

There is a strained pause before Darin speaks. "Once you hear what I have to say, I'm not sure you'll be in any hurry. Orwell lives in the heart of the Rayan Mountains. There are only two ways to reach him. One is by swimming over the mountains, which will add a day and a half to our travel time. The other is through a pass that is guarded by an Anakite crab and a giant stonefish."

Conway snorts. "Where exactly did you get this information, Aalto? Anakite crabs are the stuff of legend. Most thinking people don't believe that they exist."

I notice the muscles around Darin's mouth tighten and twist my fingers together behind my back, terrified he is going to say something that will make Conway call the guards to drag Darin off to Aquaticus in chains.

After a slight pause, Darin says mildly, "My apologies. As a 'thank you' to His Highness for setting me straight, may I suggest he leads us through the passage? Since an Anakite crab will most certainly not come down from the crags and carve him into ribbons, it seems only fitting."

Laughter bubbles up inside me, but at the sight of Conway's expression, I hastily choke it down. Ginevra smirks, clearly delighted at Conway's fury. Conway opens his mouth, but Darin forestalls him.

"Given the fact that we need to be back at the gates of Aquaticus in thirty days or an army of Nebulae will attack," he inclines his head slightly to Ginevra, who offers him a tight-lipped smile in return, "I think we must attempt the tunnel, since swimming over the mountains will add between two and three days to our travel time. I have an idea for getting through that I wanted to run by all of you. Like most predators, Anakite crabs react strongly to the smell of blood. I was thinking if we sacrificed two of the dolphins . . ."

"What?" Conway snaps. "You have no right to lay a finger on the royal dolphins. And besides," he folds his arms and raises his eyebrows at Darin, "Kai would kill you if you tried."

Darin closes his eyes, and I am certain he is beseeching the Wave Master for patience. "Would you rather I carved my initials on your forearms and sent you instead?"

Clearly, any prayers for patience he may have uttered did not work.

Conway's face tightens. Then he gives Darin a broad smile. Before I realize what he is doing, his fingers interlace with mine, sending a current of warmth up my arm. Turning, I gape at him, but he isn't looking at me. He is staring into Darin's golden eyes with a faint smile playing around the corners of his mouth. "Go on, Aalto," he says. "I'm dying to hear more about this plan of yours."

Darin's face is oddly blank. There is a moment of silence, and then as though nothing happened, he says, "If the palace dolphins are off-limits, we will need to catch creatures to use as bait. And that will take time."

"I . . ." My voice comes out as a croak. I clear my throat and wriggle my fingers out of Conway's as three faces turn toward me. Conway's black eyes dance, which sends electricity tingling to the tips of my fingers. "I could help with that," I finally say.

Darin's eyes flash with comprehension. "Of course."

Conway looks nonplussed.

Ginevra, who is staring off into the murky water, gives no sign she heard me.

"I don't understand," Conway says.

Darin smiles at me, and for an instant, my heart ceases the frantic pounding Conway's touch elicited and swells with a glowing, golden warmth. "Show them," he says.

I begin to hum. I'm not even sure where the melody comes from—somewhere deep inside—a wandering, lilting cadence that reminds me of raindrops striking the gray surface of the ocean. The thought flashes through my mind that I haven't been to The Surface in a long time.

The melody changes, becoming more consistent, a pattern of warmth and welcome, a beckoning stream of music. I open my mouth and sing, words filling my mind in the same way the tune fills my soul.

The chittering reaches me before I see the dolphin. Her sleek gray body carves through the water as she swims toward us. Even Ginevra's eyes are wide with wonder as she watches the dolphin approach, squeaking joyfully and twining her sleek body around me, butting my hands with her nose in a desperate appeal for petting.

I smooth my fingers over her snout, my heart sinking at the reality of what I've just done. "We have to kill her, don't we?" For an instant, a look I don't understand crosses Darin's face as he watches me.

"It doesn't have to be her," he says, and pity fills those golden eyes now. "But if we want to stay alive, we need to wound another living creature and send it into that tunnel ahead of us. My plan is to wound a dolphin or two and send it into the pass, hoping the scent of blood will attract a few sharks as well. If everything goes according to plan, Nimrod will jump down and attack the sharks and dolphins. His body would form a barrier, not allowing the rockfish to rise past him. Once he's distracted, we could swim

through the passage over his head. It would be an added bonus if
the rockfish impaled his underbelly and finished him off for us."

A long silence follows. I caress the dolphin's nose, heart aching
at the thought of sending several of these innocent creatures to
their deaths. But beneath the ache flows a rippling current of fear.
There are a lot of *ifs* in Darin's plan.

"I know there are holes in my plan," Darin says. "But I don't
know what else we can do. That was all I had to say. As I'm sure
you can all see, there doesn't seem to be much point in exploring
other scenarios until we find out whether or not we're going to
survive this one."

"Or we could turn around," I find myself saying. All eyes snap
to me. "Is any treasure worth dying for? Your Highness," I look at
Ginevra and shrivel inwardly at the hostility contorting her face,
"why not call it off? If you die along with us, no treasure, real or
imagined, will be any good to you. Or," I add, as her expression
remains unmoving, "at the very least, give us more time to come
up with better alternatives."

For the barest fraction of a second, I think I see a flicker in her
eyes. But it vanishes so quickly, I am sure I imagined it. "I think
not." She turns, fading into the dark water.

"What a sweetheart," Conway says. He turns to me, and I feel
heat rising in my face. "I saw a bunch of periwinkles on the other
side of that big pile of rocks where the dolphins are tethered. Fancy
a snack before bed? The rations aren't exactly overwhelming."

I glance sideways at Darin, but he isn't looking at me. The
distance between us cuts at me—the lack of our familiar, easy
comradeship leaves a gaping hole in my heart.

*I have to fix this. And I'm not entirely sure whether I want to be
alone with Conway right now anyway.*

"No, thanks," I say lightly. "That dried posidonia we had for
lunch didn't really agree with me. I don't think I should risk putting
anything else in my stomach right now."

Conway glances between Darin and me, his eyes narrowing.
There is an awkward pause as we hang suspended in a circle, all

waiting for someone else to make a move. I can feel Conway's eyes on me, but stare resolutely down into the sand, trying to ignore the patches of heat that still seem to linger directly below my eyes. Finally, I look up. His eyes are full of warmth, and I suddenly wish he wasn't wearing his tail.

"Good night," he says softly.

"Good night," I reply, my voice cracking a little.

He turns and disappears into the dark water, toward the magma hole where the rest of the group huddles. I glance up through my lashes at Darin, but he is still looking resolutely away, and the words I want to say die on my tongue at the coldness he seems to emanate.

I have to say something. We can't go on like this.

"Darin?" My timid word comes out as a question.

"Locklyn," he says, facing me at last. The expression in his gaze makes my heart ache. He looks vulnerable, broken. Impulsively, I reach out, and as his calloused fingers close over mine, he drops his head.

"You're really worried, aren't you?"

Head still bent, he gives a wry chuckle. "Man-eating crabs, giant stonefish, impossible deadlines, Ginevra and Conway at each other's throats—what's to be worried about?"

I squeeze his fingers. "At least, there hasn't been any bloodshed yet." He breathes out another laugh and squeezes back. Silence stretches between us again, but it is more like the silences I remember—comfortable silence that comes from feeling so at ease with a person. "I wanted to tell you I'm sorry," I say at length.

His golden eyes are quizzical. "What for?"

"I shouldn't have said you try to control everything. Because you don't. And it's not your fault you're a natural leader, or that the people around you look to you for solutions to their problems. I think maybe you've just gotten so used to problem-solving, you can't help trying to fix everything." I can't read the expression on his face.

"It's funny that you say that. I was planning to take the first opportunity of seeing you alone to tell you that you were right. I do try to control things. I think it makes me feel less afraid."

I gape at him. "Afraid? You?"

"Every day of my life," he says, looking away again.

"Of what?"

"Of losing the people I love. Of seeing hurt and being powerless to stop it. Of not being as strong and capable and self-sufficient as everyone thinks I am."

I grip his hand, not wanting to say something cliché, touched by his openness.

"So, I'm sorry," he says, "for trying to control your life."

"You're in no danger of losing me," I say, trying to spark a smile. "I think you should be more afraid of never getting rid of me."

For some reason, his golden eyes become shuttered, and he eases his hand away from mine. "You should get to bed. We have a long day ahead of us tomorrow."

Stung, I try to laugh it off. "Schatzi always stay up to all hours, Aalto."

"Don't call me that!" he snaps, and I can feel the connection we had moments before shattering. "You're not one of my treasure-hunting buddies."

"Darin—" I start, completely taken back.

"Just go to bed, Locklyn."

"Will you stop telling me to go to bed?" I shoot back, my frustration rising. "If you're so concerned about tomorrow, you should go to bed yourself."

"I'm not the one who could barely keep up fully rested!"

It's as though he slapped me across the face. I reel back, feeling the hot prickle of tears in my eyes.

His eyes fill with horror, and he reaches toward me, remorse twisting his face. "Locklyn, I'm sorry. I didn't mean it to come out like that."

I start to swim away, but he darts forward and catches hold of me. "Let go of me, Darin."

"Locklyn, please," he pleads. "That sounded terrible. I didn't mean it like that at all. I just know it's harder for you without a—"

"Let go!" I snap, and his hand drops off my arm as though shocked by an electric current. Water churns around me as I swim away as fast as I can, tears pouring down my face.

Why doesn't he just say he thinks I'm weak?

Poor little Locklyn. She can't even keep up.

Anger and heartache pound as I swim blindly. My thoughts swirl. As I remember Conway's hand grasping mine, realization floods me and my fury spikes higher.

He was just using me to get to Darin.

Conway knew it would infuriate him to see someone holding hands with the person who is basically his little sister.

Especially if that someone was a person Darin couldn't stand.

I veer toward the rocks where Conway said the periwinkles were, prepared to give him a piece of my mind. But just as I am about to round the corner, I stop.

Right now might not be a great time to yell at Conway. Someone else beat me to it.

16

LOCKLYN

"THIS IS JUST LIKE YOU, CONWAY! Needling and provoking Darin Aalto at every turn! It might do you good to remember that finding this treasure is all that stands between your kingdom and an attack!" Ginevra's voice quivers.

I peer around and see Conway. He leans in a bored fashion against the rocks behind him while Ginevra swims agitatedly back and forth.

"Come on, Ginny." Conway straightens slightly. "We both know what this is really about."

She stops her restless swimming and glares at him. "What are you saying?"

"You don't give two periwinkles about me provoking Aalto. Wave Master knows, you don't mind arguing with him yourself."

I shouldn't be listening in on a private conversation, so I start back toward the campsite.

"You're in a snit because of Locklyn."

I freeze at Conway's words, unable to resist listening further.

There is a pause. Ginevra's voice when she next speaks is higher than usual. "What I don't give two periwinkles about is your love life. But I do think it is in bad taste to lead that poor girl on like you're doing."

"Who said anything about leading her on?"

"You're the crown prince of Undula! You can't marry a dugong shepherdess!"

"Can't I? One of the perks of being king, Ginny, is that you get to make the rules."

Ginevra's voice is shaking again. "You are the most disgustingly immature person I have ever met, Conway." She turns to leave, and I shrink against my hiding spot.

Conway pushes off the rocks, reaching for her. "Ginny—"

"Stop calling me that!"

He sighs, hovering a few feet away, arms crossed over his chest. "Ginevra, then. We've been friends since we were kids. Why does it have to be this way?"

She remains turned away from him, shoulders stiff. "You know why it's this way, Conway."

He throws up his hands. "Just because I don't want to marry you doesn't make me your enemy, Ginny! I think you're beautiful. And smart. And ridiculously good at fighting. And scary—in a good way. I miss you. Can't we be friends again?" He holds out a hand.

Ginevra stays half turned and her voice catches when she speaks. "If you think I'm all those things, Conway, why don't you want to marry me?"

His hand drops to his side and exasperation tinges his voice. "I don't know, Ginny. I just don't, alright?"

"Well, I do know," Ginevra says, her voice rising again.

I duck down.

"You're scared. You're scared of being with a strong woman. Because you're still a boy. A boy who refuses to grow up and be a Merman and take responsibility for his life!"

Conway's voice doesn't rise, but it is cold. "I'm surprised you want to be with someone so helpless and immature. But for your information, Locklyn isn't what I'd call weak. Surviving being abandoned as an infant in a reef isn't exactly easy."

"You're just using her to get to Aalto!" Ginevra's voice has risen to a shout, and I feel prickles of anger as her words confirm my own suspicions.

"Oh, am I? Has it ever occurred to you that it might not be your strength that bugs me? Maybe I'm attracted to women who are strong without having the compassion and sweetness of a block of granite!"

I expect her to hit him. Everything I've ever heard about the warrior queen of the Nebulae makes me sure she will meet an attack with one of her own. But what happens next is so much worse.

A sudden outburst of sobs drifts over the rocks, and when I peer around them, I see Ginevra bent over, tears streaming down her face. Conway looks horror-struck, and if I were guessing, I would say he has never seen her cry before.

"Ginny—" he starts, reaching toward her, but she jerks away from his touch as though it burns.

"Stay away from me," she chokes, then swirls around and shoots away into the dark water.

For a moment, Conway hovers there, gazing after her. Then with a muttered oath, he swims in the opposite direction, directly toward where I lurk. There is no time to get out of his way, but I don't need to. He swims past without seeing me, his face set in rigid lines, and rejoins the group next to the magma pit.

I slump back against the rocks, my head falling forward so that my hair drifts over my face. I am so tired. Tired of conflict. Tired of not understanding what is going on. Tired of everything being complex and painful.

My heart aches as I think of Darin. Ever since Amaya got married and had other responsibilities, he was the one I turned to. For help. For advice. For comradeship. Now we can't seem to speak to each other without fighting.

And Conway. My heart flutters and I feel the pressure of his hand in mine again. Did that mean anything? Or am I, like Ginevra suggested, just a way for him to get under Darin's skin?

Besides the fact there is clearly something between him and Ginevra. Obviously, she is deeply in love with the prince, and my heart twists at the thought that I am contributing to the rift between them.

But he rejected her before you ever came along.

I shake my head at the little voice in my mind. He cares about her too. I can see that. I just don't know whether he's deluding himself about only wanting friendship. Part of me thinks Ginevra might have had a point about him being scared of her strength.

I lower my head into my hands.

I don't know.

I don't know.

I don't know.

Is friendship between a man and a woman completely separate from romantic love? Or is there always a hope for something more? Is it possible to love someone deeply as a friend and be incapable of being in love with them?

You and Darin have always just been friends, the tiny voice in my head says. But, unbidden, the memory of him bending over me in the palace comes to me. Tendrils of his long blond hair skimming my face. The smell of him, cold and clear like the open ocean—the smell of adventure—enveloping me as his lips pressed against my forehead, firm and steady. He awakened feelings I didn't dare to examine.

Don't, I tell myself sharply, thrusting the memory away as the thought of the scene that followed twists painfully. *Just don't. Stop it.*

Suddenly, my head snaps up. Was that a scream? A woman's scream, echoing faint and shrill through the water? Silence wraps around me, and I strain against it, listening for another sound.

Nothing comes. But instead of alleviating my fear, dread piles up, pressing heavier and heavier on my insides. Ginevra hasn't come back. And when she left, she was an emotional wreck, easy prey for whatever or whoever might attack her.

I push hard off the rocks and shoot toward the group huddled around the magma pit. Conway hovers on its outskirts, the expression on his face forbidding enough to dissuade anyone from trying to engage him in conversation. But I grab his arm and his expression lightens.

"Locklyn—"

"We have to go find Ginevra," I say urgently.

His brow darkens again, and he turns back toward the red magma glow. "Unless you fancy getting your head bitten off, I'd advise against it."

"Conway, she shouldn't be out there on her own."

"Trust me, Ginevra can take care of herself."

"I thought I heard someone scream." I give his arm an impatient shake.

His head swivels. "What?"

"It was so faint I can't be sure, but it's dangerous to be wandering around on her own. Especially in the state she was in." His eyes widen, and I feel shame prickle along my spine. "I heard you two arguing," I mutter.

He gives a rueful laugh. "That isn't exactly the way I'd have chosen for you to hear how I feel about you."

Warmth spreads up my face and neck. Now is definitely not the time for this conversation. "Are you listening? Ginevra could be in real trouble! Come on!" I turn to look for Darin and spot him on the other side of the pit, talking to one of Ginevra's Nebulae guards—Baia, I think her name is—whom I have never seen smile before. She smiles now, so widely I can almost count every one of her bright white teeth. The warmth Conway's words generated fades away into cold ash. "Darin!"

He looks over. "What?"

A coldness I've never heard before tinges his voice. "Conway and I are going to look for Ginevra. She went for a swim and hasn't returned."

Darin's face changes, and he swiftly swims through the group toward us. Unexpected resentment flares inside me at the difference in his manner now that I've brought up Ginevra. "When did she leave?"

"About ten minutes ago," I say stiffly.

"What made her go off on her own?"

I bite my lip, glancing at Conway.

He reddens, but only says brusquely, "She and I had an argument. Not that it's any of your concern, Aalto."

Darin raises his eyebrows. "Well, if you two just had an argument, it might be better for me to go with Locklyn to find her. She's probably not dying to see you right now."

The thought of how Ginevra will react if Darin—whom she clearly respects—finds her unharmed but extremely upset makes me say quickly, "I think Conway and I should go. Give him a chance to apologize."

Darin's face hardens, but his voice remains indifferent as he turns away. "Fair enough. Take a conch so you can call for backup if you run into trouble."

I look after him, my heart sinking as he swims toward the Nebulae warrior. Does he think I just rejected his help so I could be alone with Conway?

"Hey." I turn to see Conway hanging a conch shell on a leather thong around his neck. "We going?"

Pushing away all thoughts of Darin, I feel in the back of my pants for my coral knife. "Yes," I say. "Let's go."

DARIN

HE'S SEETHING AS HE WATCHES CONWAY

and Locklyn swim away.

I've known her since she was born. But as soon as the prince starts taking an interest in her, she seems happy to sink twenty years of friendship.

Darin can't take it anymore. "I'm sorry," he says to the Nebulae Merwoman, cutting off her flirtatious remarks midsentence. "I'll be back shortly." And without another word, he leaves her staring after him and swims away in the same direction Conway and Locklyn went.

As soon as he is out of sight of the rest of the group, he dodges behind a massive outcropping. With a muffled oath, he slams his fist into the rock.

He could have said something months ago. Now that Conway is so openly pursuing Locklyn, Darin has no way to express his feelings without it coming across as jealousy. No way to keep it from becoming a competition.

He imagines her, small and slight, with her creamy skin and wide, ever-changing eyes, her long hair twisting around her like a dark blue curtain. In his mental picture, she is smiling, the expression lighting up her usually serious face. The vision fades, replaced by the image of Conway, his fingers interlaced with hers, grinning with the confidence of someone who is used to getting what he wants. Pain twists in Darin's gut as he remembers her soft skin against his lips that night in the palace.

Their friendship was crumbling, as he always feared it would. He seemed unable to keep his pain and jealousy from lashing out in the form of anger and cold indifference.

Wave Master.

The name rises in his mind almost subconsciously, like the bubbles of his breath rising in a never-ending stream toward The Surface waves. But no other words come to complete the prayer.

Instead, his mind teems with other thoughts. If Locklyn were to marry Conway, she would be free of the stigma she had endured her entire life. And she would have the power to make lasting changes in the laws of Undula to protect all other Crura. Avonlea would never have to go to Atlantis.

Emotions tear into him. He's loved Locklyn all her life. First, as a little sister. Then, as his companion, his closest friend. And now, as the Merwoman he wants to cherish and be with always.

There will never be anyone else. For Darin, it has always been Locklyn, and always will be.

Rest in me.

The words echo in his mind, the voice one he has known since he was a small boy.

But what do I do?

Rest, Darin.

The words make him slump back against the rocks.

I don't know how to rest. I've always protected people. Led them. I don't understand.

The water seems to darken around him as he stays that way, head down, heartsick and weary. Seconds turn into longer moments, and when his head finally lifts, dim shapes lie on the ground around the magma pit. He must have drifted off.

He shoves away from the rock and swims closer to the pit, scanning the slumbering group for Locklyn's legs and Ginevra's distinctive tail. They are not there. His tail whips through the water, propelling him backward as he wheels around and shoots in the direction he saw Locklyn and Conway go once more. Horrific images bombard his mind.

Locklyn bleeding, sharks closing in on her from all directions, drawn by the scent of her blood.

Locklyn struggling to extricate herself from the tentacles of a giant squid as it drags her away to its lair.

Locklyn paralyzed by a sea snake bite, the rope-like black and blue creature twining around her as the venom causes her heart to falter, then stop beating entirely.

Eyes darting from side to side, Darin shoots through the water, coral knife clenched tightly in his fist, ears straining for a sound. The water remains dark and still. A shadow moves in the corner of his eye, and he wheels around, expecting to come face-to-face with some monster of the deep. Nothing.

He swims on, trying desperately not to imagine what the continued silence implies. A giant block of sandstone looms in front of him. He is about to dart around it when he notices the blue glow around the rock's edges. Pausing, he strains to listen. At first, there is nothing, but gradually the muffled sounds of deep voices and harsh laughter reach him.

Holding his breath, he swims upward until his eyes are barely level with the top of the rock. Then he peers down. What he sees makes him inhale so much water, he chokes and coughs, struggling desperately to muffle the sound.

The boulder he is hiding behind guards the entrance to a spacious cave. Scattered around the walls are bulging sacks. Crude wooden spears are piled in a corner. In the center of the cave, a group of six large, unkempt Mermen lounge on the floor, playing a game with a painted wooden board and pieces of sea glass. A single lanky Merman, with long white-blond hair tied back in a seahorse tail and a shark-tooth earring in one ear, hovers languidly near the entrance, twirling a conch shell on a cord around one hand.

It is the sight of the conch shell that causes Darin to choke. At that sound of his coughing, the lookout glances sharply upward, and Darin drops below the edge of the boulder, muscles tensed, certain any minute a white-blond head will pop over the top of the rock.

As seconds drag by and nothing happens, Darin gradually relaxes, allowing his body to drift slowly upward until he is once again able to look down on the group. Two of the men huddled around the gaming board have begun to argue while the others watch.

"Hey, Kelby," the blond man at the entrance calls, and one of the gamers, a big man with short olive hair in cornrows and a chunk missing from his nose, looks up. "Should we give 'em grub now?"

"Not sure why it matters," Kelby snorts. "Where they're going, eating is going to be the least of their worries."

"But we get paid more if they don't look like skeletons."

At the guard's glance to the back of the cave, Darin looks more closely. Illuminated by the strands of glowing blue seaweed scattered on the floor is a group of five Merpeople tied together in a clump by their wrists, mouths obscured by gags. Darin recognizes three of them.

"Give them some of the pickled walrus meat." Kelby waves toward one of the sacks. "And, Pike? I'd be careful of that one." He points at Ginevra, whose pearly tail appears to glow in the gloom. "When I was putting in the gag, she tried to bite me."

"If I have to feed the prisoners, someone else oughta keep watch." Pike sniffs, glaring pointedly at the two Mermen still squabbling over the pile of sea glass. Kelby rolls his eyes, then uses his tail to thump the Merman closest to him hard in the small of the back.

"You! Get off your lazy rear and stand guard!"

Pike smirks as the thumped Merman sulkily joins him at the cave's entrance. Swimming to the nearest sack, he opens the top and rummages inside. Glass clinks, and a few seconds later, a horrible smell greets Darin's nostrils. Pike chatters happily as he swims around the prisoners, removing their gags.

"Who wants to be first to get a lovely piece of pickled walrus? Mmm, delicious." He drifts around the circle of prisoners, pushing the jar of meat into their faces. Sounds of gagging and retching rise in his wake.

"If you don't get that out of my face, I'll add one of your fingers to it," a female voice snaps.

Darin smiles slightly to himself. Clearly, Ginevra is as sweet-tempered as ever.

"Now, now." Pike wags a finger before dipping his hand into the jar and pulling out a piece of dripping, rancid meat. He pops it into his mouth, smacking his lips. "Keep talking like that and I'll eat yer share meself."

"Please do," Ginevra says with disdain.

"Ye don't want to starve before we get to our destination, love," Pike says, helping himself to another chunk of meat. Then he pauses, hand halfway to his mouth. "Or maybe ye do."

"Where are you taking us?" Conway's voice asks next.

"Oh, but telling would spoil the surprise." Pike seems to be enjoying himself.

"Listen." Conway's tone is calm and reasonable. "If it's money you want, we can pay. As I told you before, the group we are traveling with is on a quest to recover Llyra's Lost Treasure. Think, Pike. Gold coins, rubies the size of your fist, casks of aged wine, bolts of silk softer than the finest sealskin, new metal weapons. Join us and we'll share the spoils with you."

"Llyra's Lost Treasure?" Pike begins to laugh, a squeaky, nasally sound that grates on Darin's nerves. "Next time you spin a story, boy, try to make it a hair more believable. That treasure's a myth. All that'll happen if we join yer group is ye'll slit our throats while we're sleeping or else turn around and sell us to the Guar—"

"Careful, Pike," growls Kelby.

Pike glances at him and then back to the group of prisoners. "Last chance for dinner," he says, brandishing his jar.

"I'll take some."

Darin's heart skips at the sound of Locklyn's voice.

"Good girl," Pike says approvingly, fishing a chunk out of his jar. "Open up."

"Oh, I'm not actually hungry." Locklyn's pitch is higher than usual, and she gives a nervous giggle. "I know it's silly, but . . . I'm scared of catfish."

Catfish?

Pike stares at her. "Catfish?"

"They terrify me."

Darin imagines Locklyn's eyes gazing at Pike, round and blue and innocent.

"I'm hoping the smell will keep them away."

Kelby lets out a guffaw. "Do you hear that, Pike? She's hoping the smell of pickled walrus will keep catfish away. Go on, load her pockets up. We wouldn't want the little Crura maiden getting attacked by catfish in the night."

"Oh, thank you," Locklyn gushes as Pike begins slipping chunks of meat into the pockets of her pants. "Could I sing something for you? To thank you properly?"

The Mermen around the gaming board all turn to stare at her. Kelby's question is skeptical. "You can sing?"

In answer, Locklyn begins to hum. The tune is soothing, a rippling melody that undulates and flows around the group like a current. The empty jar Pike is holding slips through his fingers and floats gently down to rest on the sandy ocean floor, but he doesn't notice. The lookout, who has been irritably whacking his tail against the cave wall, stills and looks toward Locklyn.

Words flow into the tune, and Darin recognizes the song—a lullaby she has crooned to every one of Amaya's children.

> *Moonlight on the water*
> *Shh, shh*
> *Ship rocking on wave*
> *Hush, hush*
> *King's daughter coming*
> *Shh, shh*

To fulfill the promise she gave

He knows what she is doing, and the magic of the music still pulls at him. His eyelids suddenly feel heavy, and he watches, transfixed, as the group of Mermen begin to rub their eyes, mouths stretching wide in yawns. Locklyn's voice wraps around them all, warm and soft as a sealskin blanket.

> *Blood-red rubies shining*
> *Shh, shh*
> *Locket glinting gold*
> *Hush, hush*
> *The sorceress demands payment*
> *Shh, shh*
> *For the pair of legs she sold*

It takes all of his willpower to resist the spell of Locklyn's voice and the drowsiness it invokes. Her captors don't stand a chance. One by one, their eyes are closing.

> *But, listen, king's daughter*
> *Shh, shh*
> *Wind rising, waves roar*
> *Hush, hush*
> *Is your life a fitting payment*
> *Shh, shh*
> *To settle an old score?*

> *Tempest tossing ship skyward*
> *Shh, shh,*
> *Treasure-laden decks heave high*
> *Hush, hush*
> *Prince holds his water-won lady*
> *Shh, shh*
> *Wordless last goodbye*

Pike, Kelby, and the rest of their men are slumped on the sand, snoring. The group of prisoners are all asleep as well, sagging against their bonds. Locklyn's voice is soft, almost inaudible, as she finishes her song.

> *Moonlight on the water*
> *Shh, shh*
> *Night calm, waves deep*
> *Hush, hush*
> *In the realm below the world*
> *Shh, shh*
> *The little Mermaid sleeps her final sleep.*

Silence fills the cave, broken only by the snoring of the kidnappers. Darin struggles against the lethargy Locklyn's song has engendered, knowing now is an ideal moment to help her and the rest of their companions escape. But Darin is unable to will himself to move, intrigued to watch the rest of her plan.

Locklyn reaches into her pockets, and after a moment, she begins to sing again, softly, a wordless melody, catchy and urgent. At first, nothing happens, but as Locklyn continues, he hears movement behind him. Turning his head, he sees a family of sea turtles rising from the base of the rock where he is hiding. They swim past him, heading straight for Locklyn.

Awestruck, Darin watches them peck at the ropes binding Locklyn to her companions. She must be holding the pickled walrus meat onto the ropes, incentivizing the turtles to cut through them, attempting to get the meat.

The ropes fall away, and Locklyn pulls out the last of the walrus meat, feeding it to the sea turtles as she pats their heads in thanks. Then she turns to Ginevra and places one hand over her mouth, shaking her awake. Ginevra wakes Conway and the other two prisoners, a boy and girl who look like siblings, as Locklyn swims silently over to the pile of weapons and retrieves her knife, which she uses to cut the others' bindings.

Leaving their seven captors still snoring in the sand, the group swims as quietly as possible out of the cave toward Darin's boulder. As they whoosh past the rock, Locklyn a little behind the others, he darts out and grabs her arm, clapping a hand over her mouth as she opens it to scream.

Her eyes widen, then brighten as she sees his face. He murmurs her name, gently pulls her in, and wraps his arms tightly around her. She is stiff at first, but then she melts against him, bubbles whooshing out as she releases a deep breath and relaxes.

For one glorious moment, the warm, solid reality of her pulses through every fiber of his being. Then she wriggles free, mouths, "Come on," and shoots away after the others.

Darin follows.

LOCKLYN

I SIT, HUDDLED ON THE GROUND NEXT to the magma pit. The heat is almost too much, but I am unable to stop shaking. Darin rummages in our supplies for food to offer the siblings, Arledge and Dwyn. Conway sits on a rock nearby as Kai attends to his flesh wounds. The rest of the Undulae and Nebulae guards, who had roused briefly when we returned to camp, have gone back to sleep.

Someone settles down beside me, and I look to see Ginevra stretching her pearly tail toward the glowing red strip in the sand. She doesn't say anything, and my eyes return to the smoldering liquid before me.

After a long moment, she says grudgingly, "I suppose I should thank you."

I face her, eyebrows raised. "Such heartfelt gratitude is hard to resist."

She glowers. "It's not funny. You're the last person in the world I want to be indebted to."

"Why is that?" I say, though I already know the answer.

She drops her gaze, catching her lower lip between her teeth. When she finally looks back up, the anguish in her eyes twists my insides. Soon gone, the old cynicism returns. "If I could just challenge you in hand-to-hand combat, Conway would be mine in less time than it takes to talk about it."

I bristle at the thinly veiled insult. "You didn't beat me that quickly the last time we fought."

She surprises me with a chuckle. Her next words are so low, I barely catch them before they trail away. "If I was looking for a friend . . ." Her body seems to sag.

"A Crura friend?" I do not hide my sarcasm.

She shakes her head. "I don't care about your legs."

I give her an incredulous look. "From what I've heard, Crura hunting is a sport in Nebula."

She casts me a scathing glance. "Clearly, your information sources are somewhat lacking. Crura hunting was outlawed centuries ago. I will admit, Crura aren't loved in Nebula any more than they are in Undula, but that's universal under the sea. Merpeople aren't supposed to have legs."

Surprisingly, her brusqueness doesn't sting. There is nothing hidden in Ginevra. I realize there would be something reassuring in having a friend whom you knew would never lie to you for fear of hurting your feelings.

"Why can't we be friends?" I say impulsively, stretching out a hand.

The muscles in her shoulders tense as she jerks away. "I'm not looking for friendship! I have plenty of *friends*!" Her eyes dart toward Conway, who is chatting good-naturedly with Kai. The dolphin caretaker is scowling, but the prince is ignoring his unwelcoming demeanor.

As if feeling Ginevra's gaze, Conway glances in our direction. His eyes meet mine and he smiles, his look one of complete and unaffected liking. I smile back involuntarily, the warmth of his affection balm to my soul after Ginevra's rebuff.

The smile slides off my face as I glimpse Ginevra's expression.

"You're going to take him, aren't you?" she says bitterly. "A Crura shepherdess, queen of Undula. What a chance."

Her words sear me like magma on bare skin. "I would never

marry someone for what they could give me. If I married Conway, it would be because I love him." As soon as I say it, I wonder if my words are true. As queen, I could do so much. For my family. For other Crura. If Conway asked me to marry him, would I say no if I didn't "feel" for him as I thought I should?

"Love him?" Ginevra's voice is ragged. "You've known him for less than a week!"

Her words bring Darin's to mind. For some reason, the thought of him sends unreasonable anger flooding through me. Why under the sea can't everyone just let me live my life? "You're right," I say, pushing myself to my feet and glaring down at her. "I have only known him for a few days. I don't love him. But I might. And I don't owe you anything."

I turn to swim away, wanting nothing more than to be alone, but the sound of Darin's voice stops me mid-stroke. "Will someone explain to me what happened?" He sinks down next to the lava, propping himself up on his elbows, the light turning his tail a burnished bronze. Dwyn and Arledge follow him timidly, lowering themselves onto the sand a little apart from him and Ginevra. Conway swims over, dropping down across from Darin. He looks up at me, hesitating a few feet away, and pats the sand next to him.

I hang back a moment longer, knowing that joining him will only provoke both Darin and Ginevra. The thought stings my already fragile temper. What right do either of them have to be annoyed? It's not fair for Ginevra to blame me because Conway prefers me to her. And Darin is taking the whole older brother thing way too far. He hasn't given me one valid reason to not like Conway. If it bothers him to see me sitting with Conway, then he should have made a place for me himself.

Suddenly reckless, I plop down beside Conway, giving him a quick smile. I avoid looking at either Darin or Ginevra.

Conway answers Darin's question. "Ginevra and I had a . . ." He pauses, glancing at Ginevra, who refuses to look at him. ". . . disagreement and she swam off to be alone. When she didn't come back, Locklyn and I went to look for her. When we got to the cave where you found us, Ginevra, Dwyn, and Arledge were there, tied up and gagged. Thinking they were alone, we entered the cave to try to free them, but the group of kidnappers you saw ambushed us. We fought, but there were too many of them." Darin's lips compress slightly as he motions for Conway to continue. "Honestly, I don't know about what happened next," Conway says, turning to look at me. "How under the sea did you do that?"

A brief smirk flickers across Darin's face.

"Well, I got the voice along with the legs," I say, fighting down a stab of irritation.

Conway shakes his head. "Why did we bother bringing weapons? You can just sing all our enemies to sleep."

I bite my lip and find myself glancing again at Darin. Our eyes meet for a fraction of a second. "It doesn't quite work like that," I say slowly. "There are spells—specific words in a specific order— that have the same affect every time on everyone. But the magic of singing is more of . . . I don't know how else to put it . . . an influence. So even people who don't know incantations, like me, can influence other sea creatures to a specific course of action. But I have no guarantee the creatures involved will choose not to resist my influence." I think, trying to find a way to better explain. A thought occurs to me, and I gesture to Darin. "Darin heard me singing, but he didn't go to sleep like the rest of you. Why? Because he's heard me sing that song a million times before. He knew what I was doing, and he forced his mind not to listen to my guidance."

"I still think you should try with that Anakite crab," Conway states.

I shrug. "I can try. But I don't think it will work. I don't know why, but the bigger and wilder an animal is, the harder they are to control."

Silence descends. In order to avoid looking at Darin, I stare down at my hands. A flicker of movement catches my eye, and a hand creeps into my lap and laces its fingers with my own. I turn my head and lock eyes with Conway. He stares at me with something between laughter and a challenge sparkling in his black eyes. For an instant, I study his handsome, confident face. Then I free my fingers from his and curl them into a fist beneath his hand. I can't do this right now. I have no idea what Conway wants from me.

"Why don't you tell your story to the rest of the group?" Darin's voice carries a gentleness that snaps my head up. But he is looking at Dwyn, the young woman whom the scavengers had captured before us, along with her brother, Arledge.

Dwyn glances at Arledge, who motions for her to speak, and then looks shyly around the circle. "There's not much to tell," she says. Her voice is high, but unlike Ginevra's clear, lilting tones, hers are soft and breathy. "My brother and I are from a small settlement about a day's journey west of Aquaticus. Every year, a group from our village goes out hunting needlefish sometime midwinter. This year, there was an outbreak of scale rot right before we were supposed to set out. The entire rest of the hunting party contracted it." She glances again at her brother. "Arledge and I discussed postponing the expedition until the rest of the group had recovered, but in the end, we decided to go without them. The village needed food." She shakes her head. "Clearly, that wasn't a wise decision. We were ambushed by those scavengers three days after setting out. We didn't stand a chance with just the two of us." She falls silent.

"And?" Darin prompts, his smile tender.

She returns the smile and an icy needle of jealousy stabs at my heart.

Stop it, I chide myself. Don't be a hypocrite. You were just annoyed with him for being overprotective and not allowing you to live your life.

It's not that I don't want him to live his life. It's just that it hurts to see him so effortlessly charming with every woman. Except for me. He's never like that with me.

"At first we thought they were just slave traders," Dwyn says. "But yesterday evening, when everyone else was asleep, I heard the leader, Kelby, talking to Pike who was on watch. He said we would need to hurry to reach Atlantis in time to catch the submarine going to the North Sea. And he said something about the water levels being high this year. And he mentioned a name. Lacknis?" She looks questioningly at us.

Something stirs deep in my mind. A story that Chantara told me as a child. I can't remember what it was about, but there was something named Lacknis in it. Except that Lacknis isn't quite right. "Loch Ness?" I ask tentatively.

Dwyn's face clears. "Yes! Yes, that's right! What is Loch Ness?"

I shake my head. "I don't know, it was in a story I heard as a child." I catch Darin's eyes, mutely questioning if he knows what I'm talking about.

He shakes his head, slight confusion on his face.

"I heard one more thing quite distinctly," Dwyn adds. "'The beast is hungry.' I have no idea what that means. And I don't know what a submarine is. But it didn't seem like they were just ordinary slave traders."

"I know what a submarine is." We all turn to stare at Conway. "It's a machine, made out of metal, that moves through the water even faster than a blue whale. They make them in Atlantis."

He seems uncomfortable. He must have learned about submarines when he was researching Atlantis in the hopes of swimming away from Undula and his crown.

"Well, you'd need a machine to reach the North Sea," I say, hoping to deflect the attention off Conway. "You'd be swimming for years."

I gaze into the scarlet heart of the magma pit, wishing I could infuse some of that glowing heat into my own heart. Everything inside me is cold. Cold and dull. And so very tired.

"We should go to bed," Darin says at length.

Ginevra pushes herself up immediately and, without looking at anyone, swims to the sealskin hammock her bodyguards have slung between two rocks. Dwyn and Arledge use the posidonia blankets Darin gave them to bed down near the pack dolphins.

Go, Conway. Go. Go, I chant in my mind.

I need to talk to Darin. The hug he gave me after we escaped the scavengers had regret tumbling through me like breakers. We have to fix whatever is going on between us. I care about him. He obviously cares somewhat about me. So why are we unable to speak to each other without quarreling?

But Conway seems in no hurry. I look across the glowing magma pit, trying to catch Darin's eye, but he is looking down, lifting handfuls of sand and allowing them to run through his fingers. My gaze lingers on his hands. They are big, the knuckles wide, the fingers long and broad, the palms hardened with callouses. Warrior hands. Adventurer hands. Schatzi hands.

My lips curve upward as I remember him holding Avonlea the day after she was born—those big, hard hands stroking the soft blue down covering her head with indescribable gentleness.

"Locklyn?" Conway's voice jerks me back to the present, and I glance at him, my heart skipping a beat at the intensity in his black eyes. I look quickly away. "Sing something," he says.

"Is that a command?"

"No," he whispers, the bubbles of his words tickling my ear. "But my heart will be broken if you don't."

I snort. "You should try to be more emotional. Your lack of drama is really getting to me." I look down, and my gaze catches on the strands of silver and blue, glinting in the light from the magma pit, which encircle my left ankle. The sight stings my conscience. "Darin," I say, and he looks up, the expression in his golden eyes unreadable, "pick a song."

For a fraction of a second, I think he is going to refuse, and my heart sinks. But then he says, "Rainbow Sheen," and drops his eyes back to his lap.

Conway looks between us, his eyes curious.

I clear my throat.

> *You and I*
> *Bouncing through the billows*
> *Chasing pufferfish*
> *Collecting sea glass shards*

You and I
Laughing at my sister
Playing with your little brother
Listening to your father's stories

You and I
Weaving kelp nets
Feeding the dolphins
Digging clams out of the sand

And you hold one up to me, saying
It's commonplace
So dark
So slimy
So crusted with grime

Look closer, sweetheart
It's the most beautiful thing beneath the sea
Open it up
Peer inside
Marvel at the rainbow sheen

You and him
His hand on your waist
His fingers in your hair
His lips brushing your face

You and him
Golden rings on your fingers
Glimmer of diamonds at your throat
Mother-of-pearl combs in your hair

You and him
Parents approve

Perfect couple
Ideal match, they say

Me, I'm nothing special
Dirty
Common
Boy next door

But, look closer, sweetheart
I'm wearing my heart on my sleeve
The love I've always had for you
That, dearest, is the rainbow sheen

My voice trails away into nothingness. The beautiful sadness of the song aches in my heart.

"Who did she choose?" Conway asks. "The one she'd known forever? Or the one she was in love with?"

I know what he is really asking.

But he doesn't realize there isn't a choice. Because the one I've known all my life doesn't love me. Or he'd have told me so in the four long years I've been of age.

I pull my eyes back to Conway's face. "The one she was in love with," I say, and Conway smiles.

19
LOCKLYN

THE ONLY REASON I CAN SEE THE REST
of the group is because we are swimming across a broad, flat plain.
They are so far ahead. Even if I swim as fast as I can, I will not
reach them until they stop for the night. Usually Darin would wait
for me, but for the first time in four days, he has managed to get Kai
to say more than three consecutive words by asking about his trips
to acquire dolphins for the royal herd. The result is the two of them
swimming together at the front of the group, talking animatedly
and oblivious to the world around them. *Probably immersed in
another discussion of undersea travel.*

I've been telling Darin for the last week to let me take care of
myself, but–unreasonably–his failure to notice my fatigue stings.
No one else bothered to hang back and wait for me either.

Ginevra and Conway, for once in their lives not fighting, swim
a little way behind Darin and Kai. They are both loaded down with
packets of shark meat from a recent hunting expedition, and they
are laughing. I think of a story Conway told me about how they
once painted squid ink on Ginevra's little sister's pillow while she
was sleeping so that her hair stuck. The poor girl swam through the
palace screeching with a pillow stuck to the back of her head. *Are
they reminiscing about other childhood pranks?*

The Nebulae guards, Baia and Kallan, and the Undulae soldiers, Hurley, Clyde, and Blackwell, swim out of sight, each having gone in a different direction to scout for threats to our party.

Self-pity wells up inside, and I am too tired to squash it back down.

My legs hurt so much.

I can't help carry the shark meat because I can't even keep up with nothing weighing me down.

Everyone else has someone to talk to.

This is the most boring scenery I have ever seen.

Stupid, stupid legs.

Frustrated, I kick my legs harder and let out a gasp as a cramp shoots up my left calf. Sinking my teeth into my bottom lip to keep from moaning, I halt, reaching down to massage my spasming limb. As the twitching, stabbing pains begin to subside, I hear a voice behind me.

"The props giving you trouble, love?"

My fingers dig into my calf harder than necessary. Slowly, I straighten and turn to find Blackwell hovering offensively close. Resisting the urge to dart away, I content myself with drifting backward, trying to widen the space between us, but he follows me.

"Scared, spindle-shanks? Tell me, how was your night at the city gates?"

My heart beats a dangerous rhythm against my ribs, but I keep my voice even. "I have no interest in talking to you, Blackwell. And the others will be wondering where I am." I turn away, keeping him in my peripheral vision, my fingers wrapping tightly around the handle of my knife.

"Nobody is wondering where you are, Crura. Nobody cares."

I know his words aren't true. Darin cares. And I think Conway might as well. Yesterday, I swam with Kai and the dolphins. When we parted at the camp, he had said in his gruff voice, "Not many have your gift with creatures." He'd said nothing else, but his words had warmed my heart, giving me the impression that he, at least, might not view me with the same disdain the Undulae and Nebulae soldiers do.

But Blackwell's words probe the insecurities that have been plaguing me all day. Gritting my teeth to keep in the words I long to hurl, I continue to swim in the opposite direction, forcing myself to keep going despite the residual pain in my leg.

Fingers close around my arm, and Blackwell jerks me back around. "I'm not finished with you, spindle-shanks!"

Something snaps inside me. I yank my knife out of my pants, slashing toward his face so that he drops my arm and pushes backward in the water, drawing his own knife. "Why can't you just leave me alone?" My voice is loud and I try to keep it from shaking. "I know you hate me! But why do you have to go out of your way to make my life an embodiment of Oro?"

Blackwell's visage twists, the scar on it making him look demented. "You're a freak!" he spits at me, veins standing out in his neck. "You should have died the night you were born! But somehow, you've wormed your way into normal society, blinding people to what you really are. Aalto refuses to even consider me as part of his harvesting team, but he treats you like his best friend! Prince Conway has never even acknowledged my existence, but he looks at you like the sun rises and sets in your face!"

"It's not my fault if other people aren't as bigoted and small souled as you, Blackwell," I snap back.

Blackwell's visage twists again, then his features smooth, and he says in an unrecognizable voice, "Your Highness."

I spin to see Conway hovering behind us, a wary, questioning expression on his face. "Why aren't you out scouting, Blackwell?"

"I noticed Miss Locklyn had a leg cramp." Blackwell's oily voice causes bile to rise in my throat. "I stopped to see if she was alright."

Conway glances at me, and I avert my eyes, unwilling to lie and at the same time unwilling to tell tales. I can deal with Blackwell on my own.

After a moment, Conway says, "Very well, but Locklyn appears to be fine now, so you may continue your rounds."

Blackwell gives him a deep bow, but as he swims away, he catches my eye and mouths, "Watch your back."

Conway must see my look of disgust because he turns to scowl after Blackwell's retreating form and says brusquely, "I've always hated him. Oily, conniving little suck-up."

"I'm not overly fond of him myself," I admit as we begin to swim in the direction of the main group. "Though he has never really tried to suck up to me." Not entirely true, I realize a second later. The first night he came to my hut, he definitely tried to do just that.

"Really? I thought he might be trying to come on to you just now."

I stare at Conway incredulously. "Are you crazy? Why under the sea would he be coming on to me?"

Conway rolls his eyes. "Oh, I have *no* idea."

Heat rises in my face, so I say quickly, "Well, if you must know, he did try to come on to me once, but since I cut his face open in response, I don't think he'll try that again in a hurry."

Conway gapes at me. Then he bursts out laughing. "Good to know that's how you reject your suitors. I'll have to bear that in mind. I quite like my face the way it is, but on the other hand . . ." He grins impishly, and I blush worse than ever.

"Locklyn." I look up and see Darin, his face dark. My heart sinks. I glance up at Conway and see he is staring at Darin with equal dislike. "Can I talk to you?" Darin says, pointedly ignoring Conway to address me.

"Okay," I say reluctantly, annoyance simmering. After spending little to no time with me in the last three days, he has to spoil the first lighthearted moment I've had today. I follow him, taking in the rigid set of his shoulders. He's angry about something. Apprehension gnaws with a discomfort worse than my aching legs. Are we about to have another fight?

Once we are at a distance, Darin turns to me. "Why were you so far behind the rest of the group? That's not safe, Locklyn."

There is no way I am going to tell him I was so far behind because my legs were hurting. "I'm fine, Darin."

"That doesn't change anything, Locklyn. I don't want you swimming alone again."

"Well, come and find me next time!" The words burst out, and I glare at him, blinking back brimming tears. My legs hurt, I am exhausted, and a third fight in the last four days appears to be starting. Perfect.

"Believe it or not, I was just about to when I noticed you had other company." The scorn with which he says the word *company* infuriates me.

"What is your problem?" I glare at him. "Can't you just lay off Conway? What has he ever done to you?"

Darin doesn't answer, but something has hit a nerve. The way he stares off into the water makes me say more quietly, "Darin? What has he ever done to you?"

For another moment, he says nothing, tail flicking irritably back and forth. Then he says tersely, "The first time I met Conway was when I found him stealing a sack of emeralds off a wreck I had discovered."

My heart falters. I think to ask how he knows Conway was stealing them. Then I realize the prince most certainly was stealing them to use as passage money for Atlantis. I bite my lip. Regardless of his reason, the theft was wrong. But Darin doesn't know how awful it is to be a Crura or how desperate it can make you. I say cautiously, "I think you might be misjudging him, Darin."

Darin gapes at me. "Did you hear what I just said, Locklyn? He was stealing. Stealing from his own father."

"Maybe he needed that treasure. Or thought he did."

Darin lets out a bark of derisive laughter. "Needed it? For what? A night betting at the octopus wrestling cage? A new crown?"

His ridicule touches an exposed nerve. "Mock away, Darin. You've never gone without anything you wanted in your life. Darin Aalto, the famous Schatzi whom all the Mermaids adore, with a big house in the right part of town, connections to the crown, and all the treasure he could ever want."

For a moment I think he is going to snap back at me, but

instead he says, "I shouldn't have said that. Why do you think I'm misjudging him?"

My eyes fall away from his, and I twist my fingers together, dread pooling in my stomach at the words I know I must say. "I can't tell you, Darin."

Darin's face goes blank. Then before I can say anything else, he turns and swims away without another word.

20

DARIN

HE HAD FORGOTTEN HOW TALL THE
Rayan Mountains were. He was eighteen the last time he hovered
beneath them. But that time, he wasn't trying to get across, just
hunting and adventuring.

"They're beautiful," a woman's voice says in his ear, and his heart
leaps. He turns, hoping to see Locklyn, but it is Ginevra's flint-like
eyes that meet his own.

She smiles before scanning the black wall of rock towering upward
and out of sight. The rest of the group is busy setting up camp at the
base of the towering cliff.

"I'd be able to appreciate their beauty better if I wasn't so afraid
they will be the last thing I see," Darin says dryly.

She turns her enigmatic face toward him. "And yet, playing for
high stakes always adds something to a game, doesn't it?"

"This isn't a game to me. Ten lives are in my hands. Including yours."

Her eyes flicker for an instant.

"Do you have a death wish, Your Highness? Because, like Locklyn
said, no treasure is worth dying for. And if we die, you will almost
certainly die with us."

Ginevra bites her lip, looking away. For the first time she appears
young. She must be Locklyn's age.

"Why thirty days, Ginevra? Give us more time. You might actually get your treasure then."

She begins to answer then seems to reconsider. Her face hardens. "A deal is a deal, Treasure Hunter. I was already merciful once when I spared your pretty little blue-haired friend in exchange for this treasure. I'm afraid I am all out of being generous."

Annoyance prickles at her patronizing tone, but then realization hits. "You're paying someone off."

She stills, her back to him. "What did you say?"

"You're paying someone off," he repeats. "That's why you won't move the deadline. Because you have one of your own."

"Will you keep your voice down?" she hisses, whirling to face him. She glances around, probably to make sure there is no one else within earshot.

He raises his eyebrows. "I'd be happy to go for a swim to discuss it."

"We don't have anything to discuss."

"Then you'd prefer I tell the others you're paying someone off?" His voice raises slightly at the end of the sentence.

Ginevra darts at him, seizing his hand and dragging him away. "Fine," she snaps once they are out of earshot. "I need the treasure by the end of this month. That's why we have to find it and return within thirty days."

He folds his arms. "Why do you need it?"

She purses her lips. At length she says, "I expect for the same reason Malik needed the wreck you found last month."

"To pay off Conway's gambling debts?" Darin is unable to repress a snort.

"I wish." The tone of her voice makes him want to tell her she shouldn't be eating her heart out over a reprobate like Conway.

"Then what?" Darin asks instead.

She hesitates, then says, "You know the Council of Guardians?"

"The rulers of Atlantis?"

She nods briefly. "At the beginning of this year, a delegation came to me. They demanded I choose seven young Mermen and seven young Mermaids from my people and send them to Atlantis."

His brow furrows. "Why?"

"They wouldn't say. So, I told them they could tell the Council I would most certainly not be sending any of Nebula's youth. One of them pulled a glass ball out of his pocket. Before my guards could stop him, he hurled it at a group of courtiers who were stationed along one side of my throne room." A hint of fear glistens in her dark eyes. "I don't know what it was, but it exploded. Three of my courtiers were killed instantly, and five others sustained severe burns and other injuries." Ginevra turns away, and he's unsure if she's finished. When she speaks again, it is in a tone he has never heard her use. "The side of my younger sister's face is completely disfigured. She used to be an excellent archer. Now she can't see out of her dominant eye."

The implication of her words turns his stomach. "And then they told you they would do worse if you didn't comply with their demands?"

Ginevra nods slowly, her beautiful dark face set in hard lines, as though carved from stone. "Atlantis has inventions the rest of the Undersea Realm has only ever dreamed of. There are no more feared warriors than my Nebulae maidens, but if one little glass ball can kill three of my warriors at a time, we would have no chance. And who knows what else they're planning? I couldn't risk a war. I asked if there was anything they would accept instead. The sum they named was exorbitant and I knew it would drain my treasuries. But there was nothing else I could do. So, I agreed."

"And you think they came to Malik as well?"

Ginevra snorts. "Where else would all that treasure you gave him have gone in one week?"

"Paying off Conway's gambling debts?"

"Please. Even Prince Conway," her voice is almost a growl as she says his name, "isn't capable of racking up debts that massive."

He mulls over her words. She's right. Conway would have had to lose a fortune every night of his life in order to need that much treasure to pay off his debts. The delegation from Atlantis must have come to Aquaticus too.

A chill ripples up his spine. "And they didn't say why they wanted fourteen young people?"

"No. But I assumed it wasn't for anything good. Some sick experiment they didn't want to perform on their own citizens?" Her shoulders rise and fall. "The Atlanteans worship science."

"Maybe. Or for slave labor. We should ask L . . ." His voice trails. Locklyn might not want to be asked. At least, not by him.

Ginevra's voice breaks into his thoughts. "I'm afraid the thirty-day deadline stands. Which means we should probably start swimming up or else looking for the pass—"

He glances at her sharply. All the blood has drained from her face, and her eyes are fixed on something above. He whirls to look and his throat tightens.

An enormous, pale silhouette sits crouched high on the cliffs. A silhouette with ten segmented, shiny, white legs, the front two ending in claws big enough to slice a great white shark in two with one click.

The stone corridor, hardly wide enough for their party to squeeze through single file, barely registers.

We're all going to die.

21

LOCKLYN

I CAN'T HELP IT. I LOOK UP AGAIN FROM
the net I am repairing, eyes straining through the dark water in the
direction Darin and Ginevra swam. *What under the sea are they
doing?*

"Hoping if you leave it long enough, that net will grow back
together?" a voice says in my ear, and I jump, losing hold of the
fibers I am trying to knot.

"Will you stop?" I demand.

Conway sinks next to me, black eyes sparkling with merriment.
"And miss the chance to perfect my stealth skills? Never."

I look at the net in my lap. "What do you want, Conway?"

"I thought we should talk." The uncharacteristic seriousness
of his tone causes my heart to speed up. For some reason, I can't
look at him. I concentrate on the posidonia fibers I am struggling
to twine together as I say, "Yes, I think we should."

A pause follows. Then we speak at the same time.

"Did you really steal a sack of emeralds from a wreck?"

"About the conversation you overheard me having with
Ginny . . ."

We both stutter to a halt and stare at each other.

Conway's face is set. "Aalto told you."

"I asked him," I clarify quickly. "I asked what he had against you. He didn't volunteer the information."

Conway closes his eyes for a moment. When he opens them again, their usual sparkle is gone. "It's true. But I was fourteen at the time." He lifts up a hand. "Not that this justifies it. It doesn't. But I was young. And stupid. And desperate." The next words seem to cost him a lot of effort. "I don't dislike Aalto because he caught me stealing. It's because whenever I see him, I feel the shame of what I did all over again." He sighs. "I did win a gamble once. Right after stealing from that wreck. And I left all my winnings outside the palace doors." I utter an impressed sound and he looks at me. "I'm not telling you this to blow my own conch, Locklyn. I just want you to know that I truly am sorry for what I did."

I hear the genuineness in his tone and I smile.

A hint of the old sparkle returns to his eyes.

"What was it you wanted to talk about?" I say after a moment.

"I . . ." He hesitates and then, "I enjoy being in your company, Locklyn. Very much."

Something about hearing him actually say those words to me, of all people, and sounding so vulnerable, makes my heart skip several beats. I wait for him to go on, but he doesn't say anything. "And?" I prompt.

He lets out a frustrated choke of laughter. "I must admit, I expected a slightly different response."

I draw in a long breath and force myself to look him squarely in the eyes. "What exactly am I supposed to say, Conway? I like you too. You're the only person I've ever met who can make me laugh right when I'm trying to decide whether or not to start shaking you. But what exactly does that mean?"

He shakes his head with a smile. "I've never met anyone like you."

"I imagine Crura shepherdesses are a bit rare in your social circles," I say.

He gives me an exasperated look. "I didn't mean it like that. Most girls would have been jumping up and down at being informed the crown prince had interest in them, but you immediately demand what my intentions are."

I drop my gaze to the net in my lap once more. "I'm sorry. Clearly, growing up in a reef surrounded by dugongs didn't help my social skills."

"I didn't say I didn't like it. I just said no girl has ever done that to me before."

I still can't look at him.

"Will you stop that?" he says, tugging the net out of my fingers and trapping my hands in both of his. My heart skips several more beats as my gaze slowly meets his. He lifts our hands, laughter in his eyes. "I don't usually do things like this with my friends."

I should smile back at him. Giggle even. Join in the flirting. Be flattered the crown prince of Undula has any romantic interest in a girl like me.

But I can't. Not because I think I couldn't fall for Conway. But because I don't want to if all he desires is a fling with a commoner. I've had enough abandonment to last me a lifetime.

I pull my hands out of his. I can't think clearly with him holding them. Hurt and bewilderment flash across his face. I am just about to try—somehow—to articulate the thoughts chasing each other through my mind, when a shout echoes through the water behind us.

Conway and I both whirl.

Darin and Ginevra zip through the water toward the camp. Other members of our party are jumping up, consternated as they come to a halt, gasping.

"We found it," Darin manages to get out between breaths. "The passage. And the crab. It is definitely not a myth."

I swim to them. "What's really happened? You two didn't need to come haring back to tell us that."

Ginevra, who is still spewing bubbles, chokes out, "Get weapons."

My stomach squeezes tight, and I yank my knife out of my pants, peering into the dark water in search of the threat. I see nothing.

The rest scramble for their weapons as I turn back to Darin, who has finally managed to catch his breath. He grips a coral knife in each hand.

"Darin, wha–?" I don't finish my sentence. Something moves swiftly through the water. Something unlike anything I have ever set eyes on.

A silver monster hurtles toward us, gleaming in the dark water. Its metal fins churn spume behind it. Circles of gold carve glowing portals into its insides, which are teaming with moving shadows.

Conway curses behind me. "A submarine."

Submarines only come from one place in the Undersea Realm.

And the last group we met that was associated with Atlantis was kidnapping Merpeople.

From the looks on Darin's and Ginevra's faces, I am guessing the scavengers' bosses have found us.

22

DARIN

THE SIGHT OF THE SUBMARINE MEANS
only one thing.

The Atlanteans have found a group of ten individuals, alone in the middle of the ocean, who will make excellent and convenient subjects for whatever bizarre experiment they are trying to conduct.

There is no way to swim upward without getting caught.

It is impossible to swim through the tunnel—the only place where the submarine can't follow us—without getting attacked by a monstrous, man-eating crab.

There is nowhere left to run.

The submarine slows, the stream of bubbles fading to a trickle.

"Darin!" Locklyn's voice bursts into his consciousness like a conch shell blast in his ear. "Darin, what do we do?"

She and most of the others have drawn together in a huddle behind him, the braver ones gripping weapons. Kai is off to one side, soothing the chittering dolphins.

Darin looks into her eyes, which are a navy so dark they are almost black. She is looking to him for guidance. For wisdom. For strength. And he has nothing left to give. Words won't come, but no one will touch her while there is breath in his body.

"Darin." She darts toward him, her slim fingers closing around his wrist, arresting his movement. He meets her eyes, expecting to see his own despair mirrored there, but there is something different. Hope. "You're a good leader," she says simply, and the grid of hopelessness that immobilized him shatters.

Renewed energy surges through him. "Listen to me!" Darin calls and every face swivels toward him. Out of the corner of his eye, he sees the submarine come to a full stop, floating a hundred yards away. He has minutes. Maybe seconds.

"Everyone follow Ginevra!" Turning to the young queen, he speaks to her as quickly as possible. "Take them to the mouth of the tunnel and wait for me there."

She whips around and zips toward the underside of the submarine, her white tail shining like a beacon as she shouts, "Come with me!"

The others follow her. All but Kai and Locklyn.

"Go!" Darin commands.

"You cannot fight them alone." Kai's voice is surprisingly gentle for such a large Merman.

Locklyn nods. It is clear from the look in her eyes that any attempt to reason with her will be futile.

Darin adjusts his thinking. "All right. The Atlanteans make glass spheres that explode on impact. I'm sure there are some on that submarine. To get past the crab and the stonefish, we need some. You both hide before the submarine door opens. I'll draw off the attackers who come out. Go in and steal as many spheres as you can find. Then follow the others." The round door in the submarine's side begins to jiggle. "Go!" he gestures urgently.

They both dart toward the submarine. Locklyn plasters herself to the bottom, and Kai crouches between the metal fins.

The silver door slides sideways, and a Merman emerges.

He is tall and his skin is so pale, it appears luminous in the dark water. His irises glint scarlet above the bridge of his hooked nose. His colorless, webbed feet move lazily through the water, holding him in place.

An achromos. Who is also a Crura.

Behind the first, another Merman and a Merwoman emerge. Their tails are a vivid, poisonous green, and they hover on either side of the Crura like bodyguards.

"I would drop that," the first Merman says in a conversational tone, motioning to Darin's knife. Pure white hair swirls around his surprisingly young face. He is holding a long metal rod in one hand and a fine mesh net in the other.

"That seems unwise," he replies, keeping his tone as light and casual as the other's.

"Come, come," the Merman says kindly. "We know the rest of your group swam off. So, I'd rather this was quick."

"I'm sure you would," he says.

The Merman doesn't respond. Instead, he lifts the metal tube to his lips and blows hard. Before Darin can move, something pricks his neck, right above the collar of his shirt.

He can barely see the end of the minuscule silver dart protruding from his skin. There is no doubt it is drugged. Which means he has very little time.

With one tug, the dart comes free and he flings it away. He zooms off through the water, using every stroke of his golden tail to propel him away from the pursuit he can sense rather than see.

Distance grows between him and his pursuers, the sounds of the hunt fading. But black dots crowd the edges of his vision. The movements of his tail are becoming weaker and more erratic.

He just needs to get out of sight of the submarine.

For Locklyn.

His vision turns hazy, but he can still see her face clearly. Feel the warm pressure of her fingers around his wrist, infusing him with her strength when he had none of his own. Hear her voice, repeating over and over . . .

You're a good leader.

You're a good leader.

You're a good leader.

His ears ring. It feels as though someone is closing in behind him, and he lashes out, but his fists find only water.

The ocean seems to be solidifying around him and he thrashes against it, trying desperately to move forward. The black spots swarm his eyes, but he continues to struggle, straining forward. Every inch he travels increases the likelihood Locklyn will escape.

Just a little farther.

Just a little . . .

. . . farther . . .

. . . must keep . . .

. . . going . . .

23

LOCKLYN

THE SIGHT OF THE PINPRICK OF BLOOD
swelling bigger and bigger on Darin's neck causes my stomach to
churn. I clamp my teeth together when the realization of what was
probably on that dart hits me.

Darin turns and shoots away into the dark water, pursued by
the three Atlanteans, and it takes all my self-control not to follow.
As strong as Darin is, if that dart was drugged or poisoned, he will
eventually collapse. And then he will be captured.

"Come." I turn to see Kai beside me, his face impassive as
always. "He has bought us a little time. But not much."

I follow Kai out of the submarine's shadow, and we slink toward
the door. He motions me to one side, and I press my body into
the cold metal as Kai hammers on the door and then ducks to the
other side.

For a moment, nothing happens, and I wonder if the Atlanteans
left the submarine unguarded. Then the lock clicks and the door
inches open. Kai immediately darts forward, grabbing the door
with one massive hand and forcing it wide. I flit around the open
door, just in time to see Kai reach into the submarine and yank a
Merperson out by the throat.

A slimy green tail. Olive cornrows. And a bulbous nose with a chunk missing.

Kelby's eyes meet mine, and he exhales the little air remaining in his lungs, choking. Kai gives him a shake.

"Show us where you keep your explosives." He utters no threats, and his voice remains completely monotone, but menace hovers around him like a cloud.

Kelby, still spluttering and choking, shakes his head frantically, eyes wide and fixed on me. Only one word is intelligible through his gargling. "Witch."

Kai slams him against the submarine so hard, the entire vessel sways in the water.

Kelby lets out a strangled groan.

"Where are your explosives?" Kai repeats.

Unable to speak, Kelby points inside the submarine, toward a metal chest crouched in the corner. Kai tilts his head for me to enter and I slip through the doorway. I head straight for the chest when I hear a clang behind me. Whirling, I come face-to-face with Pike, who lifts a metal tube to his lips. "Hello, *Witch*."

I am lucky. If he had sent a dart at me instantly, without pausing to speak, I would never have been able to avoid it. As it is, I use the split second he takes to taunt me to throw myself at him, latching onto the metal tube in his hands while sinking both of my feet into his stomach. He falls backward, spewing streams of bubbles, and I press my advantage, driving the metal tube, which he had half-raised to his mouth, into his teeth.

The clash of metal on bone and the sight of blood spurting from Pike's mouth as he howls in agony sets my teeth on edge.

You're not a killer, Locklyn. There's no shame in that.

The Atlanteans will return at any moment. Conway and the rest of my team are facing a murderous Anakite crab and a giant stonefish. The pain I must cause—it is for them.

With a powerful backward wrench, I tug the metal tube out of Pike's hands. Glancing at the chest, I see it is locked, and my stomach twists with fear as the sand in my mental hourglass continues to run down. We have, at most, five minutes before the Atlanteans return.

I hit Pike at the base of the skull—hard, but not quite hard enough to make him black out. "Where is the key?" I say, gesturing toward the chest. I clamp my teeth together to strengthen my resolve as Pike moans with pain.

I hate this.

I hate this.

I hate this.

Someone pounds on the door and my heart lurches. Is it Kai? Or the Atlanteans?

Pike whimpers. "It's gone. He took it." I study him as the pounding continues. He could be lying. But it is also highly probable the Atlanteans would not have wanted to leave a key with someone like him.

"I'm sorry." I hit him again, harder this time.

He slumps to the ground at my feet.

I glance at the rattling door, my thoughts churning. If it is Kai, I could really use his help to get into that locked box. But if it is the Atlanteans, every second counts.

I throw myself down on my knees before the box. I don't know how to pick locks. I am not anywhere near strong enough to break the box open using force.

I examine the front of the chest. There is no keyhole. Instead, there is a square patch of tiny, blunt, metal pins. Despair courses through me as I gaze at it, feeling time slip away, the pounding against the metal door jarring my ears. I have no idea what to do. Is this some kind of puzzle?

Hesitantly, I press the palm of my hand against the pins. They fall away, leaving an imprint of my hand in the center of the square as I hear clicking inside the box. My heart leaps and I pull at the lid. It remains firmly closed.

My heart sinks back down as I watch the pins slowly return to their original positions, erasing the hand imprint. Pike said the leader took the key to the box with him. Is there some special object that needs to be pressed into the pin pad to allow the box to open? If the Crura has it, there is no way for me to get into this box.

Unless . . .

I almost laugh as I plop down, extend my leg, and press the sole of my foot against the metal pins. At first nothing happens. Carefully, I wiggle my foot, indenting more pins around my original footprint. Just as I am beginning to give up hope, the box gives a series of clicks and the lid springs open.

The leader did have the key no one else in his group had. He had a pair of feet. And in Atlantis, Crura are the elite.

I rise and look down into the box, which contains ten clear glass spheres, filled with a murky brown liquid. I stuff two into each of my pockets, then I grab one in my right hand before darting to the door to release the bolt. I spring back as the door flies open, and I bubble with relief when I see Kai framed in the doorway.

"Thank the Wave Master," he grunts, seemingly oblivious to the explosive I am poised to hurl at him. "We have to go."

My insides twist as I realize what he means. "I found the explosives," I tell him, pointing, and Kai descends on the trunk, gathering up the remaining globes carefully in his massive arms. I follow as he flies out of the door and heads in the direction Darin sent Ginevra and the others. I am about to continue after him, but I glance over my shoulder and my limbs lock. Three figures are swimming toward us, and two of them carry a limp form with a glinting copper tail.

"Kai!" My shout arrests him and he turns. "Kai, we have to stay!"

"We can't." His monotone voice, usually so soothing, frustrates me.

"We have to!" Out of the corner of my eye, I see the distant figures pick up speed. "We have to save him!"

"Then we risk the others dying."

"We can use these." I wave the hand clutching an explosive.

"We can't afford to waste them," Kai warns. "And we might harm your friend."

Your friend.

Pain rips through me, followed swiftly by anger. Suddenly, I am so furious with Darin, tears cloud my vision.

Furious with him for sacrificing himself. Furious with him for never seeing me as more than a friend. Furious with him for getting himself captured and forcing me to leave him behind.

Kai is right. If we attempt to rescue Darin, we risk getting captured ourselves, which would leave the rest of the group with an impossible choice—end up captured or brave the passage and likely die in the process. But how can I leave him?

He would want you to. You know he would.

I feel the steaming warmth as a single tear slips down my cheek. They are close enough now that I can see his face, slack-jawed and young-looking, his neck bent at a funny angle over one of his captors' arms.

"Locklyn." Kai's voice is more urgent than I've ever heard it.

For one agonizing second, I hesitate and then turn, plunging after Kai, away from the Atlanteans and their submarine. Away from Darin.

Right now, I hate you. I hate you for breaking my heart. Don't you dare die.

24

DARIN

HE IS DRIFTING IN A WARM, HAZY RIVER, voices floating to him out of the mist.

"... you fool ..."

"Gone ..."

"How ... know ..."

"... little Crura ..."

"... amazing fighter?"

"Can't follow ..."

"... gone ..."

"Prince and princess ..."

"... both kingdoms ..."

The warm haze around him begins to fade, replaced by pain. His entire body aches as though he has a fever, and a sharp pinprick of agony lodges at the base of his throat. He tries to sit up, but someone or something jerks him back. Peeling his eyes open, Darin recoils as brilliant white light stabs his vision.

"Ah. You're awake," a voice says above him.

A shadow moves to his left as his eyes struggle to adjust, and he fights the urge to thrash against his bonds. Gradually, the figure of a tall Merman with long bleached hair and slender, white-clad legs comes into focus. Darin's gaze drifts up to his face, noting the silver chain mail shirt glinting on his chest. He inhales sharply. The Merman's scarlet irises glimmer like twin drops of blood against his chalky face. A true achromos.

"How do you feel?" the Merman says kindly.

"Other than the fact every part of my body hurts, and I am unable to move, I'm just pearly. Yourself?"

The Merman smiles. His incisors are filed to points and studded with tiny clear jewels that glint in the bright light, which comes from a glass box embedded into the ceiling. "Other than the fact you caused us to lose the rest of your group and the little Crura maiden stole the remainder of our fragor supply, I am also—what is the word you used—pearly."

His heart leaps as memory comes flooding back. Locklyn and Kai, waiting to steal the explosive globes. They must have succeeded. And if the submarine lost the others, they must have gotten through the passage. Or—his heart drops a few notches—they didn't. But the achromos and his crew only seem interested in live victims.

Please, Wave Master. Please, let them be alright.

The Merman's voice breaks into his musings. "What is your name?"

He hesitates for a moment and then decides nothing will be gained by lying or refusing to answer. "Darin Aalto."

The Merman nods. "You may call me Igor. I find that knowing the name of one's companions makes long journeys far less tedious."

Long journey?

"Where is it we're going?" Darin attempts to sound casual and Igor smiles again. The sight of the sharp, shining incisors is disturbing.

"Our ultimate destination is the North Sea."

Darin frowns, his aching brain struggling to recollect something that hovers just out of reach. Who else was just talking about going to the North Sea? His brain races as his eyes skim the cabin, coming to a figure in one corner who has begun to stir and moan.

He catches a glimpse of white-blond hair and the glint of

an earring. The soft voice of the girl they had rescued from the scavengers echoes in his head.

He said we would need to hurry back to Atlantis to be in time to catch the submarine headed to the North Sea.

That must be what the Atlanteans are doing with the treasure they are extorting from Nebula and Undula. Paying scavengers to kidnap Merfolk so they can take them to the North Sea. And then what?

"What's in the North Sea?"

Igor turns away, drifting toward the front of the submarine, where a complicated panel of levers and dials provides a way to steer the ship. "Oh, you'll see," he says. "I wouldn't want to spoil the surprise."

Darin glances around the room again, which is empty apart from himself, Pike, and Igor. "Where is the rest of your crew?" he asks, not considering how unlikely it is Igor will answer.

Igor turns and raises his pale eyebrows. "You should know I have an aversion to idle curiosity." He turns to the control panel.

Sinking back against the bench to which he is bound, Darin tries to test his reach, but the bite of the posidonia-fiber ropes around his wrists stops him. He must escape before the submarine reaches Loch Ness and whatever awaits there. Anything that requires twenty-eight young Merpeople every month cannot be good.

His mind swirls with possibilities. Some sort of mining operation even more dangerous than Oro. A trade agreement with a powerful kingdom or Sea Enchantress. Something penned in Loch Ness that needs food. But what under the sea could be big enough to need twenty-eight Merpeople a month?

His thoughts drift to Beck and his family back in Aquaticus, held hostage as security that he and Locklyn succeed in their quest. Darin's heart grows heavy. The most likely penalty for failure is that Beck's family will be offered to the Atlanteans when they return next month for payment. But that situation has slipped completely out of his hands. Even if he manages to escape, there is very little chance he will be in time to help Locklyn find Llyra's Lost

Treasure. It is up to her now. He tries to dismiss the picture of her and Conway working together.

I can see no way out of this situation.

Beck and Amaya and their children are about to be shipped off to the North Sea to die. Locklyn and Kai and the others don't have the necessary information to find Orwell. Even if they've managed to escape the crab, Locklyn is probably growing closer to Conway.

Stop, a voice that sounds strangely like Locklyn's commands inside his head. *Stop feeling sorry for yourself. You claim to love all these people. What good are you doing any of them by wallowing? Start planning your escape.*

The memory of her voice nearly causes his despair to deepen, but he refocuses. Instead of seeing the faces of his loved ones in terror or pain, he pictures them as he remembers them best.

Beck, wrapping a sealskin blanket around Amaya's shoulders, his hands lingering longer than necessary.

Amaya, gazing at her husband when he doesn't know she is looking, the adoration in her eyes obvious.

Locklyn, singing next to the magma pit, the red glow illuminating the tranquility in her face.

Zale and Ren and Fisk, pouncing on him as soon as the door to their house opens, begging for stories of treasure hunting, or clamoring to show him their latest projects.

Little Avonlea, curled up against his chest, so vulnerable and yet so trusting, sucking noisily on her thumb.

Kai, his big hands impossibly gentle as he strokes a dolphin nuzzling his side.

Ginevra, with her Nebulae guards, her normal reserve and hostility forgotten, her high, clear laugh ringing through the water.

This is for you. Darin impresses each image into his mind. *This is for each of you.*

And a plan begins to form.

25

LOCKLYN

"WHAT UNDER THE SEA ARE WE SUPPOSED to do without Aalto?" Ginevra's voice is higher than normal. "He was the one who knew where to find Orwell."

"Is that all you care about?" I snap before I can stop myself. "The stupid treasure you are forcing us to find? Darin's been captured by the Atlanteans! Who knows what they're doing to him?"

Ginevra's eyes widen and her face hardens. "Yes. Finding the treasure is all I care about."

Kai's rumbling voice pushes between us. "The submarine will reach us soon."

"He's right," Conway says.

I meet his eyes. Anxiety and pity mix together, but for some reason, his concern makes me angrier as I think of how much he has always disliked Darin.

"What are we going to do?" Dwyn's voice quavers. For the barest fraction of a second, I almost expect Darin's voice to answer—but it is Conway's instead.

"How many spheres?" he asks Kai.

"Ten."

Conway nods. "Good. I think we should use them on the stonefish," he tells us. "That will enable us to swim as low to the seabed as possible, giving us a better chance to pass between the Anakite's legs. Also, there is no guarantee the explosives will penetrate its shell."

"So, you believe it's real now?" I ask, unable to keep a hint of derision out of my voice. Conway gestures wordlessly, and I look up, up, up into the crags. Just when I am about to ask what I'm supposed to be looking at, the sight of the gargantuan, pale shadow perched on an outcropping far above causes the question to die on my lips.

A gurgling, swishing sound behind us causes everyone to whip around. My heart jumps into my throat at the submarine barreling through the water. Groping in my pockets, I pull out the four spheres and thrust two each toward Conway and Ginevra. "We have to go now!" I dart toward the gap in the rocks and squeeze through, praying the others will follow.

I swim cautiously forward in the black water, my pulse throbbing as I scrutinize the floor of the ever-widening tunnel. The ground appears to be made up of algae-covered rocks, perfect camouflage for a stonefish. I glance upward for any sign of the crab, but all is still.

The tunnel widens. I see movement out of the corner of my eye and whirl, my hands clenched around the glass ball, but it is only Conway, swimming slightly behind me and to the right, with a sphere in each hand. Glancing upward again, I search the smooth, dark walls rising above us, the shifting shadows of the water. Nothing there.

I peek back over my shoulder at the others. Ginevra swims directly behind Conway, her head swiveling from side to side as she scans the dark water, her spear in one hand, a fragor in the other. Everyone else swims behind her, weapons at the ready. No one says anything.

The silence and darkness and cautious swimming make it feel as though each second is an hour. It occurs to me that I am swimming in the center of the tunnel, which is now wide enough for ten Merpeople to swim side by side comfortably. I veer to the right, hoping to lead the group toward the shelter of one of the rock walls.

"Locklyn!" Conway's shout jolts me, and I instinctively dart downward, sure he has spotted the giant crab.

My feet skim a rough surface. My dive downward has carried me too close to the bottom, and in a split second, I realize my mistake. Pain sears my foot and I scream as agony radiates all the way up my leg.

I look down and my scream turns to a whimper. I am impaled on a footlong spine, protruding out of what looks like a giant, fuzz-covered rock. The stonefish is nearly six feet in length—its thirteen spines aggressively erect, the middle one buried in the heel of my left foot.

Moaning as pain continues to sear up my entire leg, I try not to think about the poison now coursing through my veins. I reach down, attempting to wriggle my foot free. I pull desperately at my toes, trying to slide my foot off the spine, but it is too deeply embedded. I feel the warmth of my blood on my hands and panic as I remember Darin's plan to use blood as bait for the Anakite crab.

"Locklyn!" At Conway's shout, I look up. A white shape hurtles through the dark water toward me.

Wave Master, help me! Help me!

I struggle violently, pulling alternately at my foot and the spine. But the terror pulsing through me causes my hands to shake, and I cannot get a good grip. Each slip of my fingers deepens my despair and I glance upward, fighting nausea as I see ten pale, segmented legs churning through the water as the monster nears. I freeze, staring in horrified fascination at the snapping claws, the blob-like eyes visible on its underside.

I can't get free.

I'm too afraid to move.

This is not how I wanted to die.

"Locklyn!" The urgent voice is not Conway's, and it is right beside me. Through the blank haze of my terror, I turn my head and see Ginevra at my side, her hands wrapped around the spine directly below my foot. "Swim up!" she commands. The paralyzing thought of the gargantuan crab descending from above immobilizes my limbs. "Now!" Ginevra screams, and as she pushes downward, I manage to kick up and feel the spine leave my foot as a cloud of red mists the water around us.

Something slams into me, driving my body into a fissure in the passage wall. Blinding white light flares nearby as a deafening explosion shakes the passage.

"Swim!" a voice screams and I feel hands clutching mine, pulling me back through the cloud of bubbles. Ginevra drags me through the water toward the rest of the group. The pearly scales of her tail gleam with blood.

"Ginevra," I croak. "Your tail . . ."

"No time," she snaps, dropping my hand and shoving me behind her as she raises her spear. I grope for my coral knife, but I must have dropped it when I was trying to escape the stonefish spine. Pain still radiates up my leg as I peer over Ginevra's shoulder. The taste of metal fills my mouth as my heart beats wildly. I have never felt fear like this.

The Anakite faces us from across the smoldering stonefish remains. Its enormous, pale body fills the passage from wall to wall. It stands completely still, its pasty figure gleaming in the dark water. As we watch transfixed, bulbous white eyes rise slowly out of its shell on stalks as thick as my waist.

Our horrified silence shatters as Dwyn lets out a high-pitched scream. Throwing down her knife, she streaks for the mouth of the passage. The crab's segmented legs bend with an earsplitting, grinding creak, and it launches itself, sailing over our heads and landing with a crunching crash on the ground behind us.

There is a snipping, shearing sound and one terrible scream.

Vomit rises in my throat as our group scatters. The three Undulae guards, including Blackwell, swim away as fast as they can. Conway and Ginevra dart to opposite sides of the tunnel and, on Conway's signal, hurl their spheres at the creature. Noise and white light fill the passage. Even though I know the stonefish is dead, my eyes scan the ocean floor feverishly for other threats as I dive for the knife Dwyn dropped, scoop it off the sand, and shoot upward again. Arledge hangs motionless, horror etched on his chalk-white face.

Grabbing him by the arm, I drag him toward one of the walls and push him into a crevice before darting back into the center of the passage. I only have one weapon left. I don't know if it will work, but I have to try. Before anyone else dies.

Dragging water into my lungs, I open my mouth and begin to sing as loudly as I can into the still-violent, bubble-filled water. I start with the same lullaby I used on the scavengers, willing every ounce of peace, tranquility, and rest into my voice.

The bubbles slowly disperse, and soon I am looking into the bulbous eyes of the crab. With a great rasping and creaking, it inches closer. It takes every ounce of willpower to stay suspended in the water, watching it come, pouring calm into my voice.

The lullaby ends, and the instant I pause, the crab bounds forward, its pincers raised. My voice cracks as I begin another lullaby, eyes squeezing involuntarily shut as I wait for the shearing agony of death. I keep singing.

When my eyes open again, the crab is mere feet from me. The sight of its enormous carapaces causes my stomach to clench. It sways from side to side, its segmented legs creaking slightly with the motion. I almost stop the lullaby at the sight of Dwyn's blood discoloring the insides of its pale pincers. Shaking, I will myself to go on.

The songs that would send most smaller sea creatures into deep slumber are barely holding this monster at bay. If I move or stop singing, the spell will break. There is no way I will get out of this alive. But I pray the others are using the crab's distraction to escape.

> *Be gone*
> *Fly away*
> *Escape*
> *Do not stay*

The world is hard
But sleep is sweet
Close your eyes
Let trouble retreat

Be gone
Fly away
Escape
Do not stay

I sing the chorus again and again, hoping my group has received the message and is long gone. The pain coursing through my leg is nearly unbearable, and I know that as soon as I stop singing, the crab will attack.

Wave Master. Carry me through to your Realm.
Let me see your face when my eyes next open.

"Locklyn." The word is barely a whisper. Why is Conway still here?

"Be gone, fly away," I sing, trying to infuse urgency into my tone while keeping it peaceful. One of the crab's eyes twitches and my heart jolts.

"Locklyn, back away. Slowly."

I blink. Does he have a plan? Will the crab attack if I move at all?

On the other hand, what does it matter? I have nothing left to lose.

Heart in my stomach, I drift backward, waving my webbed feet dreamily in time to my song. The crab remains motionless, still swaying, its eyes fixed on me.

A sphere hurtles straight at the crab's right eye, but the Anakite slashes a pincer through the water and knocks the small glass ball off course. It explodes against the passage wall, creating a blast that knocks me backward. I hear a second blast.

Instinct kicks in, and with a flick of my wrist, Dwyn's knife leaves my fingers, flying end over end into the swirling cloud of bubbles toward where I last saw the crab's eyes. The moment the blade leaves my hand, reality hits me and I scream in panic. "Conway? Ginevra?"

An unintelligible shout to my left fills me with relief. Conway.

Something bumps my side. "Come on!" Ginevra grabs my hand and drags me through the water.

"What about Conway?"

"He's coming! But it will follow us even if it can't see. Good shot, by the way. You got the eye Conway missed."

The tunnel narrows again as we shoot through the water, but I can hear rasping, creaking crashes behind us as the sightless crab ricochets off the tunnel walls. It is closing in.

"Can't you swim any faster?" Ginevra pulls on my arm so hard, I'm sure it is going to come out of its socket.

While I was singing and holding perfectly still, the pain in my foot was a dull, throbbing ache. Now my right leg feels as though someone is pressing trident tips into every inch of it, but I clench my teeth and churn my legs even faster. The pain is so vivid and intense, I falter. Something brushes my left leg and I kick out. A gurgling gasp follows and I wince. "I'm so sorry . . ."

"Just swim," Conway chokes out.

There is a loud grinding, scraping noise behind us, and I am stunned that the crab can still move through the tunnel, which is barely wide enough for Conway, Ginevra, and I to fit side by side. Then I realize it must be moving sideways.

Black spots begin to swarm before my eyes. The pain in my leg is too excruciating. I know I must stop swimming or I will black out. I slow and Ginevra jerks my arm.

"Come on! Do you want to be crab chow?"

"I'm sorry . . . my leg . . ."

Waves of blackness wash over me, dulling my pain. Encouraged, I begin kicking again, but both legs feel as though they are made of lead. I can't see anything. But if I stop? I shudder at the thought.

The rasping and grinding grow louder, filling my ears and pounding in my brain.

"Locklyn, it's alright . . ."
But I can hear it coming for me.
"Locklyn, we've got you . . ."
Who has me? Is it Darin? But it couldn't be.
"Locklyn . . ."
Everything fades away.
At least the pain is gone.

26

LOCKLYN

"SHE IS FORTUNATE TO BE ALIVE." A man's large, calloused hands move gently but firmly along my right calf, putting pressure on various spots. A dull ache throbs throughout the entire limb, but nothing excruciating. I lie still, eyes closed as the warmth halfway between sleep and waking wraps around me.

"You'll have to get some new guards, I'm afraid," a different voice says. "Sorry you had to finish the Anakite off."

The man whose hands tend to my leg lets out a deep, rueful laugh. "With both eyes gone, a cracked shell, and the fact he was stuck between the walls of the passage, I felt it would be a greater kindness to dispatch him. Yes, Nimrod and Scylla will not be of much use in keeping future visitors away. But I'm not too worried. Not many venture into the Rayan Mountains in any case. And, surprising as it may seem, many would rather tangle with an Anakite crab than with me."

There is a pause. Then a third voice, a woman's this time, speaks. "Why didn't you kill us when you found us at the mouth of the passage? It would have been easy enough."

"I never kill visitors without talking to them first," the man says easily. "As I said, people do not stray into the Rayan Mountains. If someone has made the effort to cross their peaks, I wish to know why." His fingers reach my foot and begin to probe firmly along the sole. Pain erupts up my leg and I gasp, jerking away as my eyes fly open.

I am lying on a smooth stone slab covered with a soft material of some kind. My head is pillowed on a cushion made of the same unfamiliar material and filled with what feels like plant fibers. Turning my head from side to side, I see I am in what looks like a large cave, divided in half by a silky scarlet curtain suspended from golden hooks embedded in the ceiling. Along one wall, a low cabinet made of dark wood with gold accents sits beneath a large oval-shaped mirror with a copper frame.

I catch sight of my own reflection as I sit up, navy hair tangling around my pale face, purple smudges beneath my eyes, which look almost black. White light spills down from a glass sphere like the one in the Atlanteans' submarine, illuminating every detail of the room. Exotic objects I have only heard described in Darin's tales jump out from every corner. A large wooden instrument with alternating black and white keys. An ivory-backed comb and brush on top of the dark cabinet. A large pot made of a reddish material painted with black designs, with what appears to be kelp growing inside it. Metal weapons of all sorts fill the brackets along the walls. A piece of thin, whitish material covered in strange black markings hangs next to the scarlet curtain.

My head begins to spin when my eyes meet those of the man drifting beside the bed. The corners of his mouth lift, causing starfish feet to pucker the corners of his deep, ocean-blue eyes. Foam-white hair swirls around his face, and his beard nearly reaches the emerald-studded belt buckle that sparkles above his tail, which is a deep scarlet.

"Hello, sleeping beauty," he says. "How do you feel?"

Someone pokes my shoulder, and I look over to see Conway glaring down at me. "You scared me half to death."

I notice Ginevra drifting next to me on my other side, looking tired and haggard. "Like she had any choice in the matter," she says.

I smile at her defense. To my surprise, one corner of her mouth tilts in return.

Confused, I look from Ginevra to Conway, then at the giant at the foot of my bed. "What happened? Where are we? How . . . ?" My voice trails as I remember. The monstrous white crab. The jagged pain of the stonefish quill embedded in my heel. The deafening detonation of the fragor spheres. Dwyn's body trailing vermilion strands of blood through the water. The certainty of imminent death.

"How am I not dead?" I say to Conway and Ginevra.

The giant releases a rumbling chuckle. "Clearly, the Wave Master has a few assignments left for you." My confusion only grows. He places a hand on my right ankle, which is swathed in bandages. "If I hadn't found you and your companions when I did, you would have had to lose that foot to contain the spread of the poison. But I heard the explosions and came to investigate. At risk of sounding like a pompous narwhal, I am excellent at treating major injuries. Wave Master knows, I've had enough experience on myself."

I stare at him, the jumbled pieces of my brain sliding around before clicking into place. "You're Orwell."

He smiles, and relief floods through me, tinged with aching regret. We would never have gotten here without Darin. And he is captured, on a submarine headed toward Atlantis and who knows what fate. At least he's alive. I won't allow myself to believe anything else.

Emotion swells, but I press it into a small, hard ball and push it to a corner of my mind. Later, when I am alone, I might let the waves of pain and loss—anger and grief and loneliness all mixed together—break over me. But not now.

"We need to know where Llyra's Lost Treasure is," I blurt.

Orwell lets out a guffaw that booms through the cavern, echoing off the stone walls. It sounds like a dozen gigantic Mermen are laughing together. He laughs so hard, his whole body shakes. "I like you," he declares, pointing a finger at me. "No pleasantries. No swimming in circles. No smooth talking. Straight to the point."

Heat fills my cheeks. I raised myself in the reef. Apparently, it shows. "I'm sorry," I begin, but Orwell waves me off.

"I prefer it this way," he says, but all traces of laughter have vanished. "You say you need to know where Llyra's Lost Treasure is. My question is: why?"

I glance at Ginevra and Conway, devoutly hoping one of them will step in and save me from embarrassing myself further.

It is Ginevra who answers, "We all have different reasons."

Orwell folds his arms, eyebrows raised. "The plot thickens. Very well, you can start. Why do you need Llyra's Lost Treasure?"

Conway and I both look at Ginevra, whose stony expression gives nothing away. "That is my concern."

I groan inwardly.

Conway does it outwardly. "For the love of everything under the sea, Ginevra!"

Orwell's expression does not change. "And keeping the greatest treasure in the Undersea Realm from falling into unworthy hands is my concern. I will ask once more: why do you need Llyra's Lost Treasure?"

I beseech Ginevra with my eyes. *Just tell him whatever it is.*

There is a moment's silence. Then Ginevra says shortly, "I drained my kingdom's storehouses to keep the Atlantean delegation from carrying off fourteen Nebulae youth. I must replenish them."

Conway and I both swivel to stare at her. My incredulous "What?" and Conway's "You didn't tell us that!" collide sharply.

Ginevra's lips tighten. "Surprisingly, I didn't feel like telling the crown prince of the neighboring country that my kingdom was weak and vulnerable."

Conway opens his mouth but says nothing.

Orwell's expression remains unchanged and his eyes find me. "And you?"

I bite my lip, trying to figure out how to condense the last few weeks into a coherent reason for this quest. "My brother-in-law is a Schatzi, like you. About a month ago, he discovered a fabulous wreck on the border between Nebula and Undula. He decided not to claim it for fear of becoming involved in an international dispute. But when my niece was born as a—" The word sticks in my throat.

"—a Crura," I finally manage, "he decided to claim the wreck in order to get enough money to send her to Atlantis where she would be safe."

The memory of the Atlantean submarine and their plot to blackmail Ginevra causes a new thought to flit through my mind— maybe Atlantis isn't the paradise we always believed. "When the treasure was disputed, Darin was blamed. In order to avoid imprisonment or death for himself and the rest of our family, he promised to find a treasure big enough for Undula to pay Nebula."

Interest flickers in Orwell's eyes, and he shifts his gaze toward the curtain dividing the room, as though trying to penetrate to the group on the other side. "Which one is your brother-in-law? I haven't spoken to another Schatzi in over twenty years."

A lump swells in my throat, so thick that I cannot speak around it.

Ginevra saves me, saying more gently than I thought possible for her, "He was captured just before we entered the pass."

"He sacrificed himself," I choke out. For some inexplicable reason, I need the legendary Merman before me to know Darin did not get captured because of some weakness or mistake on his part. "So the rest of us could escape."

Orwell gives a slow nod, and I catch a glimpse of compassion in his gaze before he turns it on Conway. "And you, Princeling?"

The title causes Conway to scowl, and I see a smirk flicker across Ginevra's face. "I am here to protect Undula's interests," he says stiffly.

Orwell's gaze bores into him. "That is not why you are here."

Conway's scowl deepens as he glares back at Orwell. "As a matter of fact, that is exactly why I am here. And I don't appreciate being called a liar."

Orwell's face splits into a huge smile, and some of the tension in the water dissipates. "I wasn't calling you anything, son. I merely meant that I don't think you give two periwinkles whether you find Llyra's Treasure."

Conway blanches. Orwell has struck a nerve. "You're right,"

Conway admits slowly. "I don't give two periwinkles whether or not we find it."

"Then what is it you are searching for?" Orwell asks.

A faint flush rises on Conway's face, and I look away, staring at my knees for fear that Ginevra or Orwell will read his secret in my eyes. "I'm not searching for anything," he responds, a little too quickly.

"Everyone's searching for something." There is an ageless quality in Orwell's expression. "I was a Treasure Hunter long enough—I should know."

I twist my fingers together in my lap, trying not to think about Darin. Or about the fact that if Orwell refuses to help us, we will never find the treasure we so desperately need. Or about how emotionally and spiritually drained I am.

"What are *you* searching for?" The question makes me glance up in surprise. Conway exudes something between a challenge and a question in his dark eyes.

Orwell stares back at him for a beat, and I am certain he is not going to answer. But then the giant bows his head and says, "Peace. I'm searching for peace." There is an extended pause before Orwell adds in a brisker tone, "I'll tell you how to find the treasure."

My breath comes whooshing out in a stream of bubbles. A rare smile lights up Ginevra's face and Conway lets out a relieved laugh, but Orwell raises his hands.

"Don't get too excited," he says. "In the fifty years I've been here, I've told three other groups the location. None of them found it."

LOCKLYN

"MMM, I'VE NEVER TASTED ANYTHING this good," Conway says as we sit, hours later, around Orwell's enormous, claw-foot ebony dining table. Orwell stipulated that we eat dinner before he reveals anything. Now our entire group—excluding Arledge, who sits outside the entrance to the cave, staring vacantly into space—is gathered around the table, demolishing platters of squid ink-soaked shrimp and fresh sargassum shoots, washed down with lecker, a potent alcohol made from the rare traub plant. I am sure that Conway must have tasted better food in the palace, but after almost a month of travel fare, this feels like a feast.

Across the table, Blackwell and the other two Undulae guards shovel food into their mouths. In contrast, Kai picks at his untouched plate, the lines of his face more stonelike than ever. We had to leave the dolphin herd at the entrance to the pass. My heart twists with sympathy as I look down at my own untouched plate. Like Kai, I cannot eat. Everything I try to swallow seems to stick in my throat.

"Will you tell us a story?" I say impulsively to Orwell. "One of your adventures?" Anything to distract me from my own thoughts.

Everyone around the table turns to the giant sitting at the head.

Orwell takes a measured sip from his wine glass and then sets it down deliberately. "Adventure is highly overrated."

An awkward pause follows before Conway says, "That is a strange position for a Schatzi to hold."

Orwell lets out a barking laugh that is completely different from his usual bubbling rumble. "Former Schatzi."

"But the fact you were a Schatzi at any point argues that you must not always have considered adventure highly overrated," Conway persists.

I want to motion to him to stop, but don't know how to without Orwell seeing.

Orwell regards Conway. Then he says with a half smile, "I've always valued persistence. It's a good quality in a future leader."

A slight flush rises on Conway's cheeks once again, and he looks down at his plate.

Orwell sighs and leans back in his chair. "I did not always think adventure was overrated. At one time, it was everything to me. Adventure and fame—I craved them above all else." He pauses and looks around at each of us. "You are all young. So very young. Infants, really. I was young when the world was young. I remember when the island of Atlantis settled onto the ocean floor. I remember when Princess Llyra disappeared, and King Triton turned his kingdom upside down searching for her. I remember," he nods in the direction of Ginevra and her Nebulae guards, "when Queen Cherith of Nebula found that her husband the king was conducting an affair with her younger sister. After killing them both, she swore on her bloody spear that a man would never again sit on the throne of Nebula."

He pauses again and then goes on. "One day, years before Llyra left the sea, I was summoned by the Conclave, the elite group of representatives from every nation under the sea. They told me there were rumors of a monster ravaging the kingdoms of the North Sea. There have been monsters in the sea since it was created, but the Conclave explained this one was different.

"Not only did it have the capability to belch a boiling,

magma-like substance that could incinerate anything in its path, but, unlike any previously discovered sea monster, this one also seemed to possess a mind of its own and a desire for destruction. It was moving methodically, from kingdom to kingdom in the North Sea, destroying villages and cities, devouring Merpeople, and collecting treasure, which it stored in a lair off the coast of Scotland. And, worst of all, they told me the creature was a baby, not yet fully grown. They told me they were assembling a team of the most promising warriors, adventurers, and sorcerers under the sea to capture the creature. And they wanted me to be the leader."

"Why capture?" Ginevra interrupts. "Why not kill?"

The lines in Orwell's face deepen. "I asked the same question. At the time, they told me they wanted to be able to study the creature, in order to cope better with other monsters like it. I believed them then. Now? I am not so sure."

He stops speaking and the look in his eyes forces the question out of me. "What do you think they really wanted it for?"

Orwell rubs his chin. "I am not certain. I have had virtually no contact with the outside world for over a hundred years. But I have heard whispers. From you," he points at Ginevra, who looks startled, "and from others who have found me here. Rumors of young people disappearing. Rumors that the Conclave is no longer content to be an advisory panel to the Undersea Realm—that they desire power. Rumors of a pan-oceanic movement gaining strength in the north." His face tightens. "Anyone who could control that monster would gain a weapon of unimaginable power."

"But you said the monster was uncontrollable," Conway points out.

"I didn't say that," Orwell replies. "I said it seemed to have a mind of its own. But I believe that makes a creature bent on evil more dangerous. Especially if it is controlled by another being equally obsessed with mayhem and destruction."

Everyone is completely sober. Even Blackwell has stopped eating.

Orwell goes on. "As I say, I believed them. I wanted to believe them. I knew if the mission was successful, I, as the leader, would go down in the pages of history. I was desperate to prove myself. So, I readily agreed to lead the team. The Conclave had already chosen certain individuals, but they gave me permission to include anyone I thought would be an asset to the mission. And I knew just the Merperson."

His eyes focus on something unseen. "Her name was Talia. And I was madly in love with her. She was a barmaid who worked in a tavern on the outskirts of Aquaticus. We met one night when I came in after delivering a load of treasure to the palace. I heard her singing. As she washed glasses, she was crooning a song about a girl whose lover took her up to The Surface to see the sunrise. She was surrounded by a swarm of little fish, transfixed by her music. I struck up a conversation with her, and she told me she had run away from home when she was fourteen to escape her abusive father. When I asked her if fish always followed her, she laughed and said, 'Only when I sing.' I began to come into the tavern every night that I wasn't gone on a quest.

"My favorite nights were the ones where Talia performed, charming hammerhead sharks, stingrays, electric eels, and blue-ringed octopi with her music. The night before I left to meet with the Conclave, I told Talia I loved her and wanted to marry her. As a symbol of my feelings, I gave her my favorite trinket—an oval-shaped, silver locket studded with sapphires and moonstones I once discovered on a wreck."

He pulls in a deep breath. Agony taints his eyes.

It makes me want to tell him to stop and not share any more. But I have too much desire to know how his story ends.

"When I came back," he continues, "I begged her to accompany me to fight the sea monster. I was certain her gift would be useful in subduing the beast. She was hesitant. Unlike me, she did not crave fame and glory—she just wanted love and security. I pressured her. I told her if she truly loved me like she claimed, she wouldn't want to be separated from me and she would help me achieve my dreams. She gave in."

His words come more rapidly. "We joined the rest of our group and traveled north. We cornered the monster near the Moray Firth. The plan was for Talia to lure it up the River Ness, while the rest of us followed and built a magically reinforced wall, trapping the monster in the lake.

"Everything seemed to be going according to plan. Talia swam up the river singing, and the monster pursued her. When we reached the lake, we hurried to build the wall. Talia swam in circles, singing to the monster. As soon as we finished, the sorcerers began to weave magic spells to reinforce our stonework. I suddenly realized that if we reinforced the gate from the outside, Talia would be trapped. I pleaded with the sorcerers to stop, then I opened the gate and called to Talia. The instant she turned, she stopped singing."

His face spasms. "In that moment, the creature's jaws opened, and it spewed magma all over her."

I can't help the little gasp of horror that escapes my lips. Orwell looks his age now—hundreds and hundreds of years old—his face exhausted and sagging. "I watched her fall. She was screaming, her body covered in the blistering red magma. I started to dart toward her, but then the creature turned, charging at the open gate. And, like a coward, I slammed it shut, ordering the sorcerers to weave their spells."

The silence around the table is so thick, it's as though the water really has solidified around us.

Orwell continues, "The fame and glory I so desperately needed? I got them. When my team and I returned to the Conclave with the tale of how we had caged the monster, my fame spread far and wide. Lief Orwell, the dashing young explorer who saved the North Sea. But I spent the next fifty years traveling to every corner of the Seven Seas, seeking a place where I could escape my soul-crushing guilt."

He pauses again, and unbidden, the memory of Darin's limp form draped over the arm of the Atlantean delegation leader sends pain slicing through my heart.

"Then one day," Orwell says, "nearly a hundred years ago, I visited one of the Wave Master's temples in the Great Barrier Reef. A prophetess lived there, one of the last under the sea. I don't know what came over me, but the moment that I saw her, I poured out every last bit of my history." He gives a short laugh. "As I am doing now. I told her about the awful regret that dogged me every single day of my life. I told her of the nightmares that came to me each night. I told her how I was beginning to contemplate taking my own life, since death refused to come for me." A sigh escapes his lips. "She told me I must return to the Mediterranean—to the Rayan Mountains. She said the largest wreck the Undersea Realm had seen would soon come to rest there, and to atone for my sins, I must guard it for the remainder of my days. She also told me I must only allow those to pass through to search for the treasure who sought neither adventure nor personal glory, but the good of the Undersea Realm and aid for others."

He looks us squarely in the eyes. "So, that is what I have done for the past hundred years."

"Wait." Ginevra stops him. "Was the crab yours then?"

"No," Orwell assures her. "Nimrod took up residence on that crag about fifty years ago. The stonefish arrived sometime later. Did the Wave Master send them to guard the treasure as well? I don't know. But they have made my job much easier."

"How have you survived here alone for so long?" Conway asks.

"The waters of the Mediterranean are particularly stormy above the Rayan Mountains. Ships wreck frequently. The wrecks provide me with what I need."

Something has been tugging at me. "You said you have let a few groups pass through before," I say slowly, and Orwell's eyes find mine, "but they never found the treasure."

Orwell answers my unspoken question. "Llyra's Treasure is a three-day journey from here. And two more obstacles remain along the way."

The dismay that ripples through us is palpable. Conway's shoulders sag. Ginevra's face darkens. Blackwell exchanges anxious looks with his bodyguard friends. My own heart sinks into my toes.

"Two more obstacles?"

Orwell's fingers caress the stem of his glass. "Yes. But before I tell you what they are, you must tell me whether you wish to go on. If not, you may turn back now. The crab and stonefish are dead. You may leave the way you came and spread tales of the impenetrability of the treasure's defenses far and wide."

"You will let us go forward?" Conway leans forward.

Orwell meets his eyes with a warmth I haven't seen there before. "Yes," he says simply and continues to gaze at Conway.

The prince reddens then bursts out, "But I didn't give you a selfless reason for why I want to find the treasure."

"Perhaps you will find your reason there," is the reply.

"I will go on," Ginevra announces. "That treasure will save my kingdom. I'm going on."

At her fiery gaze, I wonder whether I have any choice in the matter. And then I realize, even if she gave me a choice, I wouldn't turn back. Not now.

"I'm going with her," I say.

Conway nods. "Count me in."

Ginevra looks at us. A mixture of surprise, relief, and pain flits across her face.

"We go where our lady goes," says Baia in a low voice, while Kallan nods beside her.

Kai's face is set as he studies his plate. "Everyone and everything I love is dead. I might as well go as stay."

My heart twists as I think of the ten dolphins he cherished on our way here.

Orwell nods, his blue eyes full of compassion. He turns to the three Undulae guards, who glance uneasily at each other.

No one knows what to say. Then Clyde blurts, "I'm going back. I can't take no more of this." He looks at Blackwell and Hurley for support.

Hurley nods vigorously. I glance at Blackwell's pale, scarred face. Maybe, just maybe . . .

Blackwell gives a lazy shrug. "Sorry, fellas, I'm going on. It's my duty to protect the crown prince." His eyes find mine and the malicious glint in them causes my stomach to turn.

Orwell examines every face. "Very well." He gestures to the two Undulae warriors who decided to go back. "Please, follow me. The cave where I keep my dolphin herd has an upper level. That will enable us to talk into the night without disturbing you."

As Orwell leads Clyde and Hurley from the room. Conway catches my eye and mouths, "Are you alright?"

I jerk my head noncommittally, but really I'm not alright. And I want more than anything under the sea to be alone. But from what Orwell said, it sounds as though we'll be here a while longer.

The curtain covering the cave's mouth is pulled aside, and Orwell reenters the room. "Arledge will accompany you when you set out," he says to the room at large, reseating himself at the head of the table.

I look up, shocked. Ginevra's and Conway's expressions mirror my own. We were all sure that after what happened to Dwyn, Arledge would want nothing more to do with this quest. "But tonight, he needs rest and solitude." Orwell steeples his fingers on the table in front of him.

"Is there anything we can do for him?" I ask tentatively.

"There are wounds only the Wave Master can heal," Orwell says somberly. "And scars that remain until death." His tone changes. "But you need me to tell you how to find Llyra's Treasure, so listen carefully. The wreck is located three days' journey from here, high in the crags of Mount Laguna, the tallest peak in the Rayan Mountains. The swim up to it takes nearly a day and is extremely arduous. And, once there, you must pass the Guardian."

"The Guardian?" Conway asks.

"She is a siren. I have conversed with her only once. The sole reason I am still alive is because I managed to utter the name of the prophetess who sent me in time for the siren to call off her killer eels."

"Eels?" Ginevra echoes.

"She controls a group of five gargantuan electric eels," Orwell explains. "They are the means by which she kills any trespassers who cannot solve her riddle."

Now I am the one who repeats his words. "Her riddle?"

"She guards the entrance to the wreck. In order for anyone to pass, they must solve the riddle she poses."

"What is the riddle?" A bubble of hope rises. If we can ponder the riddle ahead of time, we have a much better chance of solving it.

But at Orwell's reply, the bubble bursts. "She asks a different one every time. But the one she asked me was this—"

> "Invisible am I to the naked eye
> No trace do I leave as I pass by
> Yet nothing is impervious to my touch
> Except a soul in Death's cold clutch
>
> I ripple the sea, I bring laughter and tears
> I provoke beasts to savagery, and soothe all men's fears
> No creature needs me in order to survive
> But everywhere I go, all life does thrive."

"That's all?" I say, and almost laugh out loud.

Heads swivel toward me. "Wait . . ." I say at their expressions. "You don't all know the answer?"

A bemused glint lights Orwell's eyes. "Apparently, I am a greater fool than I realized."

Heat rises in my cheeks. "No . . . I . . . that's not what I meant . . . I just—it seems so obvious to me." My eyes seek Conway's, hoping to find comprehension on his face, but his brow is furrowed. I survey the entire table and then say uncertainly, "Well, I thought the answer was singing or music, but . . ."

Murmurs of comprehension erupt around the table. "Of course," Orwell mutters to himself. Sudden sadness I do not entirely understand fills his eyes. "Is it any surprise that the Vocalese among us solved that particular quandary? But, unfortunately, the ability to solve my riddle will do you little good." He eyes me. "Though, perhaps you are naturally gifted at conundrums?"

I shake my head, embarrassment still tingling inside. "Not particularly."

"So the siren is one obstacle," Conway interjects. "You said there were two."

Orwell nods. "About a day's journey from here, you enter the domain of the sorceress Circe."

I choke on the sip I had just taken. "Circe? From the story? The Sea Enchantress who gave Llyra legs?"

Orwell lifts his hand. "It makes sense, does it not? Legend has it Llyra's plan was to dump the treasure into the sea directly above Circe's lair in order to repay her debt. Her ship wrecked before she could accomplish her goal, but it is understandable that the wreck and the witch's haunt are near each other."

Ginevra shifts. "What does Circe do to those who pass through her domain?"

Orwell's lips tighten. "The entire area is steeped in dark magic," Orwell says gravely. "The tunnel outside her cave is overgrown with enchanted kelp which causes any living creature that swims through it to fall into a deep slumber. Circe carries the sleepers into her cave, and when they awaken, she tells them they fell unconscious outside her home and offers a reviving drink. The potion she gives her unsuspecting victims causes them to forget who they are—and everything that has passed in their lives up until that moment."

As the full meaning of his words hits me, horror ripples up my spine. Forget everything? Forget Darin? Forget Amaya and Beck and their children? Forget Conway with his mischievous eyes? Forget Chantara and her songs and stories?

"How do you know this?" Ginevra says, a sharpness in her voice I am starting to recognize as her way of combating fear. "If you passed through Circe's domain to reach the wreck, why didn't she give this potion to you?"

"I don't know," Orwell admits, his voice heavy. "When I swam over the kelp, I felt drowsiness come over me and I started to turn back. But when I awoke, I was lying on the ground in a valley I had never seen. I continued on and found the wreck the next day. When the siren released me, she said that in order to avoid certain death, I must swim all the way down the other side of the mountains. From there, I was to return home by the passage you yourselves used to reach me."

Conway opens his mouth, but Orwell forestalls him. "I know about the people losing their minds because that is what happened to the individuals who have managed to reach me. A few days after they leave this place, I find them wandering the valleys between here and Circe's lair, lost and completely helpless. All any of them have been able to tell me is they met a kind and beautiful woman named Circe who gave them a drink before sending them on their way."

A school of herrings darts suddenly around the edge of the curtain, swirling above the table before reverting to their silver phalanx and streaming back outside. Then I say wryly, "So, basically, outwitting a Sea Enchantress and solving a complex riddle under the imminent threat of death are the only things standing between us and fabulous treasure. Two pearls in one oyster."

The tension breaks. Conway gives a snort of laughter, and Orwell's chuckle rumbles over us as Ginevra gives a grudging smile.

"But how under the sea are we supposed to transport the treasure back?" she says suddenly. "Our dolphins are . . ." I see her gaze flicker to Kai as her voice dwindles.

"That is the one thing I can help you with," Orwell tells us. "In my time here, I have raised a herd of fifty dolphins. I will lend you ten to carry as much treasure as you can back with you. If you succeed in your quest, I will allow you to use the dolphins to transport the treasure to your kingdoms, on the condition that you restore them to me within a month of your return."

A sudden wave of weariness washes over me and I yawn, then blush.

But Orwell instantly pushes himself up from his chair. "There is something all of you need more than any treasure on land or sea," he says. "Sleep. Come. Leave your troubles and cares for a few brief hours."

28

DARIN

"SUCH A PITY." THE WORDS ARE SPOKEN under his breath, but just loud enough that Pike, who is lounging against the submarine wall, sharpening his coral knife against a hunk of obsidian, is sure to hear.

Pike's pale eyes dart to Darin, but he pretends to be absorbed in studying his own bound hands. Igor floats at the bow of the submarine, too far away to hear anything. Hours have passed since the achromos told him their destination, though it is impossible to tell exactly how many in the unchanging white light of the submarine's interior.

When Pike resumes sharpening his knife, he lets out a long, whooshing sigh. Pike looks at Darin again. This time, Darin meets the guard's eyes. Then he glances pointedly toward Igor, making a business of straining against his bonds to lean closer to Pike.

"He hasn't paid you yet, has he?"

Pike starts and looks quickly toward his comrade. "Shut it," he hisses.

Darin sighs again and goes back to studying his bonds. After a few more moments, he mutters, "Rubies the size of your fist . . ."

A beat of silence passes, and then a hand closes roughly around his wrist, the nails hacked off and ragged. "What did you say?"

Darin faces the bow of the submarine again and gives his head a shake. Pike's fingernails bite into the skin of Darin's wrist. "What did you say?"

He leans toward Pike and says in a conspiratorial whisper, "We were so close."

"Close to what?" The bubbles of Pike's whisper tickle his face unpleasantly, but Darin leans even closer.

"What do you think? The greatest treasure under the sea."

Pike's reaction gives him the look of a surprised tarpon. "Th-the L-lost Treasure of Llyra?" he stutters, casting a quick look at Igor as excitement makes his voice rise.

"Not so loud!" Darin hisses, throwing a look Igor's way as well. "What else did you think we were doing, out in the middle of nowhere?"

Pike's mouth opens. "You know where it is?" His now quieter voice squeaks with excitement.

Darin gives a knowing half smile, then sinks against his ropes. "But it doesn't matter now."

Pike's fingernails dig into his wrist. "What do you mean?"

Darin shakes his head. "Since you're already being paid so well, you wouldn't be interested in . . . It doesn't matter."

Bitterness gouges Pike's scrawny face. "I haven't been given a single moonstone," he says resentfully, then lowers his voice to a whisper. "That spindle-shanks says since my prisoners escaped, I haven't earned anything, even though I've been chasing stray Merfolk hither and yon through this accursed sea for nearly four months."

"What?" Darin infuses as much astonishment and contempt into his voice as he can muster.

"Ye'd best be believin' it," Pike growls. The rankling injustice of it all seems to well up inside him, and he snatches up his coral knife and slashes its edge viciously along his obsidian chunk. The rasping screech causes Igor to glance toward the back of the submarine, his face taut with annoyance.

"Would you like to go for a swim in Loch Ness when we arrive at the North Sea, Pike?"

Pike glowers at Darin but does not reply.

With one swift motion, Igor yanks a long lever protruding from the floor by his feet, bringing the submarine to a shuddering halt. Then he launches himself toward Pike, the thin metal tube he uses as a blowgun raised to strike.

Pike emits a strangled cry and hurls himself backward, but the submarine wall stops him.

Igor halts directly above him, the silver tube inches from Pike's quivering cheek. "I said," he repeats quietly, "would you like to go for a swim in Loch Ness?"

"N-no," Pike quavers.

"Then I won't hear another sound until we reach the North Sea." Igor bends down and trails Pike's cheek with his long white fingers, ending with the same quick pat you would give a child. "Will I, Pike?"

"No," Pike replies, his voice barely audible.

Igor smiles, the jewels in his incisors glinting, then turns and glides back to the bow of the submarine.

Darin glances at Pike's clamped lips and trembling hands.

Time to change tactics.

"I don't know why you put up with him."

Pike glares at him. "Ye don't? Apparently those golden eyes aren't good for much other than looks."

Darin shrugs. "I mean, you could clearly take him in a fight if you weren't so scared—"

His words become a whoosh of bubbles as Pike's fist buries itself in his gut. "If ye ever dare to call me a coward again, ye golden-haired pretty boy, I'll do worse," Pike hisses.

"See?" Darin manages as soon as the water returns to his lungs. "See what I mean? You could take him in a fight any day. Why don't you knock him out and find some treasure of your own since he clearly isn't holding up his end of the bargain?"

Pike gives a sea-lion-ish bark of laughter, but Darin can almost see the propellers of his mind slowly churning. He leans over and says, so low that Darin has to strain to catch the words, "Ye know where Llyra's Treasure is? No lie?"

He looks directly at Pike. "We were this," he holds up his thumb and index finger barely an inch apart, "close before you captured me. A day's journey will take us back."

Pike glances at Igor's slender, white-clad form, then looks back at Darin. Pike's next whisper trembles with excitement. "We could take over the submarine and split the treasure. Half of unimaginable riches is still a fortune."

LOCKLYN

TEARS SLIDE SILENTLY DOWN MY CHEEKS, pooling on my pillow and congealing the hair at the base of my neck. The sound of Ginevra and her Nebulae handmaidens' even, steady breathing fills the room as I turn my face into the damp hair on my pillow, muffling my agonized sobs.

Orwell told of a horror trapped in the north.

Dwyn and Arledge spoke of their captors' plan to take them to Loch Ness.

Ginevra relayed the pressure she received from the Atlanteans to surrender Nebulae youth to them.

There seems only one plausible reason Atlanteans and scavengers are roaming the Mediterranean kidnapping Merfolk to take to Loch Ness.

A caged, centuries-old monster grows hungry.

The image of Darin, white and still, blood blossoming from the wound at the base of his neck, seems branded in my mind, and I utter a deep moan.

Even if I'm wrong about his ultimate destination, he is at the mercy of those who clearly intend him harm.

I shouldn't have left him.

Wave Master, why did I leave him?

My teacher. My crony. My best friend.

He wouldn't have left me. I know it.

And I never got the chance to apologize. No, that's not true. I did have a chance, several of them. I just never took one. Because I was sulking. Acting like the child I said he still saw me as.

The memory of him catching me in his arms after we escaped the scavengers fills my mind. He had crushed me against him, holding me so tightly I didn't think he would ever let go. The warmth of his body seemed to flow into me, infusing every particle of my being with a fiery, golden glow.

I bury my face deeply into the pillow as sobs rack my body. Painful thoughts rise to the surface, and I drown them, unwilling to confront the secret grief that has gnawed at the edges of my consciousness for four years.

He's my friend.

My friend.

Wave Master, keep him safe. Please.

If anything happens to him, I don't know what I'll do. I don't even know who I am without Darin. He's part of me. He always has been.

One of the Nebulae guards gives a grunting snore and tosses on her bed, mumbling in her sleep. Suddenly, I can't take it anymore. I throw back my own covers and slip out of bed, gliding to the curtain covering the cave's entrance and drawing it open. I slide down with my back against the outside wall of the cave, hugging my knees tightly, my tears spent.

I want Amaya. The thought might be childish, but the memory of her quiet understanding makes my bruised and battered heart ache with longing. I think of Avonlea and send up a silent prayer for her protection. She must have changed so much since I'd seen her last. The pain inside sharpens, and I bury my head in my arms, wishing the tears would return and soften the throbbing hurt.

"Can't sleep?"

My head jerks up, and I throw myself sideways, the crustacean-encrusted cave wall scraping my back.

Conway hovers a few feet away, arms crossed over his chest. He nearly scared me to death, and I am about to tell him so when it hits me. Conway's tail is gone. His legs, clad in black sealskin, are lean and muscular, fluttering lazily to keep him aloft in the water.

"Your—" my voice sticks in my throat for a moment, "your tail . . ."

"My legs start cramping up if I wear it too long." Conway settles onto the sand beside me and crosses his legs. His knee brushes mine, but I shift away, putting space between us. Everything is too complicated. And making decisions with my emotions as tangled up as they are would be a big mistake.

I wonder if he will close this distance between us again, but he just leans back against the rock wall and closes his eyes. His eyelashes make long, feathery black smudges against the pale skin of his cheeks. With his eyes closed, he looks younger, less cocky and sure of himself.

"I'm so tired," he says, his eyes still closed. "But every time I drift off to sleep, I see that crab slicing that girl in half and . . . blood in the water and . . ." His voice breaks, and he sucks his lips tight against his teeth.

The lump in my throat swells, constricting my airway so I can't speak. I don't know what I would have said anyway. There's nothing to say. Nothing that can erase the horror of what happened to Dwyn.

His eyelids flutter open, and his dark eyes fix on me. "How are you?" My face must twist, because he adds quickly, "No, don't answer that. I mean, is there anything I can do? I know you were really close with him."

You were really close with him.

I was. And then I pushed him away. For what?

My own stupid pride.

I try to answer but instead burst into tears. Gut-wrenching sobs pour out, and I curl into a tight little ball against the cave wall, as though by becoming physically smaller, I can crumple up all my pain. Maybe then it will no longer feel like an unstoppable torrent through every corner of my body.

Conway's arms envelop me, and he rubs my back, murmuring incomprehensibly under his breath. I put my face against his shoulder and cry and cry, the heartbroken wailing of a very small child.

The wailing turns into gasping, hiccupping sobs and then into silence. For a moment, I stay pressed against Conway's chest, too drained to move. Then I push away, rubbing the back of my hand across my face to wipe off the greenish slime of my tears.

"Your shirt," I say thickly, gesturing toward the ugly black smudges across the shoulder of his dove-gray top. "I'm sorry."

He shrugs lightly, his eyes fixed on my face. Something about his expression causes heat to rise in my cheeks and I say quickly, "Those stains don't come out, you know."

"I'm not worried," he says quietly.

The water seems to simmer between us, but I can't look away from his black eyes. This is how it feels to be wanted. Is it so wrong to want to be wanted?

But I want Darin.

Tearing my gaze from his, I say, "We should both get some rest. Good night, Conway."

But, as I glide past him, his fingers close around my wrist. "The way I felt yesterday almost seeing you die? I don't ever want to feel like that again, Locklyn."

Our faces are inches apart, his black eyes boring into mine. I pull my wrist from his grasp and take a shuddering breath. "The only way to get rid of feeling like that is to stop caring. Love and pain go hand in hand. So, until the day you stop caring or your mind gets wiped or your heart stops beating, shadows of that pain will follow you. Always."

As I slip into the cave, I catch the curtain before it can fall closed behind me and turn back.

"But, Conway? For the sparkling moments and thrilling seconds and golden hours of loving and being loved? It's worth it."

30

LOCKLYN

WHEN I SEE THE SOFT, BLUE-PURPLE glow illuminating the water ahead, my heart stands still. I turn to Ginevra, who I have been swimming next to for the past half a day. Despite her pointed silence and the increase in her speed, which has left me breathless and barely able to keep up, she's been good company.

"I know," she says, irritation in her voice. She looks back at the rest of the group and calls out, "We're here!"

An unintelligible shout answers her, and she faces forward again, observing the bluish radiance ahead with narrowed eyes. "I don't like this."

"Neither do I," I say, my heart racing as I watch the iridescent blue water, shimmering almost maliciously ahead. "But it's the best plan we have."

"Plan?" Ginevra scoffs. "Swimming through an enchanted forest of kelp so we can fall into a magical sleep and be captured by a sorceress? That's not a plan. That's suicide."

"What else can we do?" I protest. "There's no other way to reach the wreck—not with the time we have. And we know not to accept anything she offers us to drink. Our only hope is to somehow convince her to let us pass."

When her only answer is a disdainful shrug, my temper, already simmering, begins to boil. "Listen," I say, with a quick glance over my shoulder at the others, who are only just catching up. "I thought when you saved my life we might have grown beyond this."

She doesn't bother to look at me. "I would have saved the life of anyone on this mission," she says stiffly. "That means nothing."

I clench my jaw to keep the angry words bubbling behind my lips from spilling out.

She's impossible, Wave Master!

Turning away, I see Conway, Blackwell, Arledge, Baia, Kallan, and Kai, along with ten dolphins, drawing level with us.

"So, we're here," Conway remarks, surveying the waving blue light illuminating the water ahead. Tension seems to ripple around us. The normally cheerful chittering of the dolphins has morphed into high, strained peeping. For one mad moment, I wonder if there is some sort of enchantment emanating through the water, magnifying our fears.

"There's no point waiting around here," Ginevra says impatiently. We all look at her and she forces a grim smile. "We're all about to go to sleep anyway. What's the point of setting up camp?"

For some reason her words and her smile break the tension. I remember why I keep trying with Ginevra. Because of moments like this when I see glimmers of something genuine peeking through all her aloof surliness.

"See you on the other side," Conway says encouragingly. There is a fraction of a second where everyone hesitates, but then we all swim forward in silence.

I am riveted by the brilliance ahead, which grows brighter with each stroke of my legs. Gradually, I begin to see stalks wavering in the glow, tall and bulbous, emanating the shimmering blue light that surrounds them. My legs falter, then I force them to continue churning through the water, closer and closer to the swaying kelp forest.

Now the stalks are right in front of me. I hesitate, then plunge into the forest. Instantly, absolute silence surrounds me. The stalks are so thick that I can't see more than a foot in any direction. But as I begin to push my way through them, shoving stalks aside, a sweet, clear scent rises in the water. I pause, sniffing, trying to decide what the smell reminds me of.

Posidonia flowers.

A newborn merchild's head.

The tangy sweetness of lecker.

I breathe in rapturously, drinking in the fragrance. I know I must go on, but first I must smell for just a moment longer, inhaling this odor that is more delicious than anything I have ever encountered. I feel warm and full inside as though the aroma is something edible, filling my stomach as well as my lungs. I know I must go on, but I can't remember why. The fragrance consumes me, and without it, I will starve. It envelops me—more and more and more—and I am growing heavier and heavier, sinking through the beautiful, blue light, unable to hold myself up any longer.

"How do you feel?"

I open my eyes slowly, blinking in the soft, warm light of a small cave. A beautiful Merwoman drifts in front of me. Her eyes are large and the clear blue of the sky above The Surface. Her waist-length hair flows around her slender form, seeming to glow in the golden light coming from the small fireplace.

I blink, staring hard at the fireplace. It is full of flames. Not magma. Flames. But fire is impossible under the sea.

"I found you and your companions unconscious outside my home," the Merwoman says in her soft, sweet voice.

I stare at her, my mind churning as I will my brain to unfreeze.

The Merwoman reaches out a slender hand, placing it gently on my shoulder. "You seem disoriented," she says gently. "Let me get you a drink to soothe your nerves."

She drifts away, her aquamarine tail flicking gracefully. I turn my head slowly and see I am seated on a long stone bench, my back propped against a cave wall. The rest of the bench is filled with Merpeople. A black-haired boy with creamy white skin and inky eyelashes. A dark-skinned girl with long silvery hair and a sparkling, alabaster tail. A thin Merman with an ugly scar across his cheek. A hulking Merman with calloused hands. Two dark-skinned Merwomen lolling against each other. And, finally, a thin, nondescript boy with mossy hair and tired lines around his eyes.

"Here you are," the soft voice of the Merwoman says, and I turn to see she is holding out a simple, stone cup.

"Thank you." I take it from her, my brain swirling sluggishly. The liquid in the cup is a deep, electric blue. "Who are they?" I lift a slow hand toward the line of Merpeople on the bench beside me.

"I'm afraid I have no idea," the Merwoman says sympathetically. "I assumed they were with you. You all appeared in the kelp forest since I was last there yesterday evening."

I stare into the cup again. A shadowy reflection stares back. "Will this help me remember?" I ask, glancing up into the woman's clear blue eyes.

Her lips curve slightly. "Who knows? Its effects are unique to the individual, stimulating certain parts of the brain and veiling others."

My eyes drift back to the cup. My brain feels as though it is wrapped in octopus tentacles, being squeezed so tightly that movement is impossible. With effort, I lift the cup toward my mouth, tipping my head back. But something catches my eye and I freeze, cup suspended a few inches from my lips.

Just beyond the cave's opening, a blue light wavers. I remember seeing wavering blue light not long ago. Memory stirs. I am swimming toward a swaying forest of bluish kelp, knowing I must go through it to reach Llyra's Lost Treasure, but also knowing I am about to lose consciousness, and . . .

I slowly lower the cup and look up again into her clear, sky-blue eyes. Eyes that sparkle as they take in my dawning comprehension. "You're Circe," I say.

Circe smiles and inclines her head slightly as she drifts backward, settling herself onto a low stool carved out of coral. She surveys me with her hands clasped loosely in her lap. "Ah," she says softly. "See, it stimulates portions of the brain in certain individuals."

I set the cup down beside me and watch her with narrowed eyes. "I didn't drink any of it," I say.

"But the main ingredient in the potion is the oublier faire kelp that grows outside my front door. And it was the sight of the kelp, was it not, that caused you to remember who I am?"

"Yes," I say hesitantly, disconcerted.

"So," Circe says lightly, "why is it you have come seeking me? Clearly, you have no need for legs to win a human lover."

The comment would have stung coming from anyone else, but for some reason, the words are playful and humorous delivered in Circe's soft, sweet voice. I smile, and she returns the gesture, the expression beautifying her already lovely face.

"Llyra was my great-great-grandmother." I don't know where the words come from. Something about Circe seems to draw them from me without conscious thought on my part. I expect her to give some sign of shock, but her delicate eyebrows merely arch the barest fraction of an inch.

"Really?"

"So, I suppose you are the reason I have legs. Though I don't have a human lover."

"But you do have a lover," Circe says. And then as her gaze skims my face, she adds softly, "Or perhaps you are the one who loves."

The image of Darin's deep, golden eyes swims before me. I hurriedly shift my own eyes away from Circe, and they catch on the pale face of the black-haired boy sunken against the cavern wall, his long lashes forming dark smudges on his cheeks. Guilt swirls and I drop my eyes in confusion.

"Ah," Circe remarks. "It is complicated. I see." She tilts her head. "But why have you come to me?"

My eyes drift to the flickering blue light in the doorway, and I suddenly remember the soft blue hair on the head of a baby girl, snuggled against my breast.

"For a tail," I say, and then as her blue eyes widen, I smile apologetically. "My family can't seem to make up their minds, can they? But the tail I need isn't for me. It's for my niece."

"So, your desire is to break the curse I placed on your family."

For an instant, I hesitate. Because strangely, in this moment, when freedom from the curse is finally within my reach, I know I will not feel like myself without the legs that have shaped my entire life. But this is not about me. It is about Avonlea.

"Yes," I say.

Circe's tail sways slowly. "As the one who cast the spell, the process to remove it is relatively simple." My heart leaps. But then Circe continues, "However, your family has yet to repay me for the first service I rendered."

I lean toward her impulsively, my heart thumping heavily against my ribs. "That is why we are here," I say, gesturing to my companions slumbering on the bench. "Part of the reason, anyway. We seek Llyra's Treasure in order to save two kingdoms and," I hesitate, then go on, "so we can undo the curse that has given two of us legs."

"The boy also?" She nods toward Conway, whose head is now slumped onto Ginevra's shoulder. My eyes widen and her lips quirk. "My dear child, I have lived long enough under the sea to be able to tell a real tail from a false one. But I can claim no credit for his legs. They are not a result of my curse."

Again, her perception disconcerts me, but I force my face to remain neutral. "Are you able to give him a tail anyway?" I ask.

Circe's full lips twist. "There is very little that I cannot do, dear," she says softly.

This is it.

Time to make my own bargain with the Sea Enchantress.

I take in a breath and force confidence I don't feel into my next words. "If you let us pass, we will return with Llyra's locket. To pay for your service."

Circe pushes herself up off her stool and hovers before me, her arms crossed. "But the locket cannot be your payment. It was Llyra's payment, and by returning it, you merely even the score. In order for me to reverse the curse and take away the boy's legs, you must give me something else."

Her voice remains soft and pleasant, yet cold grips me. "But the curse was your way of evening the score, wasn't it?" I keep my voice conversational. "Once the locket is returned, justice would dictate the curse should be reversed." I stare into her beautiful, inscrutable face. "We've even paid you interest." I give a short laugh. "Five generations of Crura and their suffering." I swallow. The bitterness came out before I could stop it.

Circe's head tilts. "But, my dear, you are missing the point. Your great-great-grandmother forced me to wait five generations for what was rightfully mine. Do you really think—after all that— justice is what I am after?"

We stare into each other's eyes, and the coldness in hers causes chills to trickle down my spine. I feel as if I carry a heavy weight. "What else do you want?" I ask tonelessly.

"I don't know yet," Circe says in her sweet, quiet voice. "Let us just say that you owe me a favor. Yes. That is what I want."

My mouth suddenly feels too full of water. "A favor?" I croak.

Her smile widens. "Yes, my dear. You bring me that locket and swear, on whatever you hold dearest, you will perform one favor for me in the future, and I will reverse the curse. And throw in a bonus tail for this boy who is not your lover."

I swallow again. My heart thumps erratically against my breastbone. "You know I can't promise that."

Circe arches a brow. "Then we have a problem."

"I have to know what it is I am promising," I say quickly. "A favor could be anything. A year's supply of dugong milk. The assassination of one of your enemies. My firstborn child."

Circe laughs. "Believe me, I will not ask for your firstborn. I am not the maternal type."

"But you see what I'm saying. I would be a fool to promise a favor when I have no idea what it is I am promising."

Circe laughs again, and this time the sound causes me to shiver. "But, my sweet," she says, "at this point, you would be a fool to refuse."

"What do you mean?" I say, though I am sure I already know.

"My dear, you don't imagine I will let you or your companions leave here unless you swear to me. And you know firsthand what happens when a promise made to me gets broken."

I glance at my sleeping companions, and for one wild moment, I contemplate trying to rouse them and attacking Circe. But a heartbeat later, I know it will do no good. Even if we could overpower her, we will spend the rest of our lives sleeping in the forest of oublier faire kelp.

I meet Circe's eyes and my insides turn to stone. Her eyes are the eyes of a tiger shark staring into the terrified pupils of a cornered baby dolphin. She knows what my answer will be, because there is no other answer I can give.

I swallow. "I will bring you Llyra's locket and do one favor for you in the future on the condition that you reverse the curse you placed on my great-great-grandmother and her descendants, giving tails to Conway, me, and Avonlea. We will also need your help to reach the edge of the kelp forest in order to find Llyra's Treasure. And, upon our return, you will escort us back through the kelp forest and make no effort to detain us from returning to our kingdom."

I have tried to sound demanding, as though I am getting just as much out of this bargain as Circe is, but the satisfied look on her face and the leaden feeling in my stomach tell me neither of us is fooled.

"It is a bargain," Circe agrees smoothly. "I will reverse your curse."

My heart seems to have stopped. What have I done? What awful thing will she ask of me? Is there any way out of this?

"Swear," Circe breathes. "On the thing nearest to your heart."

The thing nearest to my heart?

Darin's face swims before my eyes, and I swallow for the third time, searching for words that will not endanger him, should I fail. "There is someone whose death would mean the death of my soul, without whom I would be a mollusk shell, empty and lifeless. It is on this Merperson I swear to bring you Llyra's locket. And I swear to perform one favor for you upon my return." I meet her icy gaze and try to keep my voice from shaking. "Whatever you ask."

31

DARIN

AS THE ROPES FALL FROM HIS WRISTS, he resists the urge to celebrate. Pike floats in front of him, pretending to check his bonds while he actually gathers the severed rope and loops it loosely around Darin's wrists to make it look like he is still bound.

"'E's strong," Pike mutters for the umpteenth time, jerking his head in Igor's direction.

Darin resists the urge to roll his eyes. "I just need you to get the blowgun away from him," he says patiently. "I'll take care of the rest."

Pike's fingers slip a little on the ropes as he glances at Igor again. "If we fail . . ." he mumbles, even lower.

"We won't fail." The words come out a little too forcefully, and Igor glances toward the pair of them.

Quick as an electric eel, Pike backhands Darin across the face and snarls, "I don't want no cheek from you! You'll stay tied up until I say different, see?"

"What is going on here?" Igor's shadow falls across their hunched forms. Pike fumbles with the ropes and one of the severed ends slips out. Igor's scarlet eyes narrow.

Throwing himself upright, Darin shoves Pike out of the way as the ropes fall from his wrists. His fist connects with Igor's jaw at the same time he slams his tail into the Crura's torso. "The gun!" he bellows at Pike.

But Pike was right about Igor's strength. The combined effect of two blows, which would have stunned a normal Merman, merely throws him backward. Hearing Darin's shout, Igor pitches himself sideways, using the force of his backward motion to slam into Pike. Pike grunts as he careens into the control lever. The submarine gives a tremendous lurch, sending all three sprawling. Something strikes Darin on the back of the head. Groping for it, his fingers close around the slim, metal rod of Igor's blowgun.

As the submarine's momentum shudders to a stop, Darin points the weapon in Igor's general direction, praying to the Wave Master it is loaded, and bellows, "Stop!"

"I wouldn't shoot that if I were you." Igor's voice is deadly. The bubbles filling the cabin clear to reveal Igor with an arm around Pike's neck, holding him as a living shield, while his other hand presses the tip of a coral blade into Pike's side. Darin hesitates, then expels all the water in his lungs into the mouthpiece.

A finned dart flies from the other end. Darin's aim is true—the projectile lodges itself in Igor's cheek. With two more hard puffs, two more darts join the first in the skin of Igor's face, forming a small, lopsided star. For an instant, he and Igor stare into each other's eyes. Then Igor slowly reaches up and, with a jerk, pulls the darts from his cheek. "I told you not to do that," he says, and buries the knife into Pike.

At Pike's bellow of agony, Darin throws himself toward Igor, swinging the thin, metal rod like a saber. Igor drops Pike and latches onto the end of the rod. With surprising strength, he jerks it hard, hurling Darin into the submarine wall.

"Aalto . . ." Pike's gurgling groan invigorates him, and Darin darts over and takes hold of the blowgun with all of his might, pulling it from Igor's hands. Then he swings it toward the achromos's face, but Igor throws himself onto the submarine floor and slithers forward, stabbing at Darin's tail with his knife. The blade glances off his scales, and Darin lashes out with his tail, dashing the knife from Igor's hands. He slams Igor to the ground with the full weight of his body and holds the end of the blowgun against the side of Igor's face.

"Why didn't the darts work?" he demands.

Despite the threat, Igor manages to smile. "You surely didn't think I'd go around carrying around a poison that could be used against me, Aalto? I'm immune to sea snake venom."

Pike moans again.

"Well, I doubt you're immune to this," Darin says and crashes the blowgun against Igor's skull.

Igor's eyes roll back in his head, then close.

Darin whirls, dropping down beside Pike. The blond Merman's fingers scrabble at the knife lodged in his side, but Darin can see the wound is clearly fatal.

"Hey." He moves Pike's hands away from the knife. "Let me."

Pike's terrified eyes bulge and he struggles to speak. Blood leaks from the corner of his mouth. "You . . . you said . . . we wouldn't . . . fail."

Guilt washes over Darin as he wiggles the blade free from Pike's flesh. He quickly pulls his shirt over his head, wadding it up and pressing it against the hole in Pike's side in a feeble attempt to stop the bleeding. "I'm sorry. Wave Master as my witness, Pike, I'm so sorry."

Pike's fingers fumble at his neck, and Darin sees he is trying to undo the clasp of a crude copper chain fastened there. Half of a clam pendant dangles from it, the mother-of-pearl on the edges flashing rainbow colors for an instant as the light from the white stone catches them.

"Here." Darin carefully unfastens the necklace, pooling the chain in the center of the clam shell and pressing it into Pike's hand.

"No." Pike pushes it weakly back at him. "Find her. Buy her freedom. That's what me half of the treasure was for."

"Find who?" Darin puts the chain around his neck, the shell

pendant resting smooth and cool against the bare skin of his chest. "Who do you want me to find, Pike?"

But the Merman's eyelids flutter, and when he coughs, blood clouds the water around them. "Find . . . her . . ."

"Who, Pike? Where is she?"

"You . . . owe . . . me . . . Aalto. Find . . . her." Pike takes a shuddering breath, and his body goes limp. Darin sinks back, eyes downcast.

Pike is right, he does owe him. So he must search and find her. Whoever she is.

32

LOCKLYN

"WHAT, IN THE WAVE MASTER'S NAME, were you thinking?"

The intense quietness of Conway's voice tells me exactly how furious he is.

"There was nothing else I could do, Conway," I say wearily. We swim a little ways in front of our group, moving swiftly along a narrow chasm between towering black peaks.

"You could have woken me! You could have told her she needed to ask for something else! You could have—I don't know—put your hands around her throat and demanded she reverse the curse!"

"Sure, that would have worked." I snort.

"This isn't funny, Locklyn! Promising her a favor was complete lunacy! She could ask you for anything! For half the treasure. For a lifetime of servitude. For your firstborn child!" I attempt to laugh and Conway glares. "This isn't funny," he says again.

I feel myself teetering on the brink of emotional collapse, and I struggle to return to equilibrium. "I know it isn't." I turn and look him full in the face. Something in my eyes causes his glare to fade.

"We have to find some way around it," he insists. "Some way for you not to give her the favor and not get cursed again."

"There is no way around it, Conway," I tell him.

"Maybe if she isn't alive to curse you," he mumbles, looking away.

"No," I say sharply.

Conway shrugs, still not looking at me.

"Conway," I say more forcefully, catching hold of his arm and dragging him around to face me. "Don't," I say again.

"Don't what?" he snaps.

"Do anything stupid."

"You know, that's rich, coming from you." We glare into each other's eyes, and I resist the urge to scream, to tell him I had no choice. That I did what I had to do. That I'm more terrified than he can possibly imagine by the idea of what favor Circe will ask of me, and that this whole situation is awful enough without him doing anything to make it worse.

"You're blocking the path." Ginevra's voice, cold as the mountains of ice floating in the North Sea, cuts in. I spin to find her directly behind us. Her face looks carved from granite, and I realize how this must appear—Conway and I with our faces inches apart, my hand clutching his arm.

"I'm sorry," I start, but she brushes past me without a word and darts away along the passage, her milky tail like a shining streak.

I turn to swim after her, but Conway takes hold of my wrist. "Why do you care what she thinks, Locklyn?"

"I could really like her if she'd let me. And I hate seeing her so unhappy."

And I know what it feels like to know the thing you want most desperately is the one thing you will never have.

"She'll get over it," Conway says, but his voice lacks certainty.

I glance at him, and for one mad moment, I want to ask him again why he doesn't love Ginevra when she would clearly give the last drop of blood in her veins for him. To me, it seems a love as strong as hers should be magnetic, attracting the object of its desire. But now is not the time. And I'm not entirely certain Conway and Ginevra together is the ending I want.

"We should keep going," I say, pulling my wrist away, as Kai, followed closely by the herd of ten dolphins, swims into view. I strike off as fast as I can, hoping against hope that he will take the hint and allow me to put some space between us.

I scan the water ahead for a sign of Ginevra's pearly tail, but she must be swimming very quickly because the minutes tick by without any sign of her. The black walls towering on either side, and the silence of the dark water, seem to press in, piling up all the fear and loss and guilt of the past several days. Memories swirl and pound against the inside of my head, and I clench my jaw, trying to push the thoughts and images away.

I just need to remember good. Something good. Anything to lighten this darkness.

I probe the images of my childhood, but in every memory—chasing dugongs, learning to read with Amaya, listening to Chantara's stories, scouring the reef for oysters with pearls inside—Darin is there, hovering like a golden shadow. First as a teenager, competitive and anxious to prove himself, but with a softness underneath. As a child, I sensed that about him but didn't know how to articulate it into words. Then as a young man, confident and good-natured, the desire of every girl in Aquaticus, but still with time to teach a shy, awkward teenager to sharpen coral knives and lasso dugongs. And then more recently, his strength weathered, his humor sharpened with edges of sarcasm. And yet, the soft underbelly remains, his carefully hidden heart as golden as the treasure he seeks.

Pain stabs with each memory and I almost despair. My heart is already too raw and lacerated to be able to take much more. Combing frantically through my mind, a memory shimmers into view, and I cling to it, dragging it to the surface.

I am about eight years old. Amaya, Darin, and Beck are all in school, leaving me lonely and bored. Boredom morphs into recklessness and I leave the reef, swimming upward. A dolphin passes after a few hours, and I give a merry warble, calling the creature toward me. Riding on the dolphin's back, I continue to rise through the ocean waters, watching them grow lighter and lighter.

Time passes and I become increasingly tired, stiff, and

discouraged. Apparently, I have forgotten exactly how long it takes to reach The Surface since the last time I rode up, when I was much younger. But just as I am about to direct the dolphin to take me home to face Amaya's wrath, I see sparkling threads of light dancing around me. Then with a whoosh, my head breaks the surface of the water, and I soar weightlessly into the cool night air, clinging to the dolphin's sleek, silver back.

All of my weariness melts away, and I laugh out loud as the wind gusts against my face. The dolphin skips across the waves with me clinging to its back. The moon is a full, alabaster orb in the navy sky, and the stars are like diamonds strung in the heaven's misty gauze that Darin says Land Dwellers call the Milky Way. Their light frosts the tips of the dark waves with glowing silver.

After frolicking in the waves for who knows how long, the dolphin and I settle down to float in the water, allowing the soft waves to rock us back and forth. I lie on my back, staring up at the sparkling sky as wisps of clouds drift across the stars, feeling a strange ache at the beauty of it all. More clouds swirl to form a barrier blocking the stars and light, and warm rain begins to fall, speckling the water and my upturned face. I close my eyes, allowing the downpour to run in streams down my cheeks and through my hair, feeling the ache inside swell and wishing, with all of my eight-year-old heart, that I could stay here, adrift with warm rain falling around me forever.

"Locklyn." Ginevra's voice jolts me from my trance.

I look up, and my heart leaps.

We've reached it.

I always wondered whether Llyra's Lost Treasure was really as fabulous as I had always heard, or if legend had gilded the reality. But, never, either above the sea or under it, have I seen a ship like this. The hulking mass of it completely obscures the blue water above. The tattered remains of crimson sails hang limply, and the hull is encrusted with barnacles, but there is no doubt it was once an extraordinary vessel.

Apart from its colossal size, it is built in the shape of a Mermaid, her torso and emerald-green tail forming the body of the vessel, her shoulders and beautiful face, surrounded by flaming red hair, forming the prow. The detail work is exquisite. The link between every one of Llyra's wooden scales is studded with a single, large emerald, and the rippling wood of her hair almost looks as if it is blowing in the wind. Her eyes have been carefully constructed from dozens of perfectly round sapphires. For a ship that has been under the sea for over a hundred years, it is in excellent condition, with the exception of one gaping hole in its side, which is where our path leads.

I turn to look at Ginevra. For once, her eyes are not hostile, but wide with astonishment. "It's real," she whispers.

"I know," I breathe back. "I can hardly believe my eyes."

We wait in silence, both continuing to scrutinize the wreck. One by one our companions join us, each of them exclaiming or simply staring in awe at the monumental ship we have come miles and sacrificed much to reach. When everyone is gathered together, Kai's dolphins jostling restlessly to and fro, Conway looks around.

"There's no point waiting," he says. "Let's go."

Moving slowly, Conway, Ginevra, and me in the lead, we approach the ragged hole in the ship's side. As we come to the edge of it, the ship growing larger and larger above us, a voice suddenly speaks from the black depths.

"Come no closer, strangers," it says.

Everyone jerks to a stop, bumping into each other. I squint at the cavity, willing my eyes to discern a figure, but the blackness is impenetrable.

Conway clears his throat. "We seek Llyra's Treasure."

"Why do you seek it?" the voice asks.

It sends a shiver up my spine.

Conway glances at me and Ginevra, clearly unsure how to respond.

"We seek to aid our families and our kingdoms," I say, deciding this is the most concise and truthful answer.

"You do not seek it for personal gain?" the voice asks.

Ginevra and I both turn to look at Conway, whose face has flushed.

"I seek healing," he says.

"For yourself or for another?"

"For myself."

"Then you may not pass," the voice says.

I glance at Conway, whose face has gone rigid.

The voice speaks again. "Does any other seek personal gain within these walls?"

I glance around. Kai's face remains unchanged. The two Nebulae women are looking at Ginevra, who gives them a small smile. Blackwell's tail flickers nervously as he stares at the ground. Arledge's expression holds the same tired pain it has had since Dwyn's death.

"Does any other seek personal gain within these walls?" the voice says again. "Be warned. If any enter seeking their own ends, they will suffer the consequences."

When no one says anything, the voice goes on, "I am the Guardian of this vessel. I protect it from those who are unworthy. If you wish to enter, you must solve the riddle I place before you. Once the riddle is spoken, you must respond. If you respond correctly, I will allow you to pass. If you answer incorrectly, my eels will attack."

Out of the darkness, five conical heads suddenly emerge, eyes staring in opposite directions, mouths open to reveal sharp, needle-like teeth. A gasp or two escapes the others, and I bite my tongue to keep from shrieking.

"If you do not answer," the voice continues dispassionately, "that will be deemed an incorrect answer. The riddle, once spoken, must be answered. So, choose now. Do you wish to hear my riddle? If not, turn and depart in peace."

My pulse is racing.

What if we answer wrong?

What if we can't figure it out?

Wave Master, help us!

I glance at Conway and Ginevra, seeing in their eyes the same terror and indecision I am feeling. But what choice do we have? I raise my eyebrows and each of them give shaky nods.

"Tell us your riddle," I say, trying to keep my voice steady as I look into the depths of the black hole. I try not to look at the five glistening, black eels.

"You have chosen," the voice announces. "Listen carefully."

> "My red mouth does not devour
> But when it opens wide
> Every creature close about me
> Ought to run and hide
>
> My saliva burns with fire
> My teeth like jagged arrows fly
> White devastation follows anger
> Crowned by a vermilion sky."

My brain seems frozen. Snippets of the rhyme echo in my ears. Vermilion sky . . . jagged arrows fly . . . red mouth . . . saliva . . . hide . . . My eyes go to Ginevra. Her eyes are closed, and her features have resumed the stonelike look they get whenever she is terrified.

I glance to my right and see Conway's face is screwed up in concentration, his lips moving soundlessly. Looking over my shoulder, I see Arledge and Kai's expressions have not changed, but Blackwell's eyes are frozen on the open mouths of the five electric eels, while the two Nebula bodyguards fiddle nervously with the handles of their spears.

It doesn't look like any of us have a clue what the answer to the riddle is.

Think.

Think.

THINK.

But my brain is failing me, and all I can think of is that beautiful night when I was eight, playing in the surf with the dolphin, and then floating in the rain until . . .

Dimly, I hear Conway say, "Could we hear it again?"

. . . until a rumbling like thunder shook the night, and miles away a huge mountain, the one the Land Dwellers call Purkagia, exploded in a shower of light and flame. And, though I was too far away for them to touch me, I could see the rocks like arrows raining from the sky, and the raindrops dissolving into sizzling smoke mixed with white flecks of ash.

"Crowned by a vermilion sky," concludes the voice. "My eels grow restless. You must answer soon."

"What?" Conway explodes. "There's a time limit?"

But his voice is dim as my memory takes me back to that night, and I see the entire sky stained scarlet and the ocean below turned into blood. I rummage in the deepest corners of my mind and a word emerges.

"It's a volcano," I say quietly.

Conway pauses his rant and Ginevra's head turns sharply toward me.

"Are you sure?" she says urgently. "If we guess wrong . . ."

"If we don't guess, those eels are still going to attack us!" Conway points out.

"Yes," I state. "Yes, I'm sure."

Conway and Ginevra are both looking at me. My throat is suddenly very dry. I raise my voice into the stillness. "Our answer is 'volcano.'"

For a long moment, nothing happens. Then the eels draw to the sides of the hole, forming a pathway through which a strange and terrible creature emerges.

Her torso is that of a woman—a woman with translucent skin under which the blue lines of her veins interlace eerily. But rather than a tail, or legs, her bottom half is that of a squid, with long inky-black tentacles wafting through the water. Tangled black hair falls to her waist, framing a pale face with a bright red mouth slashing across the bottom half. But it is her eyes that startle me.

They are black and soulless, with milky pupils that make them look almost blind.

"You have answered correctly," she proclaims.

I feel Conway exhale next to me, a soft whistle of bubbles escaping his lips.

"You may pass and take what you will," the siren says, pointing a bony finger ending in a talon-like black nail at the bowels of the ship. "All but that one." Her finger swivels directly to Conway.

Conway stills, then nods slowly. "With the dolphins, you don't really need me," he tells us, but his attempted encouragement falls flat.

"We should get this over with," Ginevra says tersely. She addresses the group. "We will take as much treasure as we can load on the ten dolphins, but we don't want to overload them, so be sure to take the smallest and most valuable objects." Everyone nods silently. Her eyes meet Conway's and I see her stone mask crack. "We'll be back soon."

"I'm going to stay with the prince." We all turn to Arledge who is hovering near the back of the group, his face pale and strained. "S-so he isn't alone."

"That sounds like a good idea," I say quickly, certain Arledge's real reason for remaining behind is to avoid entering the eel-infested bowels of the wreck, and wishing to keep the others in the group from questioning him further. "Ginevra is right. We should go."

The siren moves silently aside. Ginevra and I look at each other and then plunge into the ship's dark interior.

There is a horrible instant when I realize we forgot to bring light, but then torches flare into life along the walls. I stare, astonished at the flickering golden flames before turning to look back at the siren, who has not moved. There is magic in this place.

Ginevra's sharp intake of breath brings my attention to the room before us, and my mouth falls open. The entire belowdecks of the ship stretch longer and wider than the great hall of the palace in Aquaticus. Wooden pillars are spaced throughout, supporting the deck. And between the pillars, everything shines. Mounds of golden coins brush the ceiling. Open chests brimming with diamonds and moonstones fill the air with a rainbow shimmer. Copper suits of armor shine rosily from corners, like guardians of the fabulous treasure surrounding them.

To my astonishment, it is Kai's gruff voice which speaks first. "Let's get what we need and go. This is an evil place. The dolphins sense it. They are restless."

"Everyone spread out," Ginevra commands, coming out of her daze. "There are ten dolphins and six of us, so—"

"Wait," I interrupt her. "I—there is something I need to find. Something specific. So, I shouldn't take a dolphin." For a fraction of a second, my eyes meet Blackwell's. I resist the urge to reach for Dwyn's coral knife, which I have been using since losing mine.

I expect Ginevra to argue, but after giving me an appraising look, she merely says, "We'll each take two dolphins then. Load them with the smallest and most valuable items you can find. As soon as you are finished, return here."

As the rest of the group scatters, I remain behind, my mind racing. It would take days to search the entire vessel. And we don't have days. Today is day fifteen. To return to Nebula and Aquaticus before the thirty days are up, we must leave tonight.

My eyes skim the piles of treasure with dismay. I don't even know what the locket looks like. A trinket that small could be buried anywhere.

I close my eyes. Llyra was desperate when she set sail. She believed wholeheartedly that returning the locket to Circe and fulfilling her end of the bargain would allow her to see her son again. She wouldn't just have dumped it in a pile of treasure down in the hold. That locket was her ticket to getting her son back—the single most precious item on the ship.

My eyes fly open. I know where the locket is.

As I flit through the mounds of treasure, I catch glimpses of the others, bundling uncut rubies, tiny diamond bottles of wine and perfume, solid gold knives, combs, and other trinkets into multicolored silks and layering them carefully in the large baskets slung across the dolphins' backs.

I've never seen anything like this. Darin would be over the moon.

The thought sends a pang through me, and I swim faster, gazing around as I search for a way up to the deck above. I can't see the ceiling, which is so tall it is shrouded in shadows, but I scan the area frantically for a ladder or staircase, some way a person with legs could get down to this level. The sooner we are done, the sooner I can go find Darin. If he isn't dead. He can't be.

I finally catch sight of a neat wooden staircase tucked into the corner of the hold and make a break for it. I swim upward, following the trajectory of the stairs, marveling as I rise higher and higher without encountering the ceiling. I am just starting to wonder if the staircase is a decoy of some kind when the top of my head collides with something solid. Gingerly, I probe the knot on the top of my head before running my fingers over the surface above me. I feel wood and metal—the outlines of a trapdoor. Further explorations show the bolt has rusted. Pulling my coral knife out, I try to insert the blade between the metal edges, but the grime is too thick. Gritting my teeth, I begin to painstakingly scrape away the rust, the screeching of my knife against the metal bolt grating on my already fraying nerves.

Come on.

When the bolt finally slides back and the door opens, I burst up onto the main deck. Is it my imagination, or does the water seem slightly warmer, less dark? I swim to the railing and look down. Conway and Arledge are miniature versions of themselves, hovering a few paces away from the siren, whose eels are circling her in a ghostly dance.

The height takes my breath away.

The few times I have swum as high as this, on my jaunts up to The Surface, I have always been so focused on my destination, I haven't bothered to look down. Looking out, I see the black peaks of the Rayan Mountains stretching away below me. A school of fish circle a nearby peak, their silvery forms bright arrows in the water. Here and there, I can see scarlet trails of magma, bubbling down the sides of the rocks. I squint past the mountains to the plain beyond, imagining that, far in the distance, I can see pinpricks of light glinting through the net that surrounds Aquaticus.

Eventually, I tear myself away from the view and turn to survey the deck. It is completely clean, and I find myself wondering where the bodies of the crew are before realizing they have probably been eaten long ago by sharks and other scavenging predators. For the first time, something occurs to me.

What if Llyra's body is gone too? And the locket with it?

What if I have to return to Circe and accept a second curse because I could not fulfill my promise?

There is only one way to find out. I swim across the deck to the captain's quarters, located in the center of the ship. Heart pounding, I turn the door handle. It is unlocked. I slip inside the room, leaving the door ajar, and my heart jolts.

They died together.

Llyra's and Marcus's skeletons are sitting side by side on gilded wooden thrones in the center of the room. I can tell who they are because of the crowns, sitting at grotesquely rakish angles on their pearly white skulls. Even with the flesh gone, the bones of their fingers intertwine as though they held each other's hands so tightly as the ship went down, even death could not detach them.

I feel my throat close up, and unexpected tears well in my eyes. They never got to see their son again. But they never regretted the love that changed both of their lives. Suddenly, I catch a glint of silver and dart forward.

The locket is clasped around Llyra's neck. It is silver, with a delicate, finely worked chain. The chain suspends an oval with an intricate design of sapphires and moonstones depicting two dolphins leaping together through the waves. Almost reverently, I reach out, magic seeming to spark against my fingers as I turn the locket over. On the back, in thin, curving writing, two words are inscribed.

Forever Yours.

With trembling fingers, I reach around the skeleton and undo the locket's clasp. I gaze at the silver curled in my palms, unable to grasp one thing—the locket that has defined my life since birth is finally in my hands.

"I'll take that, Crura," says a sneering voice behind me.

33

DARIN

WONDER WASHES OVER HIM AS HE HOVERS
next to the body of the monstrous dead crab—the first emotion that
has managed to penetrate his numbness since Pike's death.

They killed it and went on. Locklyn is alright.

In reality, it is impossible to know that, but hope, impossible to
quell, swells inside Darin, like an anemone opening its soft interior
to a light touch. He scans the surrounding area for any other signs
of how the fight progressed but sees nothing. Something about the
silence and stillness of the stone passage sends prickles of warning,
and he wraps his fingers around the handle of the coral knife for an
instant before swimming onward.

The passage narrows and chalky scratches mar the smooth
black of the rocky walls. The crab must have tried to squeeze
through here, probably after escaping prey. Following the tapering
channel, the walls brushing more and more frequently against his
shoulders, he finally squeezes through a narrow opening into a
spacious valley. Looking warily around, he spots the wide mouth of
a cave covered with a heavy scarlet curtain nestled into the valley's
wall. A smaller cave with a well-constructed lattice of driftwood
before the opening looks like a dolphin stable. This must be where
Orwell lives.

"Hello?" Darin calls out.

"Hello, hello, hello." His own voice echoes back to him.

He hovers, waiting for the echoes to die, ears straining for sounds of another Merperson. But when the water is still once more, there is only silence.

Moving cautiously forward, he peers inside the stable first. It is deserted—though the piles of fresh posidonia indicate it must have been inhabited within the last two or three days. Darin catches a glimpse of a small loft above filled with a tangle of blankets. Either Orwell does not live alone, or he recently had visitors.

Swimming to the entrance of the main cave, he pauses in front of the heavy red curtain before reaching out and pulling it aside. The large room beyond is divided into two sections by a heavy folding screen. From his vantage point, Darin can see one side of the room holds a bed, a vanity, and a piano, while the other contains an enormous dark wooden table surrounded by chairs. Both sides of the room are empty.

Allowing the curtain to slide through his fingers, he turns to survey the silent, abandoned valley. Should he wait for Orwell to return? Did the Schatzi decide to guide Darin's companions to Llyra's wreck in person?

Running his fingers through his hair, he stares around the valley. He should wait for Orwell to return to get whatever information the Schatzi has regarding how to find Llyra's wreck. But Darin's emotions urge him to go on. Every moment he stays here, hovering in limbo, is another moment his companions could be wounded. Dying.

The familiar, insatiable craving for adventure whispers that if he waits, he might not get a chance to see, or help harvest, the greatest wreck in the Seven Seas.

He hesitates an instant longer, his brain warring against itself, before turning and plunging up the small, winding path that leads away from Orwell's valley, deeper into the heart of the Rayan Mountains.

Every stroke of Darin's powerful tail sends him shooting

through the water. The path winds and twists, but it remains singular, without a branch or offshoot to confuse him.

On high alert, he constantly glances around into the dark water ahead and behind, certain he is about to encounter some obstacle Orwell could have told him how to best, had he waited in the valley.

Hours pass. He scans the area for a spot to rest for the night when he catches sight of a faint blue glow illuminating the water ahead. The path has widened slightly, but towering stone walls enclose it on either side. Slowing his pace, he moves cautiously toward the light's source, his coral knife in hand.

A waving forest of glowing blue kelp blocks his way. He comes to a stop, eyeing the plants. Their eerie radiance seems evil somehow, and he instinctively glances upward, wondering if there is a way for him to swim over the forest. But the walls above have arched together, forming a roof over the passage. There is no way to go forward except through the kelp forest.

Frustration engulfs him, and his mind nags him to turn back. Orwell would certainly have information about this forest. But everything inside him revolts against the idea of turning back now. *I've been a Schatzi for my entire adult life. I've found my own way through situations far worse than this.*

Indecision gives him momentary pause, then he plunges forward into the waving blue forest. Silence instantly engulfs him. He pushes through the thick stalks, swimming as quickly as possible, every sense on the alert for an attack. What comes to him instead is a smell so heavenly, he pauses involuntarily. The scent of posidonia flowers mingles with the tangy-sweet scent of lecker, and his mind fills with memories of Locklyn and the odor of posidonia flowers lingering on her skin after a day spent harvesting posidonia for her dugongs.

Darin inhales deeply, and the fumes swirl through every part of his body, fogging his brain with a wonderful relaxation. His body begins to go limp as his eyelids drift closed.

I am falling into an enchanted sleep.

The words pierce his mind, and he jerks upright, pressing his lips together and attempting not to breathe. He whips around to go back before realizing he might already be halfway through the forest. If he can only reach the other side before passing out, he will be able to go on.

Hurling himself forward, he claws at the kelp stalks, cursing himself inwardly for his stupidity. The water in his lungs drains away, forcing his mouth to open involuntarily, and the heavenly scent again courses through him, turning his limbs to lead and making it impossible to keep his eyelids open.

I must go on.

But my body is too heavy. It won't move.

And sleep is pleasant. So pleasant . . .

"How are you feeling?"

He drags his eyelids open and stares into the face of the speaker, a beautiful Merwoman with a sweet, young face and golden hair falling past her waist. Her wide blue eyes sparkle in the blue light coming from the cave's entrance.

"I've felt better," he mumbles, dragging himself upright on the stone bench beneath him. "What happened? I can't remember."

"You fainted outside my door," the Merwoman says gently. "You must be exhausted. Have you come far today?"

He racks his brain. "I . . ." Memory stirs and he nods slowly, stopping quickly as his head throbs. "Yes, I'm going to find Llyra's wreck. My . . . my friends are there." He closes his eyes, and a face swims to the surface of his mind. "She will be there." He pauses and a name comes. "Locklyn. I have to find her. To make sure she's alright." He looks up into the sympathetic gaze above him. "I have to tell her how I feel. I've waited too long."

The Merwoman smiles, the expression beautifying her already

lovely face. "You need something to pick you up," she says softly. "The kelp's fumes are very strong, especially for someone who is already exhausted. Let me get you a drink before you go on."

She turns to the shelf behind her, and he hears glass clinking before she returns, carrying a shallow, stone cup filled with an electric blue liquid. He takes the cup but does not drink. The effort of lifting the vessel to his lips suddenly seems impossibly great.

"You will feel better," the Merwoman soothes. "This feeling you have now? Of weariness and pain and memory loss? All of that will go away."

I am so tired.

His body and brain both feel as though they've been pummeled.

With tremendous effort, he drags the cup to his lips.

The last thing he sees before draining it are the Merwoman's eyes reflecting the evil blue light from the kelp forest outside.

34
LOCKLYN

BLACKWELL LOUNGES IN THE CABIN
doorway. Cold seeps through me as he swims inside, shutting the
door with a click behind him. Involuntarily, I move the fist holding
the locket behind my back.

Blackwell laughs. "Do you really think I won't come and take it?
There's no one to hear you scream."

"You have better reason than most to know I can take care of
myself, Blackwell." My heart pounds as I grope for my coral knife.

But Blackwell lunges before I can pull it from my belt. His
impact sends us both careening backward into the skeletons. Bone
splinters, and I scream before Blackwell's fingers close around my
throat, cutting off the sound. I kick hard at his stomach with both
feet, and Blackwell doubles over, cursing, but manages to maintain
his grip on my throat.

"That wasn't your smartest move, love," he says as soon as he
can breathe again. His fingers tighten on my neck, and I choke,
blackness swimming at the edges of my vision as the water entering
my lungs slows to a trickle. I try to kick him again, but he is ready
this time and hurls his tail into my legs, so hard it feels like I have
fractured both my kneecaps.

As I sag, gasping in pain, Blackwell reaches behind me. "No," I gargle, thrashing, but Blackwell's grip on my throat firms.

Panicked, I clench the locket so hard the design feels imprinted into the palm of my hand. Blackwell must not take this and all it means away from me. From Conway. From Avonlea. Oh, why does he hate me so much?

"Why do you even want it?" I manage to get out. "There are hundreds of more valuable items down below."

Blackwell's smile widens until he looks like a shark, his face a mass of pointed teeth. "You think buying yourself a tail from the Sea Enchantress will change who you are," he breathes into my face. My heart lurches. He must have overheard me talking to Conway. "But you can't change what you're born as, spindle-shanks. And I don't want you to fool the rest of Aquaticus with black magic. I want them to see you for the trash you are."

I stare at him, gasping as the black spots dancing in front of my eyes twirl and spin, widening and shrinking. He's mad.

Wave Master, help me. Please.

Blackwell pulls at my fingers again, but I keep them clenched tightly around the locket. I won't let him take it. Not without a fight.

"I'll cut your fingers away from it, you know." He sneers. "A fingerless Crura, now that will be a siiiiggghhh—"

His words rise into a shriek. The hand around my throat tightens and then relaxes entirely, falling away. Blackwell screams, arching his back as purple-white light licks along his limbs. Frozen, I gape at him, knowing I should help him, but I have no idea what to do.

Blackwell's scream cuts off abruptly, and he collapses to the ground at my feet. It is then I see the three electric eels coiling in the water, their heads reared forward as if to strike. My heart stops. I look toward the doorway where the siren is silhouetted, the remaining two eels hovering on either side of her like bodyguards.

"Those who enter this place for selfish gain always suffer the consequences," she says, and then turns and swims away, her eels following like undulating black ribbons.

For a long moment, I remain motionless. Then I stoop down,

fumbling at Blackwell's throat for a pulse. I can find none. Horrified, I back away, darting from the room as my stomach heaves. Collapsing to the deck outside the cabin, I fight to keep from vomiting.

I had no love for Blackwell. But to watch him die like that?

I should have done something.

Numbly, I glance down at my still closed fist and slowly pry my fingers open. The locket glints up at me. I gaze at it for a full minute before opening the clasp. I slide the chain around my neck and fasten it. Then I tuck the locket into my shirt before turning to the stairs. After what happened with Blackwell, I want as few people as possible knowing what I possess.

Barely two hours later, we are swimming back down the mountain track, guiding ten heavy-laden dolphins. I hum softly to my dolphin as I lead her, trying to close my mind to images of Blackwell's body, sprawled motionless on the floor of that eerie cabin, his skeleton joining those of Llyra and Marcus.

"Locklyn?" Conway has managed to maneuver himself and his dolphins right behind me. I glance over my shoulder and shake my head, making my face as forbidding as I can.

"Not here."

"But—"

"Not here!" I hiss and speed up. I don't want to talk to Conway about the locket or about what happened. I just want to reach Circe, give her the locket, get tails for me and Conway and Avonlea, and then go find Darin. I want to forget this quest and all the pain it has caused. I want to go back to being a dugong shepherdess whose biggest worries are whether or not the castle will buy six dugongs this year. I want to see my sister again. I want to cuddle my niece and nephews. I want to talk to Darin and tell him I'm sorry for being a melodramatic, self-absorbed little fool. I want to know my best friend is alright. He has to be.

There is no good place to set up camp for the night, so we all decided we would try to make it back to Circe's. I had told everyone the enchantress would guide us and our dolphins through the kelp forest, and that we would wake up on the other side. No one but Conway knew why Circe had agreed to help us, but they all seemed to take for granted it was out of the goodness of her heart.

At long last, I see the wavering blue glow up ahead. For the past few hours, the entire group has been swimming in silence. Even the dolphins are too exhausted to chitter.

"We made it," Ginevra says, her voice weary. "I don't know if the enchanted sleep in the kelp forest will make us any less tired, but if we wake up exhausted on the other side, we'll camp there and rest before going on to Orwell's."

Everyone swims toward the swaying, luminous stalks of the kelp forest. Anxiety torments me as I push into the thick stalks, pulling a loaded dolphin behind me.

What will Circe ask for?

What if she double-crosses us?

What will it feel like to have a tail?

When my eyes open, a beautiful, golden-haired Merwoman who looks vaguely familiar, sits before me. I blink and struggle into a more upright position, my head throbbing.

"Where am I?" I mumble, squinting against the blue light flickering from the cave's doorway.

"You'll remember everything soon, dear," the Merwoman says. "I am Circe."

Circe. The name triggers a flood of memories and my hand leaps to my neck. The locket's chain slides smoothly against my fingertips. I stare wildly around and leap to my feet.

"Where are the others?"

"Sit down," Circe says calmly. "They are outside in the kelp forest. I saw no need to wake them, only to immediately put them back to sleep again."

I dart to the doorway anyway and peer out. Silvery-white hair fluttering from behind a tree, a limp hand, and a dolphin's tail are all I can see of my companions, but my fear eases away. Circe is telling the truth.

I return to my seat, meeting her mildly amused, blue gaze. "I brought you the locket," I say, unclasping it and holding the sparkling silver trinket out to her.

Something about Circe's expression shifts as she reaches out a slender, graceful hand, and I am filled with a mad desire to jerk the locket back. But I don't. Circe stares down at the silver oval in her hands, the sapphire and moonstone dolphins winking up through her fingers.

"I've waited a long time for this," she says.

Dread pools in my stomach, and I don't know why. "And the favor?" I force myself to say.

Circe does not look up. Her fingers fiddle with the clasp on the side of the locket. As it falls open, the most beautiful voice I have ever heard fills the cave. The words of the song are in some human tongue, so I cannot understand them, but my heart swells with the music, aching at the pathos of the haunting melody. Scenes begin to flash through my mind—scenes I have never witnessed before.

A red-haired Mermaid peering around a rock at a black-haired young man frolicking with a dog on a beach.

The same red-haired girl leaping through the waves with a dolphin and a sea otter.

The red-haired girl floating next to a rowboat under a star-filled sky, while the black-haired young man leans over to talk to her.

The red-haired girl cowering as a white-bearded man in a crown shouts that she is never to go "up there" again.

The red-haired girl swimming toward a forest of glowing blue kelp.

The red-haired girl waking on a beach in the black-haired boy's arms.

The red-haired girl, pale and exhausted from labor, wailing with despair as she looks down at the silent, finned child in her arms.

The red-haired girl, silver streaking her hair, standing on a cliff with tears pouring down her face as she watches her son dive down into the surf.

The singing stops and I open my eyes. Circe's face is unreadable as she clicks the clasp back into place. "Thank you," she says, looking at me. The longing in her blue eyes makes my heart stand still.

"And the favor?" I say again, struggling to keep my voice from shaking.

Circe smiles. But the expression I had initially thought beautified her face now looks hungry.

"I haven't decided yet," she informs me in that gentle voice. "I will let you know when I do."

"But how will you find me?"

"Oh, I will find you," she replies, rising as she clasps the locket around her neck. "And now for my half of the bargain. Go out into the forest."

I stare up at her and then down at my legs. Suddenly, I know I don't want to lose them. But I must. For Avonlea. And Conway. "But the curse—"

"When you awake on the other side of my forest, the curse will be lifted."

I continue to watch her without moving. How can I say I would prefer to see some proof now?

Circe's lips curve upward. "My dear," she says, "it is a little late to decide you don't trust me."

For another long moment, I stare at her. Then I rise slowly to my feet and swim to the doorway. Before going out, I glance back. Circe is looking down at the locket around her neck. I cannot see her eyes, but the expression contorting the rest of her face shocks me.

It is hatred.

35

LOCKLYN

SOMETHING IS WRONG. I AM RISING through the mists of sleep toward consciousness, but something about my body doesn't feel right. My legs have been tied together. I kick them, trying to separate the pair, but it is as if they have been cemented together.

"Locklyn!"

"Calm down . . ."

"Wake up, Locklyn!"

"She's thrashing so much. I don't want to get near that tail . . ."

Tail?

My eyes fly open, and I bolt upright. Ginevra and Conway bend over me, both looking anxious. "Are you alright?" Conway asks. "We were waiting for you to wake to start for Orwell's when you suddenly began moaning and thrashing around."

I meet Ginevra's eyes. They look tired and wan, but there is something in them besides exhaustion, an expression I have never seen there before. Is it pity?

I look down. Where my legs used to be, a long, supple, silver tail rests against the sand. I gape at it and then give it a twitch. The sight of its movement brings reality crashing down on me. My legs are gone.

"I have a tail," I say blankly, looking from Conway to Ginevra. They stare back at me, both of their faces creased with concern. The sharpness of the loss surprises me. I take a deep breath and swallow my disappointment with the water. "I have a tail," I say again. I glance down once more and catch sight of Conway's tail, no longer the fake black one from Atlantis, but forest green, with threads of gold running along the joints between the scales. He will no longer feel like he has to hide. He will be king of Aquaticus. And Avonlea. She will be able to stay with her family. She will never be an outcast.

I push myself up off the sand. "So do you!" I smile at Conway, whose face splits in an answering grin.

"But why?" Ginevra says bewildered. Her face is rigid. I glance at Conway, then back to her.

"You mean, why did Conway need a new tail?"

"No, I am aware he was a Crura now," Ginevra says. "I meant, why do you both suddenly have tails?"

"Well," I say, feeling a bit uncomfortable about not telling her the truth before, "I returned Llyra's locket to Circe, and she lifted the curse she put on Llyra's descendants."

"Locklyn also promised her an unknown favor," Conway adds sourly, glaring at me.

"You did what?" Ginevra rounds on me.

I give Conway a dark look. "I didn't have any choice," I say. "When I offered to get the locket for her if she freed my family, we were sitting in her cave. She demanded a favor as well, and she would have killed all of us if I hadn't agreed. And speaking of the locket," I continue quickly, before either of them can say anything, "it was gorgeous. Silver with a design of dolphins leaping through waves on the front made out of sapphires and moonstones . . ."

"Wait." The force of Ginevra's voice stops me midsentence. "Did you just say silver with sapphires and moonstones?"

"Yes," I say. Confused, I glance over at Conway, but he merely shrugs.

Ginevra's words are pointed. "Didn't Orwell say the necklace he gave to the girl, Talia, was silver with sapphires and moonstones?"

I scrunch my face, trying to remember. "That does sound right," I say slowly. "But Talia's dead."

Ginevra starts to say something, then shakes her head. "You're going to think I'm crazy."

"We won't," I promise as Conway prompts, "Tell us."

Ginevra looks at both of us. "What if she isn't dead? What if she survived? What if Circe is Talia? That would mean one of the most powerful enchantresses in the Seven Seas knows where the most feared monster in the Undersea Realm is."

Conway and I look at each other. Then Conway says in what is clearly supposed to be a tactful voice, "But, Ginny, even if she somehow survived, it's been a hundred and fifty years."

Ginevra glares at him. "Orwell's alive," she retorts.

"But he said himself that was extremely unusual," Conway argues. "Unusual. Not impossible."

"But, Ginevra," I jump in before Conway can respond, "if Circe is Talia and she wanted to release the monster, why is she here?"

"I don't know, maybe she needs something," she says. Then her eyes widen. "The locket!"

"Why under the sea would she need the locket?" Conway says exasperatedly, but a terrible thought has suddenly occurred to me.

"Oh, no," I say, despondent. "Llyra's voice. She used a spell to encase it in the locket. Llyra's voice was supposed to be the most beautiful voice heard in the Undersea Realm in centuries."

Ginevra's eyes widen in horror, but Conway waves a dismissive hand. "Locklyn, this is all nonsense. Talia is dead. Orwell saw her die. We have no reason to think that Circe is Talia except for the fact they both had lockets made of silver with sapphires and moonstones on them."

Ginevra starts to speak, but Conway forestalls her, "Listen, even if Talia somehow survived the monster's magma, she would be horribly scarred, and from Locklyn's description, she's gorgeous."

"All right," Ginevra says, "but even if Circe isn't Talia, what if

Circe has somehow found out about the monster and is going to use the locket to—I don't know—control it or something?"

"How would she have found out about it? Before Orwell, I had never heard of such a creature."

"Maybe Orwell told her. They live right next to each other."

"Orwell's never seen her, Ginevra!"

"We should go back to Orwell," I intervene swiftly. "We can ask him if there is any chance Talia survived. Then we can ask if he thinks Circe might have found out about the monster."

Both Conway and Ginevra are still looking stormy, but they nod briefly, and we all turn and swim to where the rest of the group huddles around a steam vent. When we set out again, Ginevra converses quietly with the other two Nebulae women at the back of the group, while Conway kindly tries to draw out Arledge, who looks paler and more distraught than ever.

I swim in silence next to Kai, dread bubbling within me. What if Ginevra is right? What if I have just handed the most powerful enchantress under the sea a deadly weapon? Scratch that, I know I have handed her a deadly weapon—I just didn't realize it at the time. Is there any way to get it back from her? Or is there a possibility she doesn't plan to use it for anything nefarious?

It isn't until we stop for a brief rest that I realize how strong I feel. Normally, after this much swimming, my legs would be aching and burning, but my tail feels perfectly fine. "Let's keep going," I say after barely five minutes of rest.

Conway smiles at me. "Liking the tail?"

"Extremely," I say, smiling back at him, masking my fears. I want to talk to Orwell and hear him side with Conway and say Ginevra and I are being paranoid—that it is impossible Talia is alive or that the locket he gave to his sweetheart had a design of— maybe—periwinkles on the front.

When Orwell's valley finally comes in sight, I speed up, streaking away from the others. "Orwell?" I call as I dart through the valley. "Orwell?"

There is a scraping sound and Orwell emerges quickly from the barn, dragging the lattice shut behind him. "Locklyn?" His face breaks into a huge smile, and he unexpectedly sweeps me into a rib-cracking hug. "You've made it! You've returned!" He holds me away to look at me, and his smile disappears. He gazes in confusion at my tail. "But, Locklyn . . ." He gestures, clearly unsure how to ask the question.

"The enchantress lifted the curse she put on my family," I tell him.

Orwell seems overjoyed. "That is wonderful, my dear. Now your niece will be safe too."

His kind tone and remembering touch me, but fear simmers just beneath the surface of my consciousness, and I can't keep back the question. "Orwell, the locket that you gave to Talia, what did it look like?"

Orwell creases his brow, but he must read the desperation in my face because he answers carefully. "It was made out of silver with an oval pendant, with a design of dolphins leaping through waves on the front. The dolphins were made from sapphires and moonstones, and on the back I inscribed—"

"Forever Yours," I whisper, my heart sinking into my tail.

"How did you—?"

"Orwell, Circe, the Sea Enchantress, she gave a locket exactly like that to Llyra. Llyra was supposed to encase her voice in the locket and return it to Circe in exchange for Circe giving her legs. The locket, with Llyra's voice in it, was on the wreck. I brought it to Circe so she would break the curse on my family."

Orwell's face tightens, the centuries of lines etched there more pronounced than ever. "You gave it to her?" His voice fills with alarm.

At that moment, the lattice in front of the stable scrapes aside, and a Merman emerges. His long, blond hair is tied back in a seahorse tail, and he wears a white shirt that contrasts sharply with his copper tail. I let out a gasping cry, and the man turns. His eyes are a deep, glowing gold—eyes I have only ever seen on one person under all the sea.

"Darin!" I rush past Orwell, closing the space between us in the blink of an eye, and fling myself into his arms. The solid warmth of his chest seems to flow through my cheek into every part of my body, and I begin to cry, my face buried in his chest, deep, gulping sobs of pure joy.

He's alright.

He's safe.

Thank you, Wave Master. Thank you.

After a long moment, I pull away, beaming up at him as tears continue to pour down my face. "Look at that," I say with a happy sniff. "I've ruined another one of your shirts."

Darin looks down at me and then up at Orwell. There is an expression in his eyes I have never seen there before.

"I'm sorry," he says. "Do I know you?"

ACKNOWLEDGMENTS

Like any great fantasy quest, my journey to publication was made possible only with the aid of many allies, friends, and mentors who helped me along the way. A huge thank you to my mother, who not only read *The Mermaid's Tale* in its earliest stages, but also watched my munchkins so I could write, flew across the country to attend a writing conference with me, and cheered me on when I despaired of ever becoming a published author.

To Bec, Helena, and Mattie, my beta readers, thank you for taking the time to peruse and critique this book in its infancy.

To Cathy McCrumb, I am eternally grateful for your kindness to an aspiring author and your tips on pitching.

Special thanks to Steve and Lisa Laube, for giving *The Mermaid's Tale* a home, answering a million questions from an inexperienced author, and helping to hone this story into the beautifully polished version readers will see.

Thank you also to my copy editor, Sara Ella, for your insightful (and always gracious) tips on how to make my world consistent and my wording flow.

And to Megan, for helping me to make the Undersea Realm believable and adding all my neglected commas, I am truly grateful.

I couldn't be happier that anyone judging my book by its cover will be looking at the breathtaking work of Kirk DouPonce— thank you.

Matthew, I so appreciate the work you put into the map of the Undersea Realm—it is stunning.

To all the incredible veteran authors who agreed to endorse this book, I am so grateful for your kind words and your generous support of a newbie.

Working with Trissina, Jamie, Lindsay, and the rest of the Enclave team has been a dream come true—the Christlike kindness with which you guided me through the publishing experience was truly remarkable.

To Kyle, the real-life reason I know that love and friendship go hand in hand, thank you for supporting my dreams, for allowing me to bounce plot ideas off you, and for holding me close through the highs and lows.

To Micah, Caleb, and Juliet, you show me the wonder of the world each and every day, and I love you more than I can say.

And, lastly, to the One whom the wind and the waves obey, there will never be enough words. Thank you for the pounding ocean breakers, for the stories that touch men's souls, and for the Sacrifice that reconciles us to You.

ABOUT THE AUTHOR

L.E. Richmond was practically born with a book in her hands (the result of being raised by an American writing teacher and a German bookseller). From a tender age, fairy tales have held a special place in her heart, leading to this spin-off of Hans Christian Andersen's classic as her debut novel. When not crafting stories rooted in lore and fairy tales, she can be found chasing three little readers-in-training, running crazy distances, and brewing homemade kombucha. She has never yet met a mermaid, but when she and her husband eventually complete an Iron Man, she plans to use the 2.4 mile swim to search for one.